THE SOUND OF

'An absorbing story . . . Marjory Alyn's first
novel is quite simply the best I have read in a
long time'
Irish News

'A droll and atmospheric novel, full of character
and humanity, and all too clearly making
understandable the tenacious roots of Irish
confict'
Homes and Gardens

'What is impressive about this book is its
authenticity of feeling . . . pleasing and
illuminating throughout'
Times Literary Supplement

'The writing is observant . . . some good
characterisation and a strong atmosphere'
British Book News

'Ms Alyn's tale abounds in honest feeling and
a civilising, wry humour. A most promising
debut'
Dublin Sunday Independent

'This richly realized first novel illuminates the
tragedy of Northern Ireland through the
unclouded eyes of a village child with unique
poignancy and humour'
Publishers Weekly

About the Author

Marjory Alyn was born in Glasgow but brought up by her grandmother and aunt in a small village near Belfast, Northern Ireland. She now lives in California where she devotes her time to writing. THE SOUND OF ANTHEMS is her first novel.

'It was a great pleasure to read such an accomplished novel. Marjory Alyn has a great ear for dialogue and also a lovely feeling for character. Grandmother is a marvellous old woman—a true product of Belfast'
Jennifer Johnston

THE SOUND OF ANTHEMS

Marjory Alyn

CORONET BOOKS
Hodder and Stoughton

Copyright © 1983 by Marjory Alyn

First published in Great Britain in 1984 by
Hodder & Stoughton Ltd

Coronet edition 1986

British Library C.I.P.

Alyn, Marjory
    The sound of anthems.
    I. Title
    823'.914[F]   PS3551.L89

ISBN 0-340-38455-7

Printed and bound in Great Britain for
Hodder and Stoughton Paperbacks, a
division of Hodder and Stoughton Ltd.,
Mill Road, Dunton Green, Sevenoaks,
Kent (Editorial Office: 47 Bedford
Square, London, WC1 3DP) by
Richard Clay (The Chaucer Press) Ltd,
Bungay, Suffolk

This book is dedicated to Isabelle Ziegler
who struck the match.

The groves were God's first temples. Ere man
  learned
To hew the shaft, and lay the architrave,
And spread the roof above them – ere he
  framed
The lofty vault, to gather and roll back
The sound of anthems; in the darkling wood,
Amid the cool and silence, he knelt down,
And offered to the Mightiest solemn thanks
And supplication.

—William Cullen Bryant
"A Forest Hymn"

THE SOUND OF ANTHEMS

CHAPTER
1

When I was eleven, Mrs. Doran's cat died and people said Mrs. Doran was very upset because she'd had Smokey a long time. When enough years had passed, most of the events leading up to the big grey cat's death became clear to me, but one thing remains a mystery. The world was full of mystery that year.

It was a year of intimacy, too, and I came to know Mrs. Doran, Uncle Dan, Aunt Madge, and a host of others with a clarity unparalleled before or since. Grandmother was something else again and remained an enigma for a long time to come.

That same year, World War II ended in Europe and since Northern Ireland was lashed to England's chariots, the victory was ours too. It seems to me the seeds of the whole affair germinated then, flowered in summer, and bore the fruit we were all compelled to taste that autumn and winter. Grandmother maintains, of course, that it started hundreds of years ago when the first Englishman set his gout-ridden toe in Ireland. And she'd wind me through the maze of bloody history which I argued was peripheral; I thought that ordinary happenstance contributed. Then she'd tack on her stock admonition that people should "remember their origins."

I don't think Grandmother ever realized how seriously I "remembered my origins" that year. I practically resurrected them! But there were certain legacies bequeathed me by my origins that I tried to bury too. I came of age to claim my inheritance the same Sunday England claimed victory over Germany.

That Sunday in May, destined to take its place with other momentous dates in world history books, dawned appropriately like a Resurrection painting, all blue and white gold. New lines were being drawn on the world atlas. In the midst of the vortex swirling around the globe, the village of Greencastle sat, seemingly untouched. But victory was to stir up dormant feelings that, once revived, were to alter the face of our village for me forever.

The spring of 1945 was a time of optimism for most people in Greencastle; a time of solidarity. Victory was imminent and people joined clubs, coteries, and cliques for the greater good of humanity. Aunt Madge volunteered to become a nurse's helper at the Mater Hospital in Belfast three nights a week as a direct result, Grandmother deduced, of three consecutive viewings of *Gone With the Wind*. Uncle Dan assumed the captaincy of the hurley team and spent Saturdays and Sundays, as Grandmother put it, "running the guts out of lads subsisting on nothing but Spam and margarine rations." Grandmother said Spam was a great equalizer. Aunt Nin headed a funding drive to strengthen the chapel balcony; Grandmother said it was nothing but an excuse to get inside people's houses to garner news.

Things were more personal then; we visited each other often for mutual entertainment and enlightenment, the sources of which were gossip, yarns, the wireless, and the newspapers—in that order. Cows hadn't yet been banished to isolated farms, and patches of cows' clap still scattered the raw tar surface of the Whitewell Road, their consistency and potency largely dependent on how soon you travelled the Whitewell after Creswell's prize bovines had been driven from the dairy byres up to the pastures. Dogs and cats were still free to remain natural enemies, and chased and spat amongst us as opportunities presented themselves. Old Coffey, the lamplighter, made his rounds; Johnny Brannigan, the coalman, hefted huge bags of slag, coke, and coal into our bunker weekly; and Constable Johnston, with the stalwart aid of a few others, pounded the beat with such deterrent effect that I believed "crime" was a Belfast word.

The official news of the British victory didn't come

through until late afternoon, but that Sunday morning first brought other news that meant victory for some and loss for others of us.

I hated Sundays. It was a matter of geography.

Greencastle sits in the lap of land that sweeps down from the Cave Hill to the shores of Belfast Lough, split in two by the Shore Road, which runs parallel with the lough all the way to Belfast. On the lough side of the Shore Road, where Aunt Nin lived, the land is flat, its sandy soil supporting lanes of tiny whitewashed row houses and four pubs (the Donegal Arms being far and away the most popular). Grandmother said publicans knew what side of the Shore Road their bread was buttered on. Aunt Nin's house had windows little bigger than postage stamps and walls two feet thick that, Grandmother said, did bugger all to keep the damp out. They'd been built over a hundred years ago, before the great famine.

Across the road, on the Cave Hill side, the land rises immediately, and rows of brick terrace houses straggle up the hill, gradually giving way to semi-detached and single dwellings off the Whitewell Road, then on up to the grand estates adjacent to the Castle grounds at the base of the Cave Hill itself.

There were three clubs: the British Legion was ensconced in a solid brick building on the Shore Road; the Orange Lodge was situated in indomitable stone block quarters near the bottom of the Whitewell Road; and the Wolfe Tone Gaelic Athletic Club was housed in a variegated tin hut pitched at the side of a field near the top of the Whitewell. Few people remembered that the great Irish patriot had been so honoured since it was never referred to as anything but the Gaelic Hut.

Greencastle had four houses of worship: Methodist, Church of Ireland, Presbyterian, and Catholic. The latter, St. Mary's Star of the Sea, had the most important vantage point since its gates were firmly implanted on the Shore Road; the chapel path curved up the first steep incline, and the chapel itself, an ancient, mossy edifice, looked down on the tiny whitewashed row houses inhabited by most of its flock.

But we didn't live in the shadow of the chapel. Grandmother, Aunt Madge, and I were stuck up on Serpentine Parade, about halfway between the village proper and the Cave Hill, and Sunday afternoons found me bereft of companions since Bobby, Pam, and the other children on our street spent every Sunday afternoon in Sunday School. Protestants took their Sundays seriously; adults didn't do any servile work that could wait until Monday, and children didn't play on the Sabbath day.

As I said, I hated Sundays.

The mornings weren't so bad, for they were filled with the rituals of attending Mass in the village chapel, followed by a visit to Aunt Nin's. I looked forward to these visits because all my school chums lived in the general vicinity of Aunt Nin's wee house, and Patsy McKenna, my best friend, lived a few doors down. They didn't hold with the no-playing notions of Protestants at Aunt Nin's.

That particular Sunday started off the same as all the others. As usual, Aunt Nin had the tea ready and waiting for Grandmother and me when we came in from Mass. I was anxious to get the ritual tea-drinking over with so I could spend some time playing with Patsy, but when Aunt Nin put a plate of her hot raisin scones, dripping butter, under my nose, I decided it would be impolite not to observe the proprieties.

Aunt Nin wasn't really related to us, but she and Grandmother had been close friends ever since they were burned out of their houses during the Troubles in the early twenties. That was a summer yarn. Grandmother's version was more dramatic because she gave the impression she actually had fled the leaping flames with Aunt Madge, a squealing infant, in her arms and my father hanging on for dear life to the hem of her nightgown. Yarns were the pulse of the people, and variations of the same story abounded so they never got boring.

There was a difference between summer yarns and winter yarns. In the long summer twilights the stories focused on the terrible doings of the B-Specials. Sad-eyed, the tellers related how Catholics were murdered by the Black and Tans in the South and their counterparts, the B-Specials, in the North. Then those same eyes would take on a zealous light as the brave exploits of the IRA were recounted; how they'd shot B-Specials (reprisals, mind you) and how those brave lads fought the whole bloody English army to win Ireland back. Well, most of it. Then the eyes would come full circle back to suffering as the martyrs were hung, drawn, and quartered with their poor old mothers looking on, right there in our living room.

But while I believed every word of a summer yarn, in all my eleven years I'd never seen anything of the sort going on, so I relegated the stories to the same netherland where I kept *Oliver Twist* and *A Tale of Two Cities*—the Olden Days. People were very cruel then and I'd cried all through the matinee.

It was the frightful winter yarns told at Aunt Nin's wee house that really made my kidneys suffer, for even if I had to go under pain of embarrassing myself, wild horses couldn't have dragged me outside to Aunt Nin's water closet. She didn't have a bathroom like ours, just a little shed rather haphazardly tacked on to the back of the house like an afterthought. The seat was a long wooden board with a hole cut out over the lavatory, and I only flushed it in daylight since I had to stand up on the bench and grope about in the dark for the chain.

Aunt Nin's house was perfect for winter yarns. The Belfast Corporation deemed it too expensive to convert the old houses to electricity, so Aunt Nin's was lit by little gas lamps that cast a greenish glow on everything and enhanced the tales of the supernatural. A howling wind leaving draughts in its wake could play havoc with the nerves of even the stout-hearted as those gas lamps flickered and threatened to plunge us into darkness. There were at least twenty tales involving the peculiar baying of a dog or the queer whingeing lament of a child "crying out" a member of its family from this world. The teller always gave his rendition of what the actual baying or whinging sounded like. "God have mercy, you couldn't even look at that chile crooked but she was whimpering and crying—for nothing a'tall, mind you! But the minute her mother died—that was it—not another whinge out of her!" Winter yarns covered a vast spectrum of the unexplainable; they told of curses and their aftermaths, of the dreadful meaning associated with wraiths, three thumps on your wall, a picture falling off its nail without earthly reason and of warning pinches from the friendly dead that someone close was on the way out. Anytime I couldn't account for the origin of a tiny bruise, I frantically sought Grandmother's diagnosis. How she was able to tell the difference between a normal earthly bruise and a dead nip was beyond me.

And the stories they told about Creswell's would have put the wind up anybody. Long ago the dairy had been a coaching inn, and the dark deeds of treachery and murder committed there had earned Creswell's second-place standing among the few ill-omened patches of earth in Greencastle. They said that the ghosts of everybody who'd ever died a violent death in Greencastle all ended up at Creswell's. And Grandmother maintained Old Coffey lit the lamps at the dairy first so he'd never be caught there in the dark. And the few lamps he lit, she said, only assured you of seeing what you didn't want to.

These stories were prefaced with the cryptic statement, "Now, I wasn't there, but I know them that were," which lent credence to the unholy events being related.

But Aunt Nin didn't need the preface; she was famous

in Greencastle, for she'd seen the Banshee with her own two eyes for a full three days before her husband died.

"Oh, they laughed at me when I mentioned it," she'd say in the telling, "for wasn't he only thirty-three and as healthy as a horse? But I *seen* her up on that wall night after night. A wee wizened-up bit of a thing . . . combing . . . combing . . . always combing that straggly hair."

I saw her, too, as Aunt Nin slowly combed the air around her head and shoulders. Then Aunt Nin would put her hands over her ears.

"And I can hear her yet. Oh, aye! Keening and wailing and carrying on. I can't do it the way she did, but it sounded something like this." Then she'd give a long plaintive "Aheee . . . ahheeeeee . . . ahheeeeee . . ."

She always did it three times. And she'd draw out those three days for us, telling of other things she'd tied in as signs of his approaching death.

"Thirty-three years of age and strong enough to fell a tree! But he dropped in his tracks—dead as a nail—right there"—she'd point to the doorstep—"over a wee bit of wood for the fire."

The village of Greencastle had quit laughing at Aunt Nin long ago.

Aunt Nin always wore black in memory of her long-dead husband, but her aprons exploded with colourful flowers or bright gingham checks. She was plump and pink and her mist of white hair always looked as if it had just been washed. There wasn't a wrinkle on her face, due, she maintained, to her liking the fat of the meat as well as the lean. Her daughter, Rosie, wasn't what you'd have called delicate either; according to Grandmother, Rosie was a spinsterly thirty-three and still trying to catch a man, God help her. Both Aunt Nin and Rosie smelled of a mixture of Devon Violets and mothballs. I thought they were the cleanest people in Greencastle, but Grandmother said, "It's stinking maids need stinking perfume."

I also thought Aunt Nin was the best cook in Greencastle, and it appeared Grandmother didn't agree with me there either, for I got nothing but grim glances from her every time I reached for another raisin scone. They were discussing Father Sheridan's sermon on intemperance and both lauded his scathing reference to "certain of the flock holding up the walls of the Donegal Arms."

"I can tell you, Nin, there was a lot of feet scuffling going on." Grandmother gave an angry slurp at her tea. "Somebody ought to put a bomb under that den of iniquity."

"Aye," agreed Aunt Nin, "that place has sent many's a mother to an early grave."

A short history of some of the doings at the Donegal Arms followed, but it was nothing I hadn't heard before. I excused myself, carefully setting the dainty teacup on the saucer among its posies of wild violets. Aunt Nin was the only person who ever trusted me with a china cup and I didn't take the honour lightly. I'd have dropped the cup at her next words.

"They put a good few away last night, I hear. Bridie McKenna wasn't expecting twins, but that's what she had. Mick got the shock of his life. Of course he played the big man and bought everybody a pint—on tick, mind you."

I only half heard Grandmother's sallying remarks about jobs not lasting forever. I was stunned.

Their names were Kevin and Theresa, Aunt Nin said, after Kevin Barry and The Little Flower. A flood of resentment hit me. Patsy McKenna already had plenty of brothers and sisters and all I wanted was one of either. Grandmother was right. "Them that don't need it, get it." Sometimes she reversed this to "Them that need it, don't get it," depending on the circumstances. Patsy had everything I wanted: mother, father, brothers and sisters. . . .

It was right in the middle of this coveting of my neighbour's goods that God drew me up short through his instrument, Aunt Nin.

"I've a bit of bad news, Maggie," she said, her eyes reflecting the tiny votive flame under the picture of the Sacred Heart. News travelled slowly in Greencastle until it reached Aunt Nin. Grandmother called her "The News of the World" after a big English newspaper that Catholics weren't allowed to buy. Grandmother said its contents were scandalous.

"Father Sheridan's leaving us." Aunt Nin's other chin settled itself. I sat down again and Grandmother halted her teacup in mid-air.

"Aye, he'll be gone in two weeks," Aunt Nin sighed.

Grandmother ruffled her shoulders. "He never gave a hint of leaving from the pulpit this morning," she said, before asking the potentially lethal question, "Who told it to you?"

Aunt Nin leaned forward, her eyes fixed on Grandmother's. "I had it from the Widow Byrne herself." Aunt Nin leaned back, folded her arms, and forced her chins into concertina pleats. Grandmother was silent. So was I. The Widow was the priest's housekeeper and that was an important charge in Greencastle. But I'd discovered the Widow Byrne rendered even more crucial services to us.

There was a subtle deception practised in the village of Greencastle. One never mentioned the sanitorium when speaking to the relative of a TB case—it was always the "hospital at Whiteabbey," and the unfortunate's condition was diagnosed as "bad health." Never were the words "consumptive" and "tubercular" to be uttered except around one's own hearth. And when one said a girl was bad, it didn't mean she stole or lied or anything. No. It meant something else, something unspeakable.

Grandmother was willing enough to explain why we didn't out and out say the forbidden words about a person in bad health; it was because their family hadn't taken good care of them and they had enough shame to bear as it was. But some instinct told me that she wouldn't be as ready to explain what a bad girl was.

There were lots of words people used that didn't really

say what they meant but *meant* the same thing anyway. Grandmother could hold a whole conversation with Aunt Nin right in front of me and their knowing eyes and head shakings conveyed understanding while I was left an ignoramus in their midst, wondering if I'd ever be adept in the coded language of adults.

No one ever said a gravely ill relative was dying either, but that's what they meant when they said in dolorous tones, "We've sent for the Widow," or "The Widow's sitting up with her." I'd caught on to that one. When the eyestrings broke, it was she who'd put the pennies in, give your corpse its final wash, and deck you out in your shroud. I kept a respectable distance between the Widow and me. Sometimes she gave me dark, quizzical looks and one day I thought she was going to pursue me across the street (I always crossed to the other side when I saw her black skirts coming at me), but she stopped at the kerb, shook her head, and continued her path.

And the Widow's words were like her presence—final. If she said Father Sheridan was leaving, then the man who held all my sins would indeed go away.

"I remember the first Mass he said at St. Mary's . . ." said Aunt Nin, and she and Grandmother began a reminiscence of Father Sheridan's unfaltering deeds. I didn't listen. I had my own thoughts to think.

I couldn't imagine Greencastle's soul under the care of anyone else. It was Father Sheridan who'd placed the first consecrated wafer on my tongue; who saw to it we renounced the Devil and all his works and pumps; helped get us all ready for confirmation into the One True Faith; meted out three Hail Marys or the Stations of the Cross to us in return for absolution. He was the only priest I'd ever really known. I'd like to be able to say Father Sheridan didn't know me any better than the other children of the parish, but he did. And ever since that unfortunate incident in the middle of spring, I dreaded going to confession.

Dark as it was in the confession box, I just *knew* he could discern me, Jennifer Marshall—desecrator of hallowed ground—from behind the grille.

Up until May, spring was just one long cold rain and the whole village seemed to hibernate. Hibernation wouldn't have been so bad if I'd had anyone to hibernate with, but Grandmother and Aunt Madge could only take limited doses of Tiddly Winks and Snakes and Ladders. Even Napoleon's Nose, the large hump of protruding rock that marked the summit of the Cave Hill, went into hiding among the big pewter clouds that just hung over us and hurled long slivers of rain that stung my face into a picture of blooming health. But I felt far from healthy. Desolation seeped through my constantly damp clothes and invaded my soul.

I made furtive studies of Aunt Madge and Grandmother. Aunt Madge was twenty-five. She had long black hair that would have been straight except at the last inch it took a soft curl inwards—Chinese hair, the colour of wet blueberries and just like the pictures in my old geography book. She looked like Grandmother, though Grandmother wore her hair slashed down the centre and clasped into a tight bun over each ear. Both were small and thin; my Aunt Madge could span her waist with her thumbs and middle fingers. They had the same eyes, too—a sort of grey with little chips of green in them. Yes, they looked alike; there was no mistaking they were mother and daughter; they belonged to each other.

Something was watching me too. I could feel it at the back of me. It crossed my mind they were making a film of the *Life of Jennifer Marshall,* every word or movement chronicled, and I wasn't supposed to know. I'd pull my face into an appropriate pose as the sad star whose parents were really the King and Queen of Mandalay and couldn't acknowledge their precious daughter for fear court enemies would do her harm. Sometimes I'd let them know I knew what they were doing. But I'd twist around to find nothing, not even a ripple in a puddle. Nobody would sit through an eleven-year-long picture anyway.

Maybe I was going into what they called "a decline." Grandmother tried to stave it off with a spoonful of treacle and an eggcupful of salt water every morning for a week. The blood needed purifying in the spring of the year, she said. Whether it cleansed my blood or not is unknown, but it sterilized my kidneys and did nothing at all for the heart of me. And the dread feeling that something had to be got through intensified.

I supposed Grandmother and Aunt Madge would miss me sometimes, but I had no brothers or sisters who'd do any grieving. And certainly no mother or father. I'd never noticed my parents were missing before; the fourth commandment had no more meaning than the fifth, and I chattered out "Honour Thy Mother and Thy Father" in the same catechistic monologue as "Thou Shall Not Kill."

I'd been too young to feel their passing, hadn't felt it, but with the event of my eleventh birthday I had the inexplicable *need* to feel it—to suffer it. Patsy and my other school chums took it upon themselves to see that I did, too. I don't know what came over them, but they "Mammy"d and "Daddy"d me to death. My "Granny"s and "Aunt Madge"s were stripped of any thrust when up against a "Mammy" or a "Daddy." And Patsy and the others looked at me funny sometimes, I know they did, like I'd never even had a mother or a father.

Admittedly, I couldn't remember all that much about them, but I *had* had them. Grandmother kept a photograph of my father on the piano—a laughing young man with Grandmother's eyes wearing a carelessly opened shirt. I didn't need a photo to remind me of my mother—Grandmother said all I had to do was look in the mirror. Now, that was all well and good, but somehow my reflection didn't do justice to the picture I had of her as a beautiful angel with long, swirling fair hair and blue eyes. I had the blue eyes, but my fair hair was a far cry from long, thanks to Grandmother's abhorrence of the National Animals. "The Irish are renowned for their love of animals," she'd say, "and they've a particular affinity for lice."

Grandmother also had a distinct dislike for cars. "If your mother hadn't had such highfalutin' notions, your father would never have bought that bloody tin lizzie. But no, nothing else would do her—she had to do her visiting in *style*." She sang the word "style."

They were buried somewhere in Scotland, where my mother's people lived, but Grandmother didn't care for the subject so it wasn't mentioned often. I'd pumped her for more information and all I got was a vexed reference to a killer fog. I'd never seen a killer fog. As far as I knew we just had plain fog in Ireland.

On my way to and from school I passed the chapel, and occasionally I'd swing off the Shore Road to say a fervent prayer for something I wanted. And I wanted a mammy and daddy, so up I went and entreated God for a miracle. But I knew He wouldn't perform this one. It would upset a lot of apple carts if He gave them back. I gave up and left the silent chapel.

It was quiet in the little chapel graveyard, and despite the angry sky the rain was just a soft drizzle that fell reverently on the grass verges and mounds. I sighed. No, the people underneath wouldn't take too kindly to God making an exception. Some of them had been here a long time. The village had outgrown the chapel graveyard years ago and most people, including my grandfather, were now buried up in Our Lady's Acre at the top of the Whitewell Road. Only a few families still had room in their original plots for the odd body or two, and still fewer had never used theirs at all.

Now, I wasn't one for walking around in graveyards, especially since I'd no kin here to visit, but some morbid fascination just took over and I sauntered around a few headstones reading names, dates, and sweet quotations. The peculiar thing was I felt comforted, and one grave led to another. Then I saw the huge slab of white marble encasing what must have been enough space for three graves. Oh, God, it was beautiful. It had a big statue of Our Lady of Sorrows looking over it, and four little angels reclined at her feet. Fluted vials stood at all four corners, but they didn't have flowers in them. You could tell it was old—one of the angels had lost a wing and moss had made inroads on the iron fence surrounding the whole thing. Whoever erected this monument must have loved the departed very much; it was just what I'd have done for my mammy and daddy. I searched for nameplates but there weren't any. And the chiselled inscription was far from eloquent. All it said was THEIR NAMES ARE WRITTEN IN THE BOOK OF LIFE. A bit disappointing, that.

Then the miracle happened. God gave my mother and father back that very instant! And they were right under this marble slab and nobody could say any different. A reverence filled me and I looked up at the heaving grey sky.

"Thank you, God," I shouted silently, and a roar of rain answered me.

In no time at all I had their grave spruced up. Close to the end of the week the moss was all but gone and the creepers given no further footholds in the grass verge. The best I could do for little One-Wing was pat his head and wash his little white face.

I couldn't let my mother and father down by stealing flowers for the vials, so I decided to ask the Sommervilles if they had any they didn't want. I liked Mr. and Mrs. Sommerville because no matter how many times our ball went into their garden they never got angry. They were delighted to retrieve it for us themselves; in fact, they insisted on it. All we had to do was ask and one or the other of them would patiently hunt in between their prize rosebeds until it was found. They were English, and all we knew about them was their devotion to the Royal Belfast Horticulture Society.

Their garden was the pride of Serpentine Parade and no matter what the season or difficult weather, they always managed to have something blooming. And instead of the usual "Good morning" or "Good evening," a greeting to the Sommervilles went something like, "How are the flowers this morning?" or "Those pansies are a sight for sore eyes this evening." Even Grandmother said, "That's one thing I'll say for the English—they know how to grow a garden."

I found out that when God worked a miracle, He did it in grand style and He didn't care what a person's religion was either. Although the Sommervilles didn't attend any church, it was generally assumed they were Protestant. But God had primed Mrs. Sommerville. She didn't even ask what I wanted the flowers for!

"Oh, you dear, *dear* child," she gushed, clasping her hands in delight.

Now, I'd have scorned this type of talk under normal circumstances, but I *did* feel like somebody's dear child for a change and I basked in her smiles. She understood.

"Flowers are a gift from God," she confirmed as she led me to a bed of narcissus. "Pluck as many as you can carry, dear"—she glanced up at the churning sky—"before this rain beats them to death."

So the vials were filled with lemon narcissus, divinely obtained. It was ready.

I invited Patsy and a few others to come see my parents' grave after school that Friday, and we all trooped up the chapel path. I couldn't have wished for a better reaction— they said it was the most beautiful grave they'd ever seen, that my mother and father were lucky to have died together in one another's arms, that they probably couldn't have lived without each other anyway. I've never been happier than I was in that graveyard.

Then we all made a tour, pointing out where some-body's Uncle Tom was and somebody else's Aunt Lucy. But their graves couldn't compare to the one where my parents lay.

"That's where they'll be putting Mrs. Quinn tomor-row," Patsy whispered, pointing to a great pile of red earth. "She used to live around the corner from me."

In Greencastle, you weren't cold on the sheets before we put you in the past tense. We all moved gingerly towards the mound. I'd never seen an open grave before so I couldn't pass up the opportunity for a quick look into the dark hole. Maybe if I'd stopped to think that there might be other coffins or skeletons in it I wouldn't have put a foot near it. As it was, my foot suddenly skidded and I was slid-ing . . . sliding in the wet red muck that gave away under me . . . clawing it, shrieking as it turned to slime in my hands and emptied me into the gaping hole.

Patsy and the other cowards fled. I didn't think. Daren't think! I was just a wild, howling animal jumping around in a pit, my hands and feet scrabbling for a hold only to have the soggy earth melt at my touch.

I don't know how long it was before I saw the big, black-cloaked figure looming over me. I nearly fainted then. But it said, "Give me your hand," and even if it had been the driver of the death coach, I would have clutched it.

I was hauled out and vaguely remember seeing Patsy's frightened face before she again turned tail when Father Sheridan started a tongue-lashing I'll never forget. But he could have beat me senseless and I'd still have been grateful to him. And to Patsy for fetching him. I'll never forget her for that. I owed her a favour. Thank God she wasn't like those other cowards.

Red muck clotted my hair, soldered itself to my clothes, and turned my shoes into two huge clogs. People stared rudely as I clomped past them. Shivering and still fright-ened, I wrapped myself in warm thoughts of a stool by the fire, a bowl of Grandmother's Friday leek soup, and her joy at my safe return as I trudged up the Whitewell Road.

But when Grandmother opened the back door she let out a keening "Aaaaahhhh" and her eyes flickered in terror. Then she crossed herself and said, "Jesus, Mary, and Joseph protect us!" I'd never seen Grandmother frightened before and the next thing I knew I was wailing.

"Don't you cross this stoop until you've washed every pick of that graveyard clabber off," she warned. And she kept me out in the rain while she filled a basin of water and then banished me to the bottom of the garden.

I slopped myself from one end to the other until the water turned the colour of blood. Grandmother shouted out the scullery window that I was to leave every stitch outside before I could get into the bath. When it came to discarding my knickers, the high hedges around the garden suddenly lost their majesty and, my degradation complete, I tore up the path as naked as little One-Wing. It'd be a while before I asked for any more miracles—the price was a bit steep.

I never saw those clothes or shoes again, never visited that grave again, and I never found out how Grandmother knew it was graveyard clabber either. She just knew. Grandmother knew all sorts of things like that. She wasn't like anybody else.

I hadn't been listening to Grandmother and Aunt Nin, but apparently they'd finished tracing Father Sheridan's devout fifteen-year tenure in Greencastle.

"He'll be hard to replace, Nin," Grandmother was saying, and Aunt Nin agreed that strict as Father Sheridan was, Greencastle needed a firm hand.

Grandmother nodded. "And those that need it the most'll be the ones dancing jigs."

Flushed with the memories of Father Sheridan's "firm hand," I wondered how Aunt Madge and Uncle Dan would take the news. I knew it didn't please Grandmother at all.

She was in league with Father Sheridan and between the two of them they kept my Uncle Dan at arm's length with regard to Aunt Madge. Uncle Dan wasn't really my uncle yet, but I knew he wanted to be.

Actually, I wanted him to have a higher title than Uncle. I'd given up on the dead as parents, but I now had hopes among the living. Uncle Dan had understood about the graveyard, had even laughed about it. And when Grandmother chilled me to the bone by saying graveyard clabber was unlucky, Uncle Dan blunted her whole theory. "If kissing a corpse is lucky," he'd said, "then it would seem to me graveyard clabber has the same quality. In fact"—he winked at me—"I'm surprised the whole village isn't smearing a little on the forehead." Oh, he was a quare fellow all right.

But when I'd ask if Aunt Madge and Uncle Dan would ever get married, Grandmother painted a bleak picture of Aunt Madge "saddled with a parcel of snottery-nosed wee children and hardly an apron to cover her nakedness" if they did.

But I knew there was a lot more to it than aprons. I'd heard them arguing late one night. Well, Grandmother and Uncle Dan did the arguing and Aunt Madge did the crying. I was in bed helping the Secret Three solve a mystery and only the rise in voices jerked me away from my chums in the *School Friend*.

They used a lot of words I didn't understand, so I just concentrated on the ones I knew. That was a mistake, for then I couldn't remember the unfamiliar one Grandmother kept harping about. Father Sheridan was mentioned a lot, too, and Grandmother held up his name to Uncle Dan like a crucifix in the face of the Devil. It was a terrible row and, ever since, Grandmother and Uncle Dan just suffered one another when he came to tea on Sundays.

I was only half listening to Grandmother and Aunt Nin, but I heard them mention Brazil and something about it being worse than Darkest Africa. I left them speculating on Father Sheridan's chances of surviving the Amazon and headed for Patsy's house.

CHAPTER
2

I found her outside, sitting in the deep recess of her windowsill. Patsy McKenna's mother hadn't blackballed long hair and she was, they said, already a Beauty with a capital *B*—a real blue-eyed, dark-haired Irish Beauty. It was Patsy who'd played the Virgin Mary in the school Christmas concert and everyone agreed with Miss McGrath she was perfect for the part. I was a shepherd boy, struck blind, deaf, and dumb when the star appeared, and restored to full faculties only upon kneeling at the crib in the final minute of the play.

Grandmother always said you could give some people the moon and they'd moan about not having the stars as well. Patsy looked like she was ready to moan. *I* should be the one with the face like vinegar.

She swung her legs down from the sill and I squeezed in beside her, steeled for the principal's account of the happy event. But Patsy just sat gazing at her feet.

"What's the matter with you?" It was an accusation.

She let out a big sigh. "Ann says we've all to get dancing costumes," she said, "and the special shoes." She rolled her big blue eyes. Patsy was the best dancer in the Irish dancing team put together and nurtured by Ann Mulholland. Ann was our cultural director and busied herself putting on plays and concerts, conducting the chapel choir and accompanying it on the organ. Grandmother called her Ann Mulhollywood.

I almost said, "So what's the matter with that?" but then I remembered Aunt Nin having reservations about how

Patsy's mother and father were going to feed, let alone clothe, any more children. I looked at my shiny patent ankle-straps, then at Patsy's black-laced brogues, still a size too big for her. They'd been handed down from someone's big sister (I'd always suspected a big brother). A rush of sympathy hit me as I remembered us all making fun of her clomping around in them. I'd have died of embarrassment. But Patsy just gave a droll laugh and said they'd make a good clatter during a hornpipe.

"I didn't even ask my mammy yet," Patsy was saying. "She's enough to bother her."

"When have you to get it?"

"By the first week in September," she said, relieving some of my anxiety. September was a lifetime away. "There's a big competition at St. Dominic's Hall away in Belfast"— enthusiasm took over her voice—"and I'm in it! I told m'mammy that bit." She changed the subject. "Grown-ups cry sometimes when they're happy—did you know that, Jennifer?"

I shook my head. The only grown-up I'd ever seen cry was my Aunt Madge. That was when Grandmother told her she'd roast in eternal Hell for the things she was contemplating.

"Oh, I forgot to tell you—my mammy had twins. Ach, they're lovely, Jennifer."

All the pints of bitter gall I'd been prepared to swallow had dissipated a bit. "Can I see them?"

She shook her head. "Not right away—m'mammy's not up to it yet and they're in the front room with her. My daddy says we've all to be quiet." She laughed. "He's a dreamer! D'ye hear that commotion?"

Patsy was the eldest of five children, not counting the new babies, and from inside their little house cries of "I'm telling on you!" and "Aw, keep your oul' comics then" were punctuated with cackles, squeals, and yells that were never heard on Serpentine Parade on a Sunday morning.

But that didn't mean they never would be. There were things I needed to know. Patsy answered all my questions and she knew a lot about babies. Yes, when people got married they *definitely* had babies. No, she was sure, no marriage, no babies. And they weren't found in cabbage leaves or roses either—Patsy said that was a lot of rot—you just got up one morning and there they were!

Dierdre and Noreen started a skipping game and we joined in, but it wasn't long before Grandmother, having gleaned all she could out of The News of the World, shouted for me to come on. She wanted to get her quilts dried, she said, since the good weather was keeping up. Sunday morning was cut short and I left Patsy and the others skipping to the age-old chants of "Tinker, Tailor, Soldier, Sailor."

The dreaded Sunday afternoon was upon me already and my sighs and scowls went unheeded as we started up the hill towards Serpentine Parade. Grandmother was more interested in whether my new black patent-leather shoes made contact with the cows' clap than in my mood or the reasons for it.

"Grandmother," I said, "are we rich?"

"What in God's name are you talking about, Jennifer?"

She always said that when she needed time to choose her words.

"Well, Patsy said we must be rich to live up on Serpentine Parade. She said only Protestants live there."

Grandmother looked annoyed. "I suppose we are rich in Patsy's eyes," she said. "Her mother doesn't have it easy rearing all those wee children on one man's pay packet."

That didn't explain anything except maybe why Patsy didn't often have a penny for the Black Babies fund.

"You and Aunt Madge bring me up on her pay packet," I persisted, referring to Aunt Madge's job at Barbour's Linen Mill.

All Grandmother said was that if we had to depend on

Madge's pittance we'd be in the poorhouse by now and that it was lucky my grandfather had had enough foresight to take out a policy on himself.

"Anyway," she continued, "we're not the only Catholics on Serpentine Parade. The McKays are Catholic and so are the Dorans."

Then Grandmother passed fiery judgment on Mrs. Doran's shadow for never darkening the door of the chapel and letting us down a bucketful in front of the Protestants.

I dragged behind her, not at all grateful for my Grandfather's prudence. It was no consolation to me that the McKays and the Dorans were Catholic. They didn't have children—at least none worth talking about since the McKay brood were grown up and married and Frankie Doran was a soldier in the army.

My melancholy deepened as I looked up at the Cave Hill.

Napoleon's Nose was clearly profiled against a brilliant blue sky. Any bad weather on the way would first have to swathe Napoleon's Nose in clouds before descending on us a few minutes later. But there wasn't a cloud anywhere along the rim of the hill. It wasn't a good day for reading.

We turned onto Serpentine Parade and if Mrs. Sommerville hadn't been hunting greenfly on her rambler, it would have been deserted.

I sat sulking on the old Jacob's biscuit tin at the bottom of the garden. "Why don't you take your doll for a walk in the pram," I mimicked Grandmother's words. I was too big for dolls now—it was a real live baby I wanted. The lifeless thing stared up at me with its glass eyes. It was beautiful all right, and to cheer me up, Grandmother had presented me with my father's christening robe. The doll was decked out in flowing silk and lace, but it wasn't any more alive than my father.

My morbid thoughts were interrupted by Mrs. Doran's

cooing voice on the other side of the hedge as she told Smokey he was the only cat in Ireland lucky enough to get liver stew every Sunday.

The idea came to me while Smokey was lapping up his stew; a few minutes later he slunk through the hedge and stretched out under our fuschia bush, just as he always did.

The wooden pram trundled noisily down the side path, alerting Grandmother that I was taking her advice.

"Don't go too far by yourself, Jennifer," she called after me.

Normally, that "by yourself" would have made me mad. She didn't have to rub it in. But today I didn't care, and even the noise made by the wooden wheels of the pram didn't mortify me. Grandmother was quite right; I shouldn't complain, and I *was* lucky to have anything remotely resembling a pram since luxuries weren't to be had in wartime.

Then I saw Bobby. Bobby McConnell had my grudging admiration. He was the only one on our street who could do everything better than me. The girls were no competition at all, and I could run faster and climb higher than any of the boys—except Bobby. He could beat me at everything even if it was only by a hairsbreadth.

He was closing his garden gate as I approached. This was the strange Sunday Bobby I didn't know too well. There were no bulges sticking out of his back pockets, though I'd bet there'd be a lump of string in them somewhere; his knee socks weren't bagging around his ankles; and he didn't slam the gate off its hinges but instead closed it properly. A black skullcap kept his ginger hair from springing out at the sides. For some queer reason, ginger hair looked all right on Bobby. Maybe it was because his fierce blue eyes were fringed with brown eyelashes instead of the sandy ones which made some red-haired people look bleary-eyed. He looked sombre and sedate in his good black blazer, and his short grey trousers had creases sharp enough to cut butter. His left hand clasped a black Bible.

"Where're you going?" I asked, just for the sake of getting an answer.

"Mars," he said, making his way around the pram.

I ignored him. "I'm taking a wee dander up to the Castle," I said with a fair attempt at nonchalance.

"By yourself?" He said it like he didn't believe me.

I shook my head and pointed inside the pram. "I've got a real live baby in there."

"Liar," he said, but he ducked his head under the hood and peered inside. Smokey let out a snarl and made a slash at him with a lace-covered paw. Bobby jumped back.

"That's not a baby," he snapped. "Smokey's as old as you are."

"He's alive, isn't he?" I said, tucking the little quilt back around Smokey. It was a pity I had to keep him strapped down, but he didn't like wearing the long white gown. I thought he looked quite nice in it.

"Does Mrs. Doran know you've got her cat in there?" Bobby had recovered enough to come up with something like that.

"Well . . . no, she doesn't."

His face took on a look of triumph and I blurted out, "I couldn't very well ask her if I could take her cat for a walk. It's not the same as a dog, y'know!"

That made him laugh. Then I laughed too. The idea of Smokey on a lead was hilarious.

"I wish you didn't have to go to Sunday school," I said, dropping all pretence.

"So do I," he said unexpectedly.

I gave him a hard look and took drastic action.

"I'm going to be the *first* one to run up the tower."

The words hit him like a shower of stones. His knuckles whitened around the Bible and as I watched the short internal struggle begin, the words of the Catechism flashed in front of me: "The Devil is delighted when we give in to temptation." Bobby looked up at the Cave Hill, his face breaking into a naughty grin. The Devil and I had a lot in common right then.

"Wait for me at Grey's Lane," he whispered, jerking his head over at Grandpa McCartney's house. "Oul' Grandpa's just itching for an excuse to get me into trouble again. See him pretending not to notice us?"

Grandpa McCartney was an archenemy. He must have hundreds of our balls in his house. We wouldn't have played near his garden at all except we liked the challenge: our deadly aim against his blackthorn walking stick.

"I'll see you after Sunday School." The whole street heard Bobby say it.

"You're a fly man, Bobby McConnell," I said with a grin and set off for the hard push up to Grey's Lane. Sunday afternoon now promised to be anything but boring.

Even in daylight Grey's Lane was shadowy. The top branches of the big chestnut trees lining it on both sides formed a canopy which only prolonged rain could penetrate with any success. The sun was hard put getting through the tangle of branches and leaves, but managed to dapple the lane with a shower of sunspots. With every breath of wind the golden spots shimmered and danced. Grey's Lane always seemed to be *moving* and no matter how beautiful it was, I wished Bobby would hurry up. Grey's Lane was no place to be alone even in daylight and, try as I might, I couldn't banish the winter yarns about it from my mind.

I wiped my sweaty hands on the quilt and screamed telepathic messages to Bobby, hoping he'd get them and get a move on. My ears, finely tuned now to pick up the faintest sound, strained for the *clip clop* of hooves and I closed my eyes to blot out a vision of Galloper Grey, our very own headless horseman.

Years and years ago, Major Grey murdered his wife and kept her bloody remains locked in a room at Greymount. I didn't understand all the ramifications leading up to her death since it seemed to me that liking a groom wasn't a viable motive for murder. Major Grey, a drunkard of the deepest dye, terrorized Greencastle for years after the murder. He galloped his big black stallion over the spacious grounds of Greymount, thundering down on any hapless villager who was trespassing. A sporting man, they said, he'd yell a warning to his intended victims, give them a bit of a start, then spur his horse to the hunt. He'd whack them with his crop all the way off his lands and many's the unfortunate turned idiot after such an encounter. Grandmother said there was ample proof that Galloper Grey still rode out often.

What really got me was the part about the children. It seems a few of them disappeared, their last whereabouts pinpointed at Grey's Lane. Neither hide nor hair of them was ever seen again. At the outcry following, even the law was forced to take a closer look at this particular scion of the landed gentry.

But it wasn't the law that caught up with Major Grey; justice, in the form of a huge slate tile, overtook him during a winter gale. It whipped loose from the roof of Greymount—some said from right over the room entombing Lady Grey—and decapitated him. Cut his head right off his shoulders!

We were left with his ghost. The golf links now sprawled over the grounds of Greymount. The links were Galloper Grey's haunt, especially on stormy nights—them and Grey's Lane, which cleaved down through the middle of the soft greens.

I think I was ready for running right then, but the "Hey!" Bobby shouted came just in time, and I quickly lounged up against a tree, legs crossed, the picture of boredom.

Bobby ran towards us and I noticed his pockets were bulging. I'd bet two weeks *Beano* comics he'd made a run through the links and swiped a couple of golf balls. The links were strictly forbidden territory for two reasons. The first was simple and easily ignored—the golfers didn't like children. But the second held a power over us few things could match.

There were three dams to the left of what Bobby said was the ninth hole rough, each dangerous in a unique way. The first was so deep it was reputed to be "Bottomless." That word made a distinct impression on me. Besides, I couldn't swim. Neither could Bobby. And even when other water was tranquil, Bottomless had wicked little waves flurrying its surface—like there was something alive in it. A blue summer sky was never mirrored in Bottomless; the closest it came to reflecting cordiality was a light grey.

The second dam, separated from Bottomless by a two-foot strip of land, was clogged with weeds which Grandmother said would drag a person down, even if they could swim.

The third, also with a little bit of a bank separating it from the others, was really a bog. Strange shrubs and trees sprang from it, and patches of dark, oily water mingled with what looked like long and very green grass. That one, they said, just swallowed you up without a trace.

On the few forays we'd made into the links, Bobby and I kept well clear of the dams.

"How many golf balls do you think are in there?" Bobby McConnell asked as he reached me. I studied the pockets.

"Two." I was definite. "Maybe three," I added when his lip curled.

"Not here—*there!*"

He pointed to the big rough in the distance. "Hundreds," he whispered reverently. "Bloody hundreds."

I got the drift of his thoughts but I wasn't having any of that nonsense. The tower was one thing, but I *could* run. Funny enough, Bobby didn't sneer and call names at me as he was prone to do on occasions like this. He just gave a lingering look at the ninth hole rough and thrust the Bible at me.

"Here," he said, "put this in the pram."

Now, glad as I was to see him I would have turned myself inside out for him, but the thought crossed my mind that Miss McGrath had been very clear in the Catechism class: Never were we to attend any Protestant services or listen to Protestant doctrine. It followed that to actually set hands on one of their Bibles might constitute contamination of some kind.

"Here," he said again, and I had to keep myself from visibly shrinking away from him.

"When did your last skivvy die?" I said. "Put it in yourself."

Bobby sighed and put the Bible at the bottom of the pram.

"I better put these in there, too," he grumbled, divesting himself of his blazer and skullcap. Then he rolled up his shirt-sleeves and rolled down his knee socks. He looked like himself again.

The Castle grounds were just across the road and I struggled with the pram, which got stuck in the tram lines, knowing full well not to expect any help from Bobby. He wouldn't be caught dead touching a pram where anyone could see him, but I knew he'd help once we got into the grounds. Smokey had fallen asleep, although it was beyond me how anyone could sleep with the noise those wooden wheels made.

In a matter of minutes we were in Sherwood Forest, and Robin Hood disappeared in search of a good branch to make a bow. Since the main path climbed steadily, it was easier to drag the pram behind me, and I wound my way deeper into the woods. Overhead, great blooms of rhododendrons splashed crimson against patches of sky, capturing my attention for a moment by their shocking pageantry.

But it was the strangely muted brilliance of thousands of bluebells that threw me into a stupor. The deep blue carpet, shading to light purple in the shadows, sprawled everywhere, around the trees and up and down the fern banks. I just stood there looking, unwilling even to call Bobby.

It wasn't as if I'd never seen them before—they came out every May—but there was a queer aching inside my chest I'd never had the other times. I plucked one, a big one with nine bells on it, and the pungent sap oozed from the broken stem, reminding me they didn't live long once they were picked. Grandmother said it was because they were wild. The fairies lived in them, and if you ever heard a bluebell ring, it was the sound of your own death knell.

"Move and you're dead."

I swung 'round as Bobby leaped from behind a tree armed with a new bow and arrow. He lowered his weapon.

"What's the matter?" he said.

"I don't know!" I flung my arms out because I didn't know what else to do with them. Then the awful thought struck that Bobby might think I was getting soppy over a bunch of flowers. "I think these bluebells are making me sick."

"Well, c'mon—we're almost there."

"There" was the crumbling remains of the stables belonging to the great Castle. The thick granite walls, engulfed with ivy that crept up over the parapet, still supported a flat roof, and that was our objective. And the only way up was via the tower.

Last year we'd made it to the seventh stair before becoming crappers and almost killing one another to get back outside. It was pitch dark in there and it had the eerie smell of a place not used to living things. I'd read that somewhere, and the tower was the only place I knew that fitted the description. God knows what would be waiting around every curve of the stairway. It did curve, but how many times or how many steps we didn't know.

We sat on the edge of what once had been a fountain, a huge bowl with a statue of a fat baby in the middle of it, planning our strategy. Bobby said he'd bring his bow and arrow just in case, and I said a lot of good that would do in the dark. Maybe we should wait until summer before tackling the tower, I thought, but I didn't dare voice this second trepidation or Bobby would have jumped on the excuse to put it off and *I'd* have been branded the scaredy-cat.

The dark green wrinkles of velvet lichen draping the fountain made a comfortable cushion, and I'd have been quite content to sit there doing nothing more exciting than stirring the stew of dank leaves in its basin until they gave off a musty smell I liked. The fountain reminded me of the baptismal font I'd seen in Whiteabbey chapel when I was there to get confirmed. Baptismal font! Inspiration seized me a second time.

"Bobby," I cried, jumping off the font, "let's baptise Smokey!"

He looked at me as if I'd grown another eye. Bobby McConnell might be better than me at everything, but he was terribly slow on the uptake sometimes.

"Look," I said, pointing at Smokey lying in the grandeur of the christening robe. "And there's the font." I nodded at the fountain.

"What'll we christen him?"

I didn't even have to think about it. "Smokey Francis Doran," I said.

Bobby frowned as if he didn't like my creation. "The Francis is for Mrs. Doran's son. He's in the army," I explained. "I think Frankie would be honoured to have Smokey called after him."

"No. I mean what will he *be*?"

I saw what he meant. This was dangerous ground we'd never treaded before. I knew it was dangerous because Grandmother often said, "You watch what you say to them, Jennifer." She didn't have to say exactly what I should watch either, anymore than she had to spell out that "Watch the road" meant you watched for trams and cars. "Watch what you say to them," instilled over the years, meant you didn't talk about *anything* akin to Catholicism when dealing with those of the opposite persuasion. It had nothing to do with differences in doctrine either. No, it got down to little things like, "On my way to Mass I saw . . ." or "Aunt Nin told us this morning that Father Sheridan's leaving Green-castle." Never in a thousand years would I have seen fit to impart that news to Bobby.

Grandmother said we'd provoke them by alluding to our Catholicism with words like "Mass" and "Father Sheridan." I knew what the consequences were if I didn't "Watch the road," but I had no idea what would happen if I didn't "Watch what I said." Protestants didn't watch what they said, for Bobby had no compunction about mentioning "church," "Sunday School," or the "Reverend Nutt."

I decided I wasn't going to just mealy-mouth my way into another subject as I normally did. Bobby won at enough things as it was.

"Well," I said, taking a firm stance, "he'll have to be Catholic."

"It's my Bible," said Bobby, equally firm, "so I say he's Protestant."

"But I know the words. I learned them from the Cate-chism." I thought that should clear things up right there. Protestants didn't learn any Catechism in their schools.

"You don't need fancy words," he said stolidly.

That was news to me. "They're not fancy," I argued. "Besides, Bobby, Mrs. Doran is Catholic so Smokey has to be a Catholic cat."

He thought about that for a minute. "My daddy says there're too many Catholics as it is," he said, and his chin jutted out.

My hackles rose. "There are far more Protestants and you know it, Bobby McConnell!"

"My daddy says he thanks God for his Gration because without it there'd be more Catholics and we'd all be ruled by Old Red Socks." Bobby laughed. "That's what he calls the Pope—Old Red Socks!" He doubled over, slapping his hand against his thigh, and I knew my face was as red as the Pope's stockings.

"That's not funny, Bobby," I huffed, but he didn't stop laughing until I asked him what his daddy's Gration was.

Bobby shrugged his shoulders. "How should I know? He just says, 'Thank God for my Gration.' But whatever it is, my daddy says it makes a lot of Catholics leave." Bobby tickled the fat baby with the point of his arrow. I was speechless for the first time in my life. Was Bobby saying Catholics didn't belong in Northern Ireland? A moment later he went straight for the jugular.

"He says, my daddy does, that Northern Ireland is a Protestant state for a Protestant people. He says . . ."

Bobby's daddy had had the arena to himself long enough. I leapt in with Grandmother.

"Well, my Granny says she wishes *you'd* all leave and go back where you came from—that you're nothing but a bunch of transplanted Scots trying hard to be English!" My lungs were sore from exertion, but I managed a last scathing, "She says Protestants aren't really Irish at all," in the same breath. He hadn't even the good grace to be insulted.

"Who wants to be? My daddy says we're British and proud of it," he said, squaring his shoulders.

"There!" I accused him. "That proves it's you who doesn't belong here. Why don't you go back to Britain?"

"I'm *in* Britain! Nothern Ireland is a part of Britain, you dope!"

Oh, God! Trapped by my own mouth. The geography book said it was; Miss McGrath said it was, although it always struck me she did so with a reticence quite unlike her. To save some face, I clung to Grandmother's misguided notion that Northern Ireland was a part of Ireland.

"Well, my Granny says it isn't," I retorted, "and I'm not a dope!"

"Only a dope would want to christen a cat," he said, poking his arrow into the fat baby's belly button.

"Just forget the whole idea." My voice was sulky.

"It was a stupid idea anyway," he said, hopping off the fountain.

I let him away with that one only because he announced he was ready to climb the tower. Anyway, there was no use trying to convince this ignoramus of anything. He didn't even know what a Gration was; that it was a Protestant word I was sure. I'd have to ask Grandmother about it. She knew a lot about Protestant words even if her geography wasn't reliable. She wasn't alone in pretending Northern Ireland was a part of Ireland either. All the Catholics of Greencastle pretended the same thing. Talk about coming to believe your own lies! I'd come a cropper by doing just that.

We left the still heathen Smokey and walked over to the tower. Bobby thought it would be a good idea to hold my hand in case I got scared, and I had an awful time deciding whether to let him make me the scapegoat. But if anyone, or anything, grabbed me in there—well, Mr. McConnell would find it hard shaking me loose.

At the count of three we made our mad dash into the blackness, and in seconds we had rounded three bends without being killed. I was shocked to see daylight so soon and we burst out onto the roof, gulping and heaving, but unscathed. Bobby tried to tell me he got on the roof first, but he modified his statement to declare a draw when he saw blue murder in my eyes. For the first time Bobby hadn't won. Neither had I, but momentarily it felt like it. Bobby wasn't invincible, and my mind was already whirring with aspiration to best him at something once and for all. We strutted about the roof surveying our captured territory and repelling invaders for quite a while before Bobby said,

"Somehow it wasn't as bad as it seemed last year."

"It was bad enough," I replied, but I'd been thinking the same thing. Of course, we were a lot older this year.

We sat dangling our legs over the parapet and I saw him eyeing Napoleon's Nose. The Throne Path, the only way up, looked like a wrinkled ribbon some unseen giant had hurled over the face of the cliff. But the sun had slipped behind Napoleon's Nose, leaving us in the shadow, and I was grateful we didn't have to conquer it today. Napoleon's Nose could be vaulted next year. And the dams the year after that.

The woods around us seemed hushed now, the trees and bushes darker, and I kept my imagination at bay, for if I hadn't I'm sure I'd have seen them slink closer. Somewhere among the rhododendrons a lone bird sang; not the trilling sound of morning, but the clear lament of evening. Maybe he didn't have a nest to go to like the other birds.

Above the tree line the lough shimmered in the distance, and suddenly I had it! Oh, it was lovely. The days of Bobby McConnell's being first and best were numbered—his reign would end just as soon as summer came. I was going to learn how to *swim!*

Fragmented glints of the dams showed through the tops of the trees, but I certainly wasn't daft enough to use them as swimming pools.

I shivered, knowing full well the sudden spasm wasn't from cold. It was the strange shiver people said you got when someone tramped over your grave.

"We're going to catch it, Bobby," I said. "We've stayed too long."

CHAPTER
3

We ran that pram all the way down the road and stood panting at the top of our street.

"*Hey, you!*" The words cut through the muffled thumping in my ears. Bobby, in the midst of cramming himself into his blazer, froze in a good imitation of a scarescrow. Constable Johnston wasn't to be trifled with, and if he said "Hey you," you snapped to attention and said "Yes, Mr. Johnston," which we did.

He was the tallest man I'd ever seen, even taller than Uncle Dan. His face seemed set in a perpetual frown because his black bushy eyebrows met over the bridge of his nose. And he always looked at Bobby and me with grave suspicion.

The thumping in my ears was no longer muffled.

"You," Constable Johnston said, glaring at Bobby, "were supposed to be at Sunday School." He left the statement hanging there long enough for a fleeting vision of Grandpa McCartney's gumsy old mouth to materialise in my head.

The inevitable "Where have you been?" followed, and Bobby caved in immediately. Not that I blamed him, no, indeed; I'd have done the same thing. Constable Johnston had no interest in my whereabouts at all for he just growled, "Get away on home wi' ye" to both of us. In reply, Constable Johnston got a venomous snarl as Smokey alerted his deliverer. I thought my knees would give way and I looked wildly at Bobby, but he declined to look at me.

Constable Johnston reached inside the pram, and he had the strange notion Smokey was wearing God's nightgown for that's what he said when he picked up the squirming christening robe. I told him no, that it was my daddy's christening robe, and at that point Bobby disassociated himself from me and declared he had had nothing to do with the taking of Smokey.

"You get home, McConnell—I'll see to you later," said Constable Johnston, and Bobby took off at a right clip.

Smokey was fighting mad now and Constable Johnston's big fingers couldn't get a grip on the tiny pearl buttons. He hoisted Smokey up under his oxter. This was the last straw for Smokey, and he sank his teeth into his gaolor's arresting hand.

"Vicious bugger!" yowled the Constable as he clamped his other hand under Smokey's chin. "Get thisss bloody thing *offff*." The words came at me like a long hiss, and I jumped into the fray. Those buttons were hard to undo, but Smokey's natural state was eventually resumed when I drew off the offending gown.

"There we are," I said, making light of the whole thing, "Smokey's as right as rain." But Constable Johnston wasn't in the mood for chatter—he just glowered with his beetle-brows and pointed down the street. The pram became a tumbril leading me to the guillotine, its wooden wheels trundling over the pavement just like in *A Tale of Two Cities*.

Constable Johnston gave our knocker a few thuds and Grandmother opened the front door. In all the time I'd lived with Grandmother and Aunt Madge I'd never crossed the threshold by way of the front door. That was reserved for visitors we didn't know. Grandmother didn't invite us in so the trial was conducted right on the steps. Most of the whole story came out without much help from me.

But we didn't get to the sentencing because Mrs. Doran came barging through the gap in the hedge, yelling to Grandmother, "It's all over, Maggie! It's really over. Oh, dear God in Heaven, it's all *over!*"

I'd never seen Mrs. Doran in such a state. She'd forgotten to take the wave grips out of her hair and was actually outside in her slippers! If it had been anyone else I wouldn't have noticed, but Mrs. Doran was very particular about how she was seen in public. She actually got all rigged out in her good tweed costume and felt hat just to do her shopping.

She gave another yelp and her round brown eyes got rounder when she saw Smokey. Constable Johnston quickly dumped Smokey on her chest.

"Oh, Smokey, you're a bad wee article to scare me like that." She held him up to her face. "Where *did* you get to?"

I thought, "Here it comes—they're going to tell her," but Mrs. Doran was already urging Grandmother to turn on the wireless. It was official—the war was over! I thought it was wonderful news.

Mrs. Doran shooed me in our front door, but I didn't have time to savour the experience for another unprecedented event took place—Constable Johnston followed after us and took up a stand by the front window. No Protestant that I knew of had ever been in our house before, and Constable Johnston's vast form made our living room seem as small as Aunt Nin's.

I squeezed in between Aunt Madge and Uncle Dan on the settee, somewhat comforted that Uncle Dan was between me and the constable. Uncle Dan looked like a formidable match for anyone. His chin was granite hard and stubborn and his eyes could take on a flinty blue glare sometimes when he answered Grandmother.

Then Mr. Doran came in by the back door and sat near the scullery—another first—and I realized that the news was more significant than I had thought.

Mr. Doran had "won a bit on the pools" and gave his winning strategy to anybody who'd listen. He maintained the only way to pick the pools was to fortify oneself first, then proceed with a kind of ritual which somehow involved sticking a pin in the coupons. Grandpa McCartney was the only one to avail himself of Mr. Doran's expertise. The two held weekly sessions that thus far had yielded "nothing but sore heads in the morning for them," Grandmother said.

Everyone was hushed as Grandmother fiddled with the knobs on the wireless. It let out a few of its screaming *aiaiee*s before picking up the chimes of Big Ben.

"What've ye got on there, Maggie?" said Mr. Doran, winking a red eye at Grandmother. "Tarzan?"

I thought that was funny, but then I always thought Mr. Doran was funny. He winked and nodded a lot when he talked and Grandmother had dubbed him "The Gentleman Bricklayer" because nobody would ever have known he was near muck or cement by the look of his clothes. He wore a tweed suit, a bit droopy in the knees and backside, and a shirt and tie to work, and he carried his tools in an attaché case. If it weren't for the level, which was too long to fit in the case, his trade would have been guessed as an architect or something.

But he was a far cry from gentility tonight as he sat puffing away on a Woodbine, actively courting Mrs. Doran's furious glances at his collarless shirt and bare braces. I wished I could tell him the strict "No talking" rules that Grandmother enforced while the news was on. She was the only one who had licence to dissent or agree with the commentator, and Aunt Madge and I endured her interpretations and grumblings in total silence. To Grandmother, the news was a serious business.

She didn't grumble as much when Lord Haw Haw gave us the news from away over in Germany every Sunday night. Now I didn't understand him at all. I knew he was an Englishman because of his snooty accent, but it seemed to me he was on Germany's side, always extolling the virtues of Hitler and denouncing Churchill for deluding the British people. Sometimes he addressed himself to the Irish, as if he had a special affection for us, and told us that the Fuehrer—that meant Hitler—had great admiration for the Irish people's long struggle against English aggression and oppression. I suppose that's why Grandmother liked him so much.

Mrs. Doran didn't like him at all. One day when I re-peated something he'd said, she held her hands over her ears and said it was treasonous to listen to that man and that I was never, *never* to mention him in the presence of the ladies of the British Legion. I didn't mention this to Grandmother, for I didn't like the sound of the word "trea-sonous." I didn't say anything about Mrs. Doran's member-ship in the British Legion either. Actually, I felt it was the appropriate club for Mrs. Doran since her son was a soldier fighting in the war and the ladies of the Legion assembled first-aid kits and knit socks and mufflers for the veterans. But a primeval instinct, handed down from some canny an-cestor, warned me Grandmother wouldn't like it. Anything with the word "British" in it was anathema to Grandmother.

I had broached the subject of peace.

"What's peace like, Granny?"

"Peace?" She looked confused. "Sure, how would I know—I've never had any."

"Mrs. Doran says the Germans are beat and that peace is just around the corner."

"Haahh! She'd better hope she's wrong. This is as much peace as we've ever had—one man's war is another's peace."

God, but I didn't understand Grandmother at all. And she didn't touch spirits either!

Lord Haw hadn't been on for weeks now and I knew Grandmother missed him.

I snuggled deeper into the settee and Uncle Dan put his arm around me and bent his head to say something, but Grandmother put up a warning finger and shushed him.

"This is the BBC Home Service—and here is the news." Mr. Liddell, his distinct voice familiar to every British sub-ject, broke his tradition of emotionless pronunciation and allowed a ring of ebullience to permeate his diction as he told us England had been delivered from the jaws of the German war machine. Then Winston Churchill's voice came through and said the same thing. I liked the way he said "waugh" when he meant war, although Grandmother felt his pronunciation was affected because his mouth was always stuffed with cotton wool. When he'd finished, pandemonium broke out in our living room and everybody was talking at once.

"The first thing *I'm* going to do is burn that bloody blackout curtain," said Mr. Doran, snapping his braces with his left thumb. "And don't give me any more of that pink lint on my piece," he added, looking at Mrs. Doran without the hint of a wink or a nod.

"But Sammy, I thought you liked Spam." She looked hurt and I thought everyone had taken leave of their senses when they busted out laughing. Then it dawned on me. The "pink lint" he meant were the square pieces of fine flannel cloth used as first-aid dressings. They *did* look like slices of Spam, and apparently Mr. Doran felt Spam tasted the same, too. I suppose everybody did. We were sick of the sight of it, for even with Grandmother's black market endeavours, Spam was all too often on the table.

Uncle Dan's eyes had a thoughtful look about them. He tapped his pipe into the old tobacco tin he carried with him. "There'll be a building boom, Sammy, and good bricklayers like you and me could make a mint."

Aunt Madge chimed in, "And no more clothes coupons! If you have the money, you can buy as much as you like."

"Aunt Madge," I said, putting two and two together, "if you don't need coupons for clothes now, does that mean I'll be able to get sweeties without sweetie coupons?"

Aunt Madge gave me a big hug and said, "Yes, love." That was the best news yet and I made mental plans to set new records for the consumption of clove rock, bull's-eyes, and brandyballs. The taste of cloves, peppermint, and burning brandy was almost real. Yes, indeed, life without the war sounded promising.

Mr. Doran shook hands with Constable Johnston. "Now, Constable, let's you and I nip through the hedge for a wee drap of something that's not buttermilk and celebrate properly," he said. But Mrs. Doran interrupted before Constable Johnston had a chance to answer.

"You've celebrated enough this weekend . . ." She cut herself short suddenly, and her bottom lip began to flutter. "My Frankie will be coming home," she wailed, and she burst into tears as we all sat there with our mouths hanging open, especially me.

Aunt Madge rushed over to her with a hanky. "It's all right, Mrs. Doran, the war has rattled everybody's nerves. Everything will be all right now it's over."

"Oh, Madge," she quivered, "I've been upset all day. Smokey disappeared and I couldn't find him." She blew her nose. "And I just *knew* something had happened to Frankie!"

My heart stopped! I know it did.

"Ach, Christ, wumman—not *that* again," exclaimed Mr. Doran, and he turned back to Constable Johnston. "That buggering cat—if it eats something it shouldn't, she gets it into her head the cat's dying and it's an *omen* that Frankie's lying shot to hell."

Mrs. Doran's shoulders shuddered and she wailed again into the hanky.

Constable Johnston said, "Aye, women are like that," and gave me a chilling look. "Well," he said to everyone else, "I've got to get on home. All the best, now." He tipped his cap and left.

Mrs. Doran bobbed her head in answer to Aunt Madge's soothings. She raised her reddened nose suddenly and her eyes, tight from crying, peered after Mr. Doran, who was following Constable Johnston.

"Sammy! Sammy! Where are you off to?"

Mr. Doran gave her a wink and a nod and said he was running through the hedge for some sustenance.

"Oh," said Mrs. Doran as if the wind had been knocked out of her. "Well, don't you forget, Sammy Doran, you've got your work to go to in the morning."

Grandmother hadn't said anything since Churchill, but

no sooner had the door closed on Constable Johnston's back than she announced that Britain was bankrupt.

Uncle Dan's eyes twinkled. "I knew you'd brighten up as soon as the B-Special left," he said.

B-Special! So that's why she'd put a muzzle on her mouth—she was minding her own rule of "Watch what you say to them." It was Grandmother's conviction that B-Specials, those malevolent creatures in summer yarns who hunted and killed Catholic prey under cover of darkness, were the same men who posed as policemen during the day.

I didn't for one minute think Constable Johnston was a B-Special. A B-Special would have up and told Mrs. Doran I took her cat. That's just the kind of low trick they'd pull. No, Constable Johnston was as nice as ninepence in my book, but I was glad he was gone.

"What was he doing here anyway?" Uncle Dan asked Grandmother.

"He brought Jennifer home," she said, and I waited for the addendum "with Smokey," but it didn't come. She was already attacking Churchill, who I knew was stigmatized by virtue of being his father's son.

"Did you hear the great praise Churchill had for Northern Ireland and his attack on the Free State for not letting them use the ports down there?" Grandmother's lips disappeared she'd clamped them together so hard. "That's him making sure the Orangemen here remember how to vote next month. His father over the back! Anytime the Tories are in trouble, just dig up the old bones of contention in Ireland and the loyal Orangemen of Northern Ireland will vote them in!"

"Ach, Maggie," exclaimed Mrs. Doran, "you're reading things in that aren't there. Winston Churchill is a great man—a great man." If it hadn't been for him, we all might have ended up speaking German."

"There was a time when the Irish spoke Gaelic," snapped Grandmother.

Mrs. Doran rolled her eyes as if summoning patience with a stubborn child. "Maggie, that man—Hitler, I mean—wanted to rule the world!"

"And England never did, I suppose?"

Mrs. Doran had no answer for that, but Uncle Dan said something under his breath about England's sense of fair play being involved. Mrs. Doran confirmed that, yes, Dan was right, only England had stood up against Hitler to help those other poor countries. "That's why my Frankie joined up," she said, and her round brown eyes were proud.

"Fair play, is it?" Grandmother ignored Frankie's sacrifice and her eyes swept past Mrs. Doran and impaled Uncle Dan to the settee. "And just where was this fair play hiding when it came to Ireland?" she said with a civility I always held suspect.

Mrs. Doran gave a nervous little laugh. "Ach, Maggie, sure that's all past. That's the trouble with us—we're always dredging up the past."

"The past in Ireland is never past," Grandmother replied to no one in particular before she lit on Uncle Dan again.

"Some scholar *you* turned out to be. No wonder the Christian Brothers got rid of you. God rest your poor mother, for she'd turn in her grave if . . ."

Aunt Madge came through the scullery door carrying a nervous tray of rattling teacups. "The Christian Brothers didn't get rid of him, Ma. He got rid of them."

"Either way," Grandmother said stoically, "he's not teaching history for the good Brothers now, is he?"

Mrs. Doran's head swivelled round to face Uncle Dan.

"Well, now, Dan—a history professor!" she said, as if speaking to a priest.

I mean, it was like Uncle Dan had undergone the same metamorphosis Raymond McVeigh had. One day the village spoke of Raymond as "that sleekit McVeigh twerp" and the next, after the wand of ordination waved, we said with veneration, "The *Father* is up from Maynooth visiting his mother, God bless him."

"Well, now," Mrs. Doran said again, "I'd no idea."

Mrs. Doran missed a lot of what went on since she didn't frequent the village much and preferred to do her shopping up in Belfast.

"And what in the name of God are you out labouring for?"

"Nobody tries to tell me what way to dig ditches," was all Uncle Dan said, and he gave full attention to keeping the belly of his pipe glowing.

"Oh, I see," said Mrs. Doran, but she didn't look as if she saw at all. Then she lowered her eyes for an instant. "You know, Dan, my Frankie is going into a profession, too. Aye, the army's using him in the Signal Corps, you know, and it'll stand him in good stead when he gets out. Of course"—she gave a little squeak of mirth—"he always was good at his sums."

Then she went into a detailed account of the struggle to keep Frankie in school past fourteen years of age, and this innocuous talk might have gone on, but Grandmother was unwilling to loosen her death-grip on Churchill.

"Aye, he'll go to all lengths to discredit the Free State." She gave the dying coals a few stabs with the poker.

Mrs. Doran came to Mr. Churchill's defence. "Well, he didn't have to go to any lengths a'tall," she said hotly. "Closing the ports was a vindictive act and—well, when I think of my Frankie—well," she said again, "it doesn't endear me to Mr. De Valera or the Free State, I can tell you that!"

I watched Grandmother's knuckles tighten around the poker until they were bloodless. Mrs. Doran had really done it now. To us Catholics in Northern Ireland, the Free State was a magic kingdom—the real Ireland, they said, won back from the English in 1916 by the blood of Irish sons. In my geography book, the Free State was coloured an appropriate emerald green and covered most of the map of Ireland,

and Northern Ireland was just a dot of orange in the northeast corner. I knew Protestants didn't see the Free State in the same revered light, but this was the first time I'd heard a Catholic say anything less than venerable about it.

It was Uncle Dan who broke the silence. "Now, Mrs. Doran," he said, "I don't see eye-to-eye with old Dev on a lot of things, but the smartest thing he ever did was to declare the Free State neutral and close the ports to everybody. No, it wasn't vindictive, though Maggie's right"—he gave a grave nod at Grandmother—"it'll be taken and used that way here."

Grandmother smoothed her apron as if wiping off Uncle Dan's conciliatory gesture. "If it'd been up to me I'd have let Hitler use them like he asked," I heard her mutter. Mrs. Doran heard her, too.

"Maggie! It's talk like that that keeps things stirred up." She looked at Uncle Dan as if she expected him to second her, but Uncle Dan just covered his mouth with his hand. "Catholics bring a lot of trouble on themselves talking like that and acting as if everything English or Protestant was poison." She looked a bit helpless. "I mean, you see it all the time—even in little things—people running out of the picture house so they won't have to stand up for the King . . ."

Uncle Dan laughed. "Right you are there, Mrs. Doran, I don't think there's a Catholic around here who's ever seen the end of a picture. Bloody frustrating sometimes."

I agreed, although I didn't say so. I hated being rushed out of the cinema right before the end so we wouldn't have to stand up for the English anthem.

Once, when Bobby and I attended the Saturday matinee, I just couldn't desert a beleaguered D'Artagnan, who was defending a staircase single-handedly while his mates sat drinking at the inn unaware their leader was taking the "One for all" pledge seriously. The next thing I knew, the ominous roll of drums started and everyone got to their feet. I was caught. I knew I couldn't make a run for it once the anthem started. There was an unwritten rule that if you were fool enough to get caught you'd bloody well have to squirm your way through it.

I stood up while King George saluted his minions from the balcony of Buckingham Palace and the deliberate, plodding "God Save Our Gracious King" surged through the cinema. Bobby stood very straight, head back, shoulders square, eyes riveted to the screen, while I shifted from one foot to the other, grateful he couldn't see the thick flush on my face in the dark. I thought my shifting feet had clomped down on Bobby's toe when he let out a baying "Gaw-wid," but he was just joining in the pleading last line and finished the *"save our king"* in budding Caruso style.

Now, I liked the King. In fact, I liked the Queen and the Princesses, too, and nothing would have pleased me more than to join in the anthem with Bobby. But, had they known I harboured such sentiments, the Catholics of Greencastle would have treated me as a direct descendant of Judas Iscariot. They maintained it wasn't our anthem; that our anthem was the "Soldier's Song" they sang in the Free State.

"Well, I think it's low behaviour," sniffed Mrs. Doran.

Grandmother took a violent pinch of snuff. It always amazed me that snuff didn't make her sneeze. When I had a cold and my nose was all bunged up, Grandmother prescribed a pinch of Leahy & Kelly's Regent mixture, which acted on me like a stick of dynamite.

"And you don't think the Orange parades are low?" Grandmother's voice was simpering, and I thought something was the matter with her.

"Of course I think they're low!" declared Mrs. Doran. "But the Protestants have *quit* their Orange carry-ons. They haven't walked on the Twelfth since the war started."

I'd never seen the Orangemen celebrating the Twelfth, but it was given bitter mention in a lot of summer yarns.

"We should let bygones be bygones too," Mrs. Doran

continued. "This time Catholic boys volunteered right along with Protestant boys, and we fought the same fight. And that," she added emphatically, "is going to make a difference."

"They'll use anybody for cannon fodder," Grandmother said, and Mrs. Doran's shoulders flinched. "Mark my words, Mary Doran"—Grandmother's eyes glinted as she spoke—"it doesn't do to forget."

The clock on the mantelpiece ticked very loudly for a few seconds. Then somebody said Johnny Nod was in my eyes, and I took advantage of the excuse and headed for the stairs. Nobody else knew what Grandmother meant when she said she'd speak to me in the morning, and I felt her eyes boring through my shoulder blades until I got out of her sight. They were still talking and I heard Uncle Dan say, "I hope you're right, Mrs. Doran," but there wasn't much hope in his voice.

I padded up the stairs, grateful that Constable Johnston and Grandmother had screened Mrs. Doran from the truth about Smokey. Oh, God! God! What if Smokey had been lost? A gruesome picture, dredged up from some matinee, showed me Frankie Doran lying bleeding on a battlefield. Would Mrs. Doran's superstition about Frankie have become reality? Uncle Dan said superstition was a Catholic disease and that people should quit scaring themselves with such nonsense. Well, nonsense or not, Smokey Doran could rest in peace under our fuchsia bush ever after, for he had nothing more to fear from me. I swore I wouldn't lay hands on that cat again if my life depended on it. Then I took the swear back. They said God sometimes tested swears.

I got beneath the covers, stretched like a corpse, and put my hands under my head, all ready to dissect the peculiar happenings of the day.

They seemed to think—well, at least Aunt Madge and Mrs. Doran did—that things would be different now. That was no great revelation. People could rest easy in their beds in the future without being scattered out into air-raid shelters. Belfast had been lucky, they said, for with the exception of one deadly Luftwaffe raid away back in 1941, we were nowhere near as harassed as the people in England, Scotland, and Wales. Perhaps the Fuehrer did like the Irish.

But something was up—I could feel it. Although the dark, siren-screaming days of the war were gone, Grandmother and Mrs. Doran seemed to be pitching battle standards in anticipation of some other fray. I inclined towards Mrs. Doran's camp. Bygones, she'd said. Did Bobby's daddy . . . ?

It'll be a long time before I go to sleep on an empty stomach again! Bobby's daddy and Grandmother kept changing faces with each other, and I dreamt all night about the cat. Smokey changed faces, too, spitting and girning at me with a wizened old baby's face.

Grandmother didn't have a chance to resurrect the past before I left for school the next morning, and by the time I got home she was slitting the white throats of leeks and grousing to herself as she flung them into the pot. I didn't care what the reason for her bad temper was as long as it didn't have anything to do with me. But before we'd finished tea that evening, I cared very much.

CHAPTER
4

Aunt Madge came home from the mill about six o'clock and the three of us sat down to tea at the scullery table.

"They're going to have a Victory Party to celebrate." Grandmother might as well have announced her bunions were throbbing. She said "They're" in the tone she always used for Protestants. "Aye," she continued, "they're getting the whole street out next Saturday morning."

My mouth was crammed with buttered barnbrack but I still managed to ask, "Us, too?" Instinctively, my "us" was inflected with Catholic reference. The dimensions of personal pronouns expanded when accompanied by a certain, though undefinable, stress on the words.

When Grandmother said they'd deigned to include us, I just wanted to kiss her. But Grandmother didn't go in much for kissing so I shoved another hunk of barnbrack into my mouth. Grandmother baked the best barnbrack I'd ever tasted, no question about it, the sweet, raisiny bread was almost cake.

Then the barnbrack stuck in my throat.

"They want to hang bunting on all the houses."

If our scullery had been an empty cathedral, those words couldn't have reverberated any more than they did.

"Oh, no!" Aunt Madge exclaimed. She looked dismayed but she didn't say anything else.

I gave a monumental swallow and the barnbrack painfully cleared my throat. "What's bunting, Granny?"

"Wee Union Jacks all strung together."

"Oh."

I wished I could think quietly about the implications, but I knew they were bad just from the first quick feeling of dread that hit me. My brain summed up the whole thing in one lightning instant, made its conclusions, and then left me in the dark with only the gnawing warning that the news was not to my advantage.

All Aunt Madge said was, "Who was telling you this?" and Grandmother lunged into an attack on Mrs. Doran. I was afraid Mrs. Doran would hear her over the hedge.

"Oh, she's in it up to the hilt! On the decorating council, indeed." Grandmother drew her lips into a thin line. "I tell you, that woman would turn her coat the day before tomorrow if she thought she could get in *their* good graces." A deaf man could have heard the inflection in the personal pronoun now. "But when she got up and told me that the

McKays had given their consent as well—they're in their dotage anyway—I stopped her dead in her tracks."

Aunt Madge picked little pieces of flax off her blue overall, and when there were none left, she still picked at it.

The green chips in Grandmother's eyes came to life. "Stopped her dead in her tracks, I did! Says I, *You* debase your house if you have a mind to, but there'll be no bunting on this house." Grandmother snorted. "Let her run back to her decorating council with that."

"Oh, Ma," Aunt Madge cried, "you should've just put them off nicely." Her eyes were as green as Grandmother's. Yes, they looked alike, but Aunt Madge didn't like strife.

"There's no way you can put people off nicely if you've got something to say they're not going to like."

I was inclined to agree with her there, but I didn't want to. Grandmother's philosophies suited me sometimes, depending upon what side of the fence I was on, but since the Victory Party sounded like a grand do, as far as I was concerned they could hang bunting from one end of our house to the other.

Aunt Madge rolled a little ball of flax between her fingers. "They're not going to like it, Ma."

Something niggled at me. If they didn't like it, would Grandmother's "no bunting" stance bar us from attending? But surely there was some way to say no to a request without grudges being stored up by the malcontents, ready and waiting in remembrance. Mind you, I had to admit that every time Grandmother said no to my pleas for a sweetie coupon—and sometimes she really said it as if she wished it were yes—I was still mad at her. But although I swore retaliation, my grudges had as much backbone in them as a snake.

Adults were quite a different kettle of fish. They took their grudges and stored them up, waiting to pounce. I never got bawled out only for the trangression just committed; Grandmother dredged up things that happened weeks ago and tied them all up in a lump.

Grandmother poured herself another cup of tea and the *thruup* of the boiling water as it gurgled through the spout sounded as angry as she was. "And Mary Doran didn't like what I said, I can tell you."

The all-important question was right on the tip of my lips, but some leftover remembrance warned me it would brook ill tidings if I asked it now, so I excused myself from the table and headed for the biscuit tin.

There was still some sun at the bottom of the garden enticing the unwary pink and white candytufts to pop tiny flowers out of their buds. Although it was only May, they thought it was summer already because of the good weather, and Grandmother complained it would bugger up the whole garden. And this bunting business was disrupting the whole lovely idea of the Victory Party. Why was Grandmother making such a fuss about it anyway? All those little flags would brighten up the whole place.

The word "bunting" was bandied about in summer yarns when they talked about the great Protestant celebration they called "the Twelfth"—the same one Mrs. Doran had mentioned last night. It used to be held every year on July 12, and all the Orange Lodges—Uncle Dan said some even came from Australia and Canada—met and marched through the streets of Belfast singing their songs to the skirl of Scottish bagpipes, feisty flutes, and the great boom of the Lambeg drums. Grandmother said the drummers became so incensed their knuckles bled and that Orangemen felt unless the blood spattered the drum they weren't doing it right.

A cold hand wrenched at my insides. That's what my brain had summed up in an instant. Union Jacks and bunting were associated with Orange celebrations! And Grandmother said the Orange Order was dedicated to the persecution of Catholics. Persecution! Visions of Nero throwing Christians to the lions came and then went. I'd never seen an Orangeman, but even I knew Orangemen didn't do *that*, whatever else they did. Now, from all I'd heard, they didn't like us, hadn't a good word to say about us, but our summer yarns about them weren't what you'd have called praise either.

But this *wasn't* an Orange affair. They didn't even have their old celebrations anymore. This was a Victory Party celebrating the winning of the great World War. And Northern Ireland was a part of England no matter what Grandmother said, so we were entitled to share in the victory too.

But Grandmother hadn't been all that pleased about England's victory. She mystified me. She wasn't German; we didn't even know any Germans, yet she took their side and venerated their leader. She'd never missed an opportunity to argue with the BBC's version of the news, and Aunt Madge and I listened to her pooh-pooh the Allied victories as "luck" and trumpet Hitler's advances as "strategic" right up to the end.

Aunt Madge said not to heed her, that it was just talk and Grandmother's way of continuing her father's war with England. "If the Devil himself was making war on England, I think she'd take his side," Aunt Madge confided.

Well, that was nothing to do with me. England had won the war and that was perfectly all right in my book. My thoughts stubbornly returned to the prospect of attending this unique celebration. Victory certainly was unique to Catholics, for I'd learned from Uncle Dan's stories of ancient Irish heroes—and they were all Catholic since that's all they had then—that even when it sounded like we were trouncing the enemy, I'd better brace myself for the knell of defeat that inevitably crept into his voice.

And this victory embraced *both* Catholics and Protestants! Now, *that* was a rare one for you all right. A sudden spasm of resentment shook me. That bloody Bobby *never* came out a loser; he was a *drawer* at worst. I could hear him now. "Ho-hum, just another Victory Party to attend."

But, used to victory as Bobby was, I'd bet two weeks *Beanos* he'd be just as fired up as me about this party. Yes, my blue organdie would be all right, and I could wear my new patent-leather shoes; they weren't even scuffed yet. Despite Grandmother's odd fondness for Germany, I had no qualms whatever about celebrating its defeat with our neighbours, except . . .

I put my elbows on my knees and squeezed my hands against my head trying to squash out the nasty little thought that crept out of Grandmother's words. They'd *deigned*. I knew what that meant, and my face burned my hands. Then I felt a sly smile cross my mouth. Two could play at that game. If they could deign, so could we. We could deign to put up the bunting! A vision of me in a cloud of blue sitting down at the table conversing with Bobby in sedate tones, fawned over and petted by the neighbours, abruptly dissipated when I got to the part where I casually flicked my two long golden plaits over my shoulders. That's when I remembered Grandmother wasn't in favour of deigning anything of the sort. All because of a bit of bunting I had about as much chance of going to the Victory Party as I did of growing those imaginary plaits. Now, if the Orange Order had had any imagination at all and made up their *own* flag for their parades instead of borrowing the Union Jack, there wouldn't have been a problem. Well, not as much of one anyway. Grandmother didn't let loose of problems too easily; she seemed to thrive on them.

I got up from the biscuit tin, lingering just long enough to take in its ravaged condition. A skin of rust covered the once shiny black and gold lettering. The winter rains had won that battle. I might as well tackle the first hurdle and get it over with. If you had something to say to someone you knew they weren't going to like, it made no difference how, or *when*, you said it.

The shell path crunched beneath my feet and I felt like a giant crushing faceless little skulls all the way to the back door.

"Can I go?"
The all-important question was answered by a waspish

"Yes." Four words, and not one over three letters in our whole conversation, and I was right in tune with the instantaneous flash of joy that came on the heels of Grandmother's "Yes."

Now all I had to worry about was them, and how well they stored their grudges. My only hope lay in Mrs. Doran's ability to find a nice way after all to relay the "no bunting" edict to her friends on the decorating council.

A sort of alienation set in between Grandmother and me on Tuesday. I think she would have liked me to up and say I wasn't going to the party. Now, she never said that; it was just there. Of course, she might just get her wish—about me not going—but it wouldn't be any of my doing.

"What if they come to the door?" Aunt Madge brought my fears into the open. That was adult pig Latin for "What if they *demand* our compliance?"

Grandmother's answer dashed any hopes I had of her being coerced. "There'll be no bunting on this house. They'll have to burn me out first!"

Burn us out! My eyes threatened to pop out on the floor. "They wouldn't, would they?" My voice was just little puffs of breath.

"Oh no, love. Granny's just being melodramatic," Aunt Madge said, but when she looked at Grandmother the green splinters in her eyes were very noticeable.

And the long, anxious wait set in for any rap on the front door.

I didn't dally on my way home from school, nor was I interested in proving my superiority in hopscotch and skipping, our perennial preludes to summer. Uncle Dan called in every night that week on his way up to the Gaelic Hut to play hurley. He'd never done that before, and Grandmother didn't complain to Aunt Madge about him hanging around either.

I asked all sorts of questions hoping he'd end up missing the hurley practise, but he just stayed long enough to smoke a pipe and say a few things about the grand hurley team they had this year and speculate on their chances for the All Ireland Championship. The smell of that pipe wafted about our living room and curled around me like an eiderdown—a safe, warm smell. I wished Uncle Dan would hurry up and marry Aunt Madge whether Grandmother liked it or not.

The long Irish twilights weren't conducive to early sleep so I read a lot by the front window and watched the bunting transform the houses around us. I had a good view of the goings on at Mrs. Doran's since the living room window had two angled side panes. Grandmother called it a bay window.

Mrs. Doran had no more notion of how to hang bunting than we did so I suppose that's why Pam Boyd's two big brothers got the job of stringing the long lines of red, white, and blue flags on the Doran house. They scrambled up and down the ladder, expertly hammering in nails at strategic points to keep the bunting in place. You'd have thought they were crucifying Christ to hear Grandmother, for with every thud of the hammer she'd go into a near tantrum, shouting "Abomination," "Turncoat," and "That Judas."

"He must have had to work late," I heard Mrs. Doran tell Morris, who steadied the ladder while his brother, Reggie, stretched precariously to hammer in the last nail at the gable end. "With the light nights upon us again, he likes to get in a few extra hours. Makes up for the time he loses in winter," she said with a little pat on Morris' shoulder. "Here," she added, "Mr. Doran said to give you and Reggie this for your trouble."

Morris grinned and took the note from her, but our window was just too far away for me to tell if it was ten shillings or a pound. Reggie and Morris, after a bit of discussion on just where to hang the last string of flags, framed the front door with it and waved "cheerio" to Mrs. Doran. It was done.

Mrs. Doran closed the front door and I didn't know whether the lump in my throat was there because Mrs. Doran had allowed flags on her house or if it was because Grandmother hadn't.

I was having a little trouble with my eyes, too, so I couldn't see how Bobby's house was coming along. He lived further up the street on the same side as us, but I knew his house was a part of the great red, white, and blue blur that stretched into the sky. I bent my head into my book and spent the rest of the evening with the Famous Five in a haunted castle. Being scared witless was more comfortable.

I read until the light from the window showed the first inklings of the dark lavender that gave a brief showing before it turned to purple. Grandmother was already sleeping the sleep of the just in front of the fire, and I was about to head for the stairs when I heard it.

I banished my first fearful thought and listened again. It was singing. *"Hello, Patsy Feagan—You're the apple of my eye . . ."*

I peered out the window as the figure gave rather wide berth to the lamp post at the corner of the street. Good God! It was Mr. Doran, and he seemed to be having trouble with the latch on the gate.

"Hello, Patsy Feagan—You can hear the girls all cryyyy. . ."

He let it rip with great feeling at the same time as he lurched forward and ended up in a heap at the bottom of the steps. He sniggered to himself, then took up again, *"You're a harum, scarum, devil-me-carum daycent Irish boy!"* He tried to slap his knee, but he kept missing. He was *drunk*, that's what he was.

Now, I'd seen Mr. Doran with a few jars in him before—every Friday night to be exact—but never in this state, and *never* on a week night. Mr. Doran had a bit of the Jeykll and Hyde in him. He was good as gold all week, saying very little to Mrs. Doran any time I'd been around, but come Friday night he came into his own, as if he'd stored up all his conversation just for the weekend. Mr. Hyde had taken over this evening.

I was trying to make up my mind if I should go to his aid when the star of this little show was spotlighted. Mrs. Doran opened the front door and switched on the hall light. *"You're the apple of my eye"* died on his lips and he blinked up at her, his blue irises adrift for a second before focusing.

"You've done it this time, Sammy Doran," she mumbled as she hurried down the steps and tried to hoist him up.

"No!" he shouted, disdaining her helping hand and getting to his feet. *"You've* done it," he said, and marched up the steps past her with remarkable dignity. He went through the front door without a glance at the bunting. Now, I don't know how he could have missed it. A blind man could have seen it. I wondered if that's what they meant when they said someone was blind drunk. Mrs. Doran had a furtive peek to see if anyone was watching, but I knew she couldn't see me in our darkened living room.

Grandmother had roused herself and stood at my elbow. "That woman would drive a saint to drink," she said, shaking her head.

Talk about turncoats, I thought, remembering the many times she'd referred to Mr. Doran as "that drunken oul' blert next door." Now it was all Mrs. Doran's fault just because she hadn't followed Grandmother's lead in the matter of a few flags.

CHAPTER
===5===

All week long my head jerked at every footstep, so when Grandmother mentioned a quick run down to Aunt Nin's on Thursday I was only too glad to abandon my post by the window. Aunt Madge must have felt the same way, for when Uncle Dan suggested she might like to watch the hurley practise, she just threw a coat on top of her overall and away she went to the Gaelic Hut without as much as a lick of lipstick. And hurley was a bit too bloody for Aunt Madge's taste.

Bunting followed Grandmother and me all the way down the Whitewell Road; Serpentine Parade wasn't the only street planning celebrations. But the little row houses where Aunt Nin lived showed no signs of victory, their plain whiteness broken only by a few unruly nasturtiums someone had let get out of hand.

The tea tray, with its china cups, winking cut-glass sugar bowl, and milk jug, sat on the heavy sideboard that was Aunt Nin's pride and joy. It took up the whole wall that hid the stairs; its glinting dark wood was anointed weekly with paraffin polish. It had been her mother's, and Aunt Nin didn't know how she'd managed to hold on to it through the years. Grandmother sometimes told a funny tale about the big sideboard and how Aunt Nin had rescued it single-handed during the burning out.

Aunt Nin brought out a big plate laden with savoury sausage rolls—my favourite.

"I made them for Rosie coming in," she said, "but the mill can't get enough spinners to keep up, so she's getting all she can while the going's good."

Poor Rosie, I thought, as I prepared to do those rolls justice. A spinner had the worst job in the mill, and I was glad Aunt Madge wasn't in the Spinning Room where the women sloshed about ankle deep in water wrestling the raw flax.

Grandmother shook her head and held up her hand at the plate.

"No, no, Nin. You put those back for Rosie. We had sausage rolls not so long ago."

Aunt Nin mouthed the usual "You're sure now, Maggie? I've got plenty," but her hands were already on the rim of the plate to whisk it away. Then I knew why Grandmother had refused them. It was all part and parcel of the same village code that called a consumptive a victim of bad health; you couldn't serve tea without a bit of a morsel to go with it—that was low. So Aunt Nin was prepared to sacrifice Rosie's dinner, knowing full well Grandmother, adept in all the vagaries of the code, would refuse it. It was like me offering my last bull's-eye to Aunt Madge or Uncle Dan; the gesture afforded me high praise and at the same time I could rest assured of retaining the bull's-eye. Now, I wouldn't ever make that kind of gesture toward Bobby McConnell.

The proprieties had been observed; Rosie would get her dinner; Aunt Nin wasn't shamed; and Grandmother could bask in Aunt Nin's silent gratitude. She'd wait until we got outside before saying, "God forbid I ever have to offer a cup of tea to anyone without as much as a slice of bread."

Aunt Nin poured the tea while Grandmother rumbled on about the Victory Party and the constant traipsing of the decorating council in and out of the Doran house. When she got to the part about "There'll be no bunting on *my* house," Aunt Nin's steady hand wavered for an instant and she set the teapot down.

"You're not as young as you used to be, Maggie," she said as she covered the teapot with a yellow tea-cosy.

"There you are!" said Grandmother tartly. "That's the attitude we've taken all along, Nin Rafferty. Just take whatever they care to dish out, but for God's sake don't say anything and"—Grandmother threw her hands up in mock horror—"God forbid, don't *do* anything!" She banged the teaspoon around in the cup, stirring her tea into a whirlpool. "If I was Brian Boru himself, you'd be telling me I wasn't big enough or strong enough!"

Try as I might, I couldn't picture Grandmother as anything like the brave Brian Boru Uncle Dan told me stories about.

Grandmother slurped the white, sugary tea. "Well, I've stood a lot in my day, but they're not draping me with a bloody flag that promotes my destruction!"

God, but she was exasperating. She'd got it all wrong! If she'd just put up the flag, she'd *prevent* any destruction! As it was, I thought bitterly, we were right on the brink of an updated version of the summer yarn describing the "burning out" of Aunt Nin and Grandmother, and this time it'd be *me* hanging on to Grandmother's skirts.

I think Aunt Nin sided with me. "The meek shall inherit the earth," she said, her eyes resting on the exposed and bleeding heart of Our Lord above the mantelpiece. I expected Grandmother to take that as a slap in the face, but she just said, "Ach, I know—I know all about that."

She knew about it all right, but I could tell she didn't believe it.

"Nothing's changed, Nin—nothing at all," Grandmother said, and the light went out of the green chips in her eyes. The flesh around them seemed darker. I'd never noticed before, but Aunt Nin was right, Grandmother wasn't as young as she used to be, and I didn't want to pursue that line of thought at all.

I drained my cup without studying the pattern of tea leaves at the bottom, for Grandmother said people who practised the reading of tea leaves got their answers from the Devil, and I didn't want any answers right now.

I got up to go to Patsy's house. Aunt Nin said not to ask to see the new babies yet; that Patsy's mother wasn't as well as she might be. And Grandmother told me not to be gone longer than ten minutes.

Patsy hadn't bought a sweetie or a piece of honeycomb in two weeks. Every penny she got she'd lit a candle to Our Lady.

"Oh, Jennifer, it was a miracle right enough!" she said, showing me the bottle-green dancing costume. It was a bit late for me to tell her my new knowledge about miracles now, so I kept mum. The serge had been given to the Widow Byrne by a woman she'd "sat up with" through an illness. Rosie had contributed a piece of amber satin to line the cloak, and Aunt Nin had done the intricate collar lace-work. The widow was still working on the gold cord piping.

I told her I was attending the Victory Party on Serpentine Parade.

"We never celebrate anything down here," Patsy said peevishly. "I mean, even Marie McNulty's wedding wasn't much of a do. It was very quiet." She lowered her voice. "M'mammy says she *had* to get married—the whole place was talking."

I told her about the lavish food preparations and what Grandmother was contributing (I didn't tell her Grandmother didn't know about her generosity yet).

"I wish we lived on Serpentine Parade." Patsy sighed. Then she brightened up. "But my daddy says it shouldn't be too long now before it's our turn to get moved to a new house."

"My Uncle Dan says they'll be building lots of new houses now the war's over," I said helpfully. This was as much for my benefit as hers—we might need a new house, too. I hadn't told Patsy about the bunting problem because I thought it would put a dampener on my description of the event. Besides, I wasn't sure Patsy would have approved of my participation if she knew I was sanctioning the Union Jack.

"My daddy says ten years on the list ought to put us near the top."

"What list?"

"The Corporation Housing List," Patsy replied as if I hadn't been listening to her. "You have to be on the list before you can get a new house," she explained. "Well, rich people don't have to—they can just go out and buy one. Just like that." Patsy snapped her fingers. "Just like your Granny did!"

The impact of Patsy's words left me staggered. Grandmother had been rich enough to scorn the housing list once, but if we were burned out, would she be rich enough to do it again? Ten years? Almost a lifetime!

"Does everyone have to wait that long?" You'd have thought the death rattle was in my throat my voice was so hoarse.

"Not if you're Protestant, you don't," Patsy said sourly. "My daddy says *their* names are juggled to the top of the list."

I didn't have a chance to digest this information right then because Grandmother was calling. I hastily promised Patsy a full accounting of the party when I saw her on Sunday after Mass. I might have to invent some eloquent lies if I didn't get to go—after all, it was only Thursday. I wondered briefly if premeditated lies were more serious than spontaneous ones. Well, Father Sheridan could just take these last lies of mine with him to Brazil—nobody knew me there. Actually, it wouldn't be a bad idea at that to start off fresh with the new priest, make a good impression, like. It was getting harder to be a Catholic all the time.

It wasn't until we got home that I discovered I'd missed something at Aunt Nin's. Aunt Madge had me up on the stool so she could see where the hem on my blue organdie should hit my legs.

"A *lodger!*" Grandmother said to Aunt Madge. "Can you imagine that? A lodger!"

Aunt Madge pulled the dress over my head. "So what's wrong with that? They could be doing with the extra money."

"Pah!" Grandmother spat. "It's not the money Nin's looking at—it's a *husband* for the big heifer she's after!"

Rosie's not the only big heifer, I thought, as I strained into the suffocating blue mist.

"You should have heard her! 'Ach, Maggie, isn't it a lonely washing that doesn't have a man's shirt in it?'" Grandmother mimicked Aunt Nin. "*I* know what she's after all right!"

Aunt Madge stopped tugging. Perhaps she, too, was comparing Aunt Nin's endeavours to help Rosie find a man to Grandmother's efforts to dissuade one.

"Where's he from?"

"Dublin," replied Grandmother with a finality that meant the word "Dublin" should tell us everything we needed to know.

"What would a Free Stater want up here?" said Aunt Madge.

"*Exactly!*" Grandmother pounced on the word. "There's nothing up here for a Free Stater. He must have been drummed out of Dublin!"

"Ach, Ma, maybe the man has a job up here."

"And just who would give a job to a Free Stater?" Grandmother gave a scoffing laugh. "Not on your life! I'll not say what I *think* he's up to, but I know they've just opened the jails down there."

Aunt Madge gave a final jerk and I emerged panting.

"Talk about the Protestants being suspicious of Free Staters," Aunt Madge said. "You're as bad as *they* are, Ma."

"Say what you like, but Nin Rafferty may well rue the day she takes him in."

My insides protested the tourniquet of blue organdie.

"It's no use. I can't *breathe!*" I fretted to Aunt Madge as she helped me struggle back out of the shrunken dress. The water had already sprung to my eyes and my mouth stretched like a gargoyle's ready to bemoan this final agony. But Aunt Madge hadn't conceded defeat. "A few wee gussets out of the sash will fix that, love." She smiled at me. Then she studied the limp dishrag that once had been my pride and joy. "Aye, you'll do a few more turns," she told the dress. I'd never thought of Aunt Madge as a fighter before.

The delegation from the decorating council never arrived. It was Grandmother's opinion the Protestants were sated on German blood right now, so they were feeling magnanimous and putting on a show of propinquity.

"What's propinquity, Granny?"

"Kinship," she said. "They're putting on a show of kinship with us."

I didn't say so, but I thought the Protestants were showing better manners than Grandmother and that propinquity was one of the nicest words I'd ever heard.

But those four worrisome days had taken their toll on me and even though I could now rest assured of my attendance at the party, by Friday night I was cross and tired. And I didn't feel all that well either. Maybe I'd caught something. And it might *rain*. Aunt Madge said I'd better get plenty of sleep or my eyes would look like two burnt holes in a blanket. I knew I couldn't sleep, but I went to bed anyway.

The blue organdie hung on the bedroom door and I lay there marvelling at Aunt Madge's miracle. She'd put starch in it and it stuck out crisp and full, as good as new. It fit too!

I watched the moon chase a few ragged clouds until I remembered Aunt Madge's remark about my eyes.

The window in my room faced the garden and Napoleon's Nose, and I only needed to sit up in bed when Saturday morning dawned to see if Mother Nature was still benevolent. She was. Only a few white puffs of cloud broke the vast blueness and they were high above Napoleon's Nose. I liked to think of Mother Nature controlling the elements even though Miss McGrath once made me scratch out "that pagan goddess" all the way through a composition and put in "God" instead.

Grandmother put a plate of porridge in front of me and told me I could use the cream on top of the milk. She was benevolent, too, this morning! Normally she'd shake up that bottle of milk like a cat with a rat making sure the cream was thoroughly distributed. But when she produced the box containing good creamery butter, tins of red salmon, and paper parcels marked "Tongue" and "Venison," I just didn't know what to make of it. There was sugar, too, and a big pound package of Orange Pekoe and Pekoe tea.

"Take that in to Mrs. Doran for the party," she said, as if she did the same thing every day.

This was the best of her black market hoard and she didn't part with it lightly. Grandmother relished her forays into Belfast and she had several sinister shops she frequented, sometimes dragging me with her to queue up for hours for as little as a dozen eggs or a pound of butter. Aunt Madge didn't like her "keeping those crooks in business," but Grandmother said it would be a bad day when she had to resort to ruining good bread by putting margarine on it.

I was almost duped into thinking Grandmother was getting into the spirit of the victory celebration until she said, "I'll not have them saying you went to their party empty-handed and ate all their rations." She patted the box. "And some of them have lived on Spam and margarine for so long, they'll not know what to do with *this*." Grandmother had a curious air of victory all her own, as if she had won some battle all by herself.

I skipped through that hedge to Mrs. Doran, and Grandmother's motives didn't detract one bit from the pride I felt handing over our contribution.

"Oh, this is just grand, Jennifer," Mrs. Doran said as she inspected the box. "I'm so glad your Granny's coming around."

I didn't know how to answer that without fibbing a bit, so I just put on an idiot smile to remind her she was speaking to one who hadn't a grasp on these intricacies. She smiled back and said she'd made me a place beside her at the victory table.

Serpentine Parade dazzled in a blaze of red, white, and blue. The saucy bunting stretched from house to house, fluttering now and then in the gentle breeze. Narrow tables, covered with crepe paper, formed a long red, white, and blue spine down the middle of the street, and vases of red and white carnations spiced the air. Everyone's ration book must have taken a gruelling depletion, for the bounty spread before us was fit, someone said, for the Royal Family themselves.

"They're not eating like this in Berlin," somebody else shouted, and a roar of approval rent the air. I sat between the Dorans and the Sommervilles, enjoying the banter and camaraderie between the neighbours.

"Now there's a man with something to cry about," Mr. Doran said quietly to Grandpa McCartney at his elbow as Constable Johnston wheeled his daughter, Sarah, up to the table. Bobby's daddy took out a chair to make a place for her wheelchair. I could have told Grandpa McCartney differently, but Bobby and I had pledged to keep Constable Johnston's terrible secret to ourselves. We'd discovered he *smiled* a lot when he wheeled Sarah out into their back garden. It was a nice smile, too, and Bobby and I were flabbergasted watching the two of them talking and smiling and nodding.

I remembered that Sarah had laughed at something Constable Johnston said, but the laugh was cut short when she took a fit of coughing. We thought she'd never stop, and Constable Johnston just stood there running his fingers through his hair until Sarah lay back gasping and wild-eyed. He wheeled her back into the house and we waited to see if he'd come out again. When he did, he had a bottle of Bushmills and a tumbler, and Bobby and I watched him for a long time. But he wasn't doing anything, just filling the tumbler and drinking it, so we got bored and sneaked away.

Sarah was about twelve—Bobby said thirteen—but since she couldn't come out to play with the rest of us, the only thing we really knew about her was that she was ailing. Sarah wore her brown hair in two plaits that fell past her waist and which I coveted.

"Aye," said Grandpa McCartney, his new delft teeth clattering. "I'm afeared that wee girl is going the way of her mother before her."

The two bright pink spots on Sarah's cheeks matched her dress and her eyes had an odd lustre I passed off as excitement. Contrary to Grandpa McCartney, I thought she looked a lot better.

"These bloody teeth," Grandpa wailed. "I can't get used to them. But Julia insisted I'd put people off their food if I sat down without them." He gave a clattering chuckle. "And I told *her* I'd not put them off half as bad as that snottery-nosed wee bugger of a boy she has."

I knew just what he was talking about. His grandson, William, checked the constant flow from his nose with a flickering tongue. Mr. Doran commiserated by promptly pouring a dollop of amber liquid from a very solid paper bag into their teacups. Mrs. Doran pretended not to notice. Everyone was having a grand time. Bobby shouted over that I shouldn't miss the raspberry tarts, and I didn't feel it necessary to tell him I'd had three. He'd only take it as a challenge. Pam Boyd was happily spearing pickled eggs from a big jar filled with beetroot juice, and I turned away from the scene because I didn't like the idea of eating old eggs.

Mrs. Boyd plied me with meringues that promised the sweetest sweetness only to dissipate the minute my tongue touched them. There was something unfulfilling about meringues. My mind loved them, for it savoured the promise of the sweetest sweetness from the first glimpse of the frothy balls right up to the moment I bit into them. But my mouth was left wanting. Now Mrs. Sommerville's English trifle was something else again, and I yelled back to Bobby.

The Reverend Nutt called for order—I couldn't remember if he was Church of Ireland or Presbyterian—and led us in what he called the Lord's Prayer, which was nothing more than the Our Father with a little tacked on to the end. He thanked the good ladies who had worked so hard to prepare this feast and asked them to stand up. Mrs. Doran blushed and beamed.

As we showed our appreciation to these women who flitted around with laden plates, I wished Aunt Madge or Grandmother was one of them. Aunt Madge had sought sanctuary at Aunt Nin's with the feeble excuse of seeing Rosie, and Grandmother—Grandmother just stayed in the house behind closed doors.

The first quick pang of yearning hit me then. All week I'd only been concerned whether *I* got to join this exultant throng; now my lone participation wasn't enough.

Grandpa McCartney's discarded teeth grinned up at me from the table and a little gust of wind rustled the bunting. I stared over at our house, the only one not bedecked with gay flags. I hoped Bobby wouldn't notice, but that was like wishing a meringue wouldn't dissolve at the first hint of saliva. It was unnerving; a naked gap in the midst of the bright symbols of Britain's victory, and a stark reminder that this was an uneasy propinquity between them and us.

Them and us. Why couldn't it, even just this once, be "we?" Why weren't we ever "we?"

The bare bricks on our house slapped me harder than Miss McGrath's cane ever could. What our house said was that it wasn't happy with the victory; that the people living in it weren't on the same side. I looked around the friendly, flushed faces of our neighbours and I thought of Grandmother—Grandmother spurning their attempts at propinquity, contemptuous of everything they stood for—and I resented her for the first time in my life.

Then the chastizing emotions of love and loyalty battled

the resentment and a cry filled my throat; a long, silent cry thrust out to the bricks. They couldn't answer my "Why" and I was *afraid* to ask the people around me. They'd think I was simple! I knew I wasn't simple, but perhaps I was *demented*. Everyone was either "them" or "us"; everyone else accepted that, was *content* to belong either to "them" or to "us." I was far from content.

I looked over at Bobby jumping up and down between the bulwarks of a mammy and daddy. Egged on by comradely shouts, he waved a Union Jack and pranced about stabbing the air with it. That little flag took away all question as to what side *he* was on.

Every country had a flag symbolising its people, and the Union Jack was the flag of Northern Ireland. But Catholics just wouldn't have anything to do with it if they could help it. Grandmother said the Union Jack *wasn't* our flag; our flag was the green, white, and orange one they flew in the Free State. Fine and dandy, but we didn't *live* in the Free State and never had—we lived under the red, white, and blue. I didn't care what *colours* made up the flag—I just wanted a *flag!* Wanted to be able to stand up waving it like Bobby—*with* Bobby.

Shamed and bewildered, I turned to see why Mrs. Doran was nudging me.

"Isn't it wonderful, Jennifer?" she said as the Reverend Nutt called for a rousing "Hip Hip Hurrah" for the brave lads who'd fought and won.

"Oh, yes," I answered this other person who sat beside me. "Oh, *yes!*" I breathed again, remembering Mrs. Doran wasn't all that content with the Protestant "them" and the Catholic "us" either. And my spirits soared as another realization struck me. Her son was one of the "us," and he'd *fought* to keep that Union Jack of Bobby's flying. Frankie Doran was one of the brave lads "they" were cheering! That was as near to a "we" as I could get.

I loved Frankie Doran right then. I couldn't remember

what he looked like, for any distinguishing features had evaporated and melted into one uniformed face, any soldier's faceless face. But I loved Frankie Doran right then. He'd taken the bare look off us Catholics and given us the right to victory.

Bobby threw me a flag. I picked up the Union Jack for the first time and it didn't sear my hands. I waved it at him as the vibrant and victorious roar went up. I cheered louder than Bobby, louder than anyone. For Frankie Doran—for whole armies of faceless faces. *"Hip Hip Hoooray! Hip Hip Hoooraay! Hip Hip Hoooor-Raaaay!"*

Although I didn't know it then, before that last hurrah had faded, my feet were in a springing stance ready to leap over the other side of the fence into a treacherous summer of apostasy.

CHAPTER
6

Although the Victory Party was well over, only the Dorans, the McKays, and the Sommervilles stripped their houses of bunting. May approached its end and the bunting was a permanent fixture. I thought they were afraid to take it down in case it meant the end of victory, but Grandmother said no, they had more victories they meant to celebrate during the summer.

Perhaps she'd been "victoried" to death and was sick hearing about it. All I know is she took to clicking off the wireless in the middle of the news with shouts of "Lies" and "Propaganda." Several words cropped up, but "Ouch" and "Wits" were particularly offensive. These and "Jews" heralded the immediate silencing of Mr. Liddell and my exile to the scullery right after that with orders to do my homework and close the door.

But I knew if I whipped that door open I'd find her

with her ear up to the wireless hanging on to his every word. Suffering Duck! She'd go to all lengths to pretend she wasn't interested in what he had to say about the Jews. As if I cared. For that matter, I'd never known her to care what Jews did either. She'd never had that much truck with them, and what's more, she didn't want any. They were the chosen people, she said, and while it didn't do to question the wisdom of Our Lord, it seemed to her He'd chosen a bunch of usurers. Didn't the handful of them own all the big shops in Belfast?

"Oh, don't be deceived by the respectable names they have over their doors," she'd say. "They *change* them."

They could sell you tuppence worth and make you believe it cost them a shilling. The way she said this, you'd have thought this was a fault!

But it was her cloaked intimations of a curious fondness they had for leading good Catholic girls astray that prompted my resolve to be wary of Jews just in case I ever met any. Grandmother could make a simple word like "astray" take on sinister meanings that defied the dictionary.

"But I'll give them this," she said with surprising charity; "they'll give a Catholic a job just as quick as they will a Protestant. Aye, I'll give them that—they're not bigoted."

I didn't like being cooped up in the scullery even though it was quiet. Long ago I'd trained myself to read or do homework with the wireless blaring and Grandmother arguing with it; at the same time I could keep an eye on Bobby and the others just in case they had anything of interest going on.

I got my place by the bay window back on Thursday, and it took me a while to realise something was missing. The wireless, normally full of life, was silent; the living room was quiet. Grandmother's bellowings of "Lies" and "Propaganda" had trickled into a silence unnatural to her and she answered Aunt Madge's attempts at conversation with token ayes and a few half-hearted nos.

Another curious thing happened that night. Uncle Dan turned evangelist on us! He came in on his way up to the Gaelic Hut.

"So, you've heard," he said, casting a grim eye on Grandmother.

She returned his look and nodded. That piqued me because I hadn't a glimmer of *what* she'd heard. Uncle Dan sat down on the settee and laid his arm along the back of it.

"Well, I just hope Frankie Doran got in a few good shots at the Jerries for me," he said.

Aunt Madge stopped ironing her overall and set the iron up on its end. "They think the figures will run into the *millions*," she said. She wet her fingers against her tongue and brushed them against the flat of the iron, it popped and hissed in answer.

Millions! That was a lot of shots and I felt Aunt Madge was exaggerating even Frankie's capabilities. I wasn't the only one.

"Millions?" Grandmother got out of her slump. "Where'd you hear that?"

"Mrs. Doran said it was on the six o'clock news," said Aunt Madge.

My hero took on Herculean proportions. Mrs. Doran had told me Frankie was up for bravery. "As near to the Victoria Cross as you can get" was the way she described the medal he'd been awarded. But the six o'clock news!

"I don't believe it," Grandmother said ungraciously. "England's always been good at lies. . ."

"Somebody's coined a new word for this—it's called genocide," Uncle Dan said, banging his pipe against the heel of his hand. "England knows genocide when it sees it, Maggie, and Ireland can't claim to be the only victim of it now."

There they went again! Always changing the subject on me and using words I'd have to go to Oxford to learn!

"Even the wee children!" Aunt Madge put her hands to

her head as if she were in pain. "Oh, God have mercy on us all," she cried.

I'd never seen Uncle Dan look at Aunt Madge with anything but warmth before, but tonight his eyes could only be described as blazing, and the thought fluttered through my head that I wouldn't want to be the poor devil who had to face him on the hurley field this evening. He leaned forward.

"Run! Placate Him!" he commanded Aunt Madge. "Grovel on your knees and beg mercy! There'll be those who'll say He didn't have much on the Jews!" Uncle Dan sounded like those men who went around Belfast brandishing Bibles and shouting, "Repent! The End of the World is at Hand!" Bible Thumpers, we called them. Uncle Dan struck his forehead with his fist instead.

"Aye, there'll be a run on the confessional! Some good Catholics will beat their breasts and beg forgiveness for daring to ask why He allowed this to happen—for questioning His very existence!"

Grandmother cut in sharply. "I'll have none of that atheist talk in this house! Don't you question God in *here!*"

"Oh, Dan! You promised. . ." Aunt Madge bit her lip.

Uncle Dan held up his hands. "Hold your horses and let me finish," he said. "The strange thing is, I *am* questioning His existence."

"So? What's so strange about that, Dan O'Neill?" Grandmother's eyebrows arched up. "You've said all along. . ."

"Ah, Maggie, Maggie—you're missing the irony." His mouth turned down in a wry smile.

He sucked thoughtfully on his pipe and his eyes followed the trail of blue smoke up to the ceiling. "Believing God is responsible for this, that He felt it necessary for some grand purpose we aren't privy to, would be a whole lot easier than facing the fact that *people* can hate each other to this degree." His eyes descended the line of smoke and stopped level with Grandmother.

Grandmother ruffled her shoulders. "Well, don't look at me! *I've* never hated Jews," she said.

Uncle Dan gave a weary sigh. "*Who* we hate isn't important, Maggie." He said this as if he was thinking out loud, and I thought Grandmother would pick up the gauntlet and give him an argument, but she just burned him with her eyes and turned her face to the fire. She wasn't at all well.

I disagreed with that last statement. I thought it was very important. What if you hated the *wrong person?* I was glad I'd at least understood this much out of the whole rigmarole they'd just conducted. Thank God I had a good few years to go before being *expected* to understand anything they said! I'd heard some of it before and hadn't understood then either; something that had to do with Uncle Dan. It was time I found out.

The springs in the settee *ping*ed as Uncle Dan got up and Aunt Madge walked him to the back door. I let them get a bit of talking done before following. Halfway through the scullery, I heard Aunt Madge say, "Did you mean that in there, Dan?" But I wasn't quick enough to see if he nodded or shook his head.

"Can I watch the hurley practise tonight, Uncle Dan?"

He gave me grave consideration for a minute. "You'll stay back off the field?"

"Oh, aye," I said, "I'm not *that* daft!"

Uncle Dan let out a great roar of laugh and said, "Come on, you wee twister." I liked Uncle Dan to call me a wee twister. When he said it, it meant he liked what I'd said. Grandmother used the same term, but when she said it, it meant the opposite.

The hawthorn bushes were white with blossoms, so I got my first crown of the year on the way up to the Gaelic Hut. I watched Uncle Dan twist the supple branches into shape, his big hands hardly ever knocking off a flower. Uncle Dan was the only person I knew who could weave a hawthorn crown free of thorns. Despite Grandmother's conviction that "Pride felt no pain" I knew exactly how Our Lord felt at the "Crowning with Thorns" when I had to make them myself.

"There you are, milady," he said, putting it on my head. "Behold Maeve, Queen of the Fairies!" he said to the bushes.

"Was she really Queen of the Fairies, Uncle Dan?"

"Some people think so, Jennifer," he said. Then he had a furtive look around to see if any fairies were listening. "But between you and me," he whispered, "I think Maeve was no more than a Queen of Ireland and"—he lowered his voice even more—"I'm told she was given to stealing cattle!"

Uncle Dan was pleased with the effect his words had on me, and he laughed too. But I put paid to mine in a hurry for I knew the fairies didn't like being scoffed at and Uncle Dan had shown scant respect for their Queen. Poor Uncle Dan. If it wasn't Grandmother who didn't like what he was saying, it was the fairies. I wondered if this was atheist talk, too. That was the word I'd heard during the big row between Grandmother and Uncle Dan long ago, the one Grandmother attached so much importance to, and the one I couldn't remember until I'd heard it again tonight.

"Uncle Dan, what's an atheist?"

It took him a while to stop clearing his throat so I knew I'd come up with a good one.

"Someone who doesn't believe in God, Jennifer."

There were times when I just couldn't grasp things—I mean, I didn't get their full significance right away. But right on the heels of Uncle Dan's words I knew it would have been a lot better if he'd said he was—well—if he'd said he was a plain old Protestant, or even a B-Special.

There were trifling venial sins and grave mortal sins. I'd even heard vague mention of something called cardinal sins, which I assumed were exclusive to the Princes of the

Church. But this was the Supreme Sin. Miss McGrath had explained this by way of the Black Babies Box. The pennies we sacrificed to it were sent to the African missions and brought the Word of God to those poor little unbaptised darkies. But, once they heard it, if they denounced it, they were damned! Not only had Uncle Dan heard, he could *expound* on it sometimes. My distraught mind conjured up Aunt Madge by the back door saying, "Did you mean that in there?" but hope was quickly stamped out by the spectral figures of Grandmother and Father Sheridan looming between me and Uncle Dan. I tried desperately to scatter them.

"But you *can't* be an atheist!" I cried. "You're a Catholic."

Uncle Dan shook his head. "No, love, I'm not a Catholic."

The evening sun had sucked all the colour out of the sky around his head and left it white. Something was being drained from me, too. I couldn't put a name to it, but whatever it was I didn't want to let it go.

"But . . . but . . ." My confused brain reduced me to the stammers. "But you're one of *us!*" It was a desperate attempt to keep him aligned to our side, to me.

Uncle Dan smiled down at me. "Yes, love, I'm one of you."

Now, we weren't given to kissing and cuddling, but I flung my arms around him and would have kissed his startled face if I'd been able to reach it. "I knew you were," I lied, my heart bursting with relief. I could have told Uncle Dan right then I had proof there was a God.

He took his pipe out and patted his pockets, looking for his tobacco tin.

"I'm in no hurry to knock hell out of someone tonight," he said. "Here—sit down a minute, and I'll have a bit of a smoke."

We sat on a grass bank by the side of the road, watching the sun tease Napoleon's Nose. He tamped his pipe and struck a match on the sole of his shoe. The rich fumes of Dunhill's Special overpowered the scent of the hawthorn. He squinted at me out of the corner of his eye.

"I'm going to let you in on a secret, Jennifer," he declared.

I was suitably awed. Aunt Nin's china teacup was one thing, but for Uncle Dan to include me in an adult secret— and he hadn't even bothered with the distrustful "Can you keep a secret?" that prefaced other people's confidences— well, I'd never forget him for it.

He let out a great billow of smoke. "It wouldn't do to let this one out, love, for it's one of the best kept secrets in the world," he said. "So secret, in fact, that only a few people are onto it."

I straightened my face to match his gravity. I was a bit apprehensive that he was going to build his case about there not being any God, for I'd have had to hurt him by telling him I couldn't listen to heresy. I needn't have worried.

"You see, love," he said between puffs, "in Northern Ireland, a man is born either Catholic or Protestant. The lines of demarkation"—he looked at me to see if I was following—"are drawn *then*, never to be erased. The title of Protestant or Catholic doesn't denote what *God* you worship, it identifies your *race*. Here"—his arm swept the fields— "Protestant stands for 'of English or Scottish' descent, and Catholic stands for 'of native Irish' descent. Now take me," he said, stabbing himself with his thumb. "The odd deviate like myself can cease believing in God and spurn Catholicism to beat the band, but he can't shrug off the *people* he belongs to. Do you see what I mean, Jennifer?"

"Oh, I see," I said brightly, "you're a Catholic atheist!"

Uncle Dan gave a deep chuckle. "Well put, you wee twister," he said, patting my hawthorn crown. "In Northern Ireland, there are no plain atheists—you're either a Catholic atheist or a Protestant atheist. Well put indeed," he said again and gave me a delighted smile.

I waited for him to tell me the secret, but he didn't say

another word and I wasn't about to make a mug out of myself by asking what it was. For all I knew, it was contained in what he had said, hidden in the elusive language of adults. And if he found out I didn't know all the intricacies yet, he'd think twice about imparting any more secrets to me.

"I've got a secret to tell you, too," I said, returning the compliment. "Father Sheridan's going off to Brazil and we're getting a new priest!"

Now, I didn't expect him to get up and dance a jig or anything like that, but I thought he'd at least show some interest. After all, maybe the new priest wouldn't be as down on him marrying Aunt Madge as Father Sheridan was. But Uncle Dan had no imagination as far as priests were concerned, for he just said they were six of one and half a dozen of the other.

"But if you and Aunt Madge could get to the new priest *before* Granny poisons him and just not say anything about being an atheist . . ."

Uncle Dan put his arm around me and kissed the hawthorn crown. Then he said Catholic conscience was an exclusive and terrible thing, and he was glad I didn't have one yet.

"Granny's just looking out for Aunt Madge's afterlife," he said. "You know, like the ancient Egyptians did by putting food and trinkets in the tombs . . ."

I think he would have gone on in this vein but I wasn't interested in an ancient Egyptian afterlife right now and asked him what about this one?

"There are a lot of people in Greencastle, Jennifer, who exist in this 'vale of tears' as they call it with the sole thought of getting into heaven. And if anything should make them enjoy their sojourn on this earth, they pluck it out—destroy it—for it must be a sin." He glanced up at the Cave Hill. The sun had struck Napoleon's Nose and fiery prisms now pierced the white sky. Then he looked at me, really looked at me as if he'd forgotten I was with him, chucked me under the chin, and said, "Right, love. Now let's go knock the hell out of somebody."

I was worried about Grandmother. Perhaps she listened to the news while I was at school, but she and Mr. Liddell had had a definite falling out, for the wireless remained dead in the evenings. She just wasn't herself these last few days; something weighed her down, and my attempts to liven her up were met with listless appreciation. I'd gone through my entire repertoire from the Mad Conductor to the Bow-Legged Ballerina and the nearest she came to dropping her subdued facade was to give me a mild chastizing for my "vulgar display" of the Constipated Opera Singer.

So on Saturday night when she said she'd go with me to confession, I jumped at her offer. She'd feel a lot lighter for it. Confession was an uplifting experience after you got the confessing over with. I always felt that great black weights had been physically removed from my soul when I came out of the confessional and by the time I'd said my three Hail Marys penance, I was in grand form—a crusader for good, my soul a shining white shield again. I don't know why I pictured my soul as a shield. Perhaps it was because I felt mine was constantly on the defensive. I wondered what kinds of vile sins adults committed that they were never sentenced to anything less than a *decade* of the rosary. You could tell how bad they'd been by the length of their penance. I'd seen some worrying the beads of the whole rosary!

I was going to make this confession a good one. I'd tell all, even some things that had been hanging over me for a while that I considered borderline between mortal and venial. It was peculiar the way these sins continued to bother me even after I'd spent hours convincing myself they were venial, thus eliminating the need for them to be confessed. Now was my chance to rid myself of them once and for all. And the beauty of it was, I'd never have to face Father

Sheridan again. The unworthy thought crossed my mind that Grandmother felt the same way.

I linked my arm through Grandmother's all the way down the Whitewell Road. The sharp smell of beached seaweed met us halfway, beckoning us to the shore. The grey spring tides had ceased their relentless battering and the sea calmed itself into a sparkling blue ripple. The lough was ready for summer. So was I, and I chattered away about school ending, about the upcoming summer holidays. But Grandmother couldn't join in that conversation with much exuberance since it didn't affect her directly, so I led the talk around to something that did; something I thought would give her a bit of comfort.

"You know," I said, drawing her out, "Miss McGrath was telling us Hitler might not be dead—that they're not sure at all."

I'd struck the right mark! Grandmother's eyes got light in them for the first time that week, and the buns over her ears shook.

"Well, they'd better make bloody sure he is and not let that fiend loose on the world again!"

I was stunned. Baffled. Now, I could see her being angry with Hitler for not beating the hell out of England, but it seemed unnecessarily harsh to call Germany's vanquished leader a fiend! And her face—well, when she'd said it, I could see her temples pulsing with anger. God help me, but I'd never, never understand that woman.

She lengthened her stride so I had to trot to keep up with her. She stopped at Katie Keenan's wee shop. Normally she called in at Katie's after chapel because she didn't want to lug her purchases into the chapel. I didn't mind the deviation at all since I always got two ounces of bull's-eyes from Katie's. I'd already mastered the art of speaking intelligibly while nursing a bull's-eye in my cheek, and Father Sheridan would never know the difference from behind the grille.

Katie's shop was sparse in stock, but rich in aromas. She sold things like cinnamon sticks and cloves, and sometimes she made her own honeycomb, which melted into honied toffee in your mouth. Most of the time I missed the honeycomb since Patsy and the other village children depleted the supply the minute Katie set the tray out. Whiffs of snuff added to the exotic smells. Katie sold a limited variety of snuffs, none of which Grandmother liked, but which she bought sometimes anyway to tide her over in an emergency.

Katie was the newsagent for the daily editions of the *Irish News*, which Grandmother also bought, although "There's nothing in it I haven't already read." She hated to admit it, she said, but the Protestant *Belfast Telegraph* gave more news of the goings-on in the world than the *Irish News*.

"Then why do you buy it?" I once asked her.

She spluttered a few "Because"s, then she said, "We have to take care of our own, and the *Irish News* is all we have in the way of a Catholic paper. And poor Katie ekes out very little in her wee shop, for she can't stock all the things the bigger shops can."

But Katie stocked something no other shop in Greencastle sold. Mass cards. When someone died it was to Katie Keenan you went.

I nearly dropped when Grandmother asked to see them. So that's what had been bothering her all week! Someone had died. No wonder she'd been acting peculiar.

Katie bent beneath the counter and brought up boxes of Mass cards and spread out the sombre array. Most of them were just white with black edging and a stark black cross under the "In Memoriam" lettering. Only a few had a discreet fleck of purple violets growing out of a corner or an embossed cream lily saying "In Deepest Sympathy." I wanted to help Grandmother pick one, but when she asked Katie to give me my two ounces of bull's-eyes, my attention went in that direction. And not because I was more interested in the sweeties either; rather because I always had an anxiety attack when Katie had to get my sweeties. She had to struggle a heavy glass jar off the shelf and it staggered her frail little body every time. And Grandmother said she was on the far side of eighty, so I went through an agony of waiting while she maneuvered it over to the tin scale. There was a momentary relief as she rattled the hard bull's-eyes into it and added or subtracted until she got it to come out to two exact ounces. Then came the worry of whether she'd manage the return trip to the shelf without mishap.

By the time Katie got the jar back to the shelf, Grandmother had already picked a Mass card. I saw her tuck a pound note into it, but I couldn't see what she'd written on it.

"And I'll take an *Irish News*, Katie," she said, pocketing the Mass card.

"Aye, aye, right you are, Maggie," Katie said as usual. "God bless you."

The tin bell rattled as we went out.

"Who's dead, Granny?" I said, without allowing my distended cheek to interfere with my diction.

Grandmother shrugged and patted me on the shoulder.

"Never you mind, love," she said, "you wouldn't know them."

I waited at the chapel gates while Grandmother handed the Mass card in to the Widow Byrne at the Parochial House. The bull's-eye pleasantly numbed the inside of my cheek while I wracked my brain trying to think who Grandmother knew that I didn't. Then the absurdity of that struck me. How *could* I know them if I didn't know them? I laughed out loud and nearly ended myself. I hadn't yet mastered laughing with a bull's-eye in my mouth. It served me right anyway—death wasn't a laughing matter.

I wished Grandmother would hurry up, for it looked like half of Greencastle wanted to unburden themselves tonight and they scurried up to the chapel path past me, which meant in *front* of me in the queue.

I don't know how he knew, but Uncle Dan was right. There was a run on the confessional!

CHAPTER
7

Whether it was the trip to confession that cured Grandmother, or the news that the Labour Party had a good chance of winning the General Election, I don't know, but I was glad of her fevered interest and feigned some of my own just to get her going.

During the last few hours of May, I got proof her recovery was complete.

Grandmother hadn't spoken to Mrs. Doran for two weeks, not since the bunting affair, and she'd subtly stressed this was by choice and not accidental by drying her dishcloths and muslins on the opposite hedge. I was helping her spread the clothes when Mrs. Doran's voice sounded at the back of us.

"Morning, Maggie," she said.

Grandmother rummaged in the basket for another muslin while I turned around to acknowledge the greeting.

"Is there any particular reason you've taken to using that hedge for drying?"

"Aye," said Grandmother, "there is."

Mrs. Doran waited expectantly. So did I, but nothing happened.

"Well, what is it then?" Mrs. Doran's face was getting a bit pink.

"What's what?"

Horrified, I saw what was going on but Mrs. Doran didn't seem to get it yet.

"The *reason*." Irritation finally tinged Mrs. Doran's voice.

Now I knew Mrs. Doran already knew the reason. I also understood this was her way of acknowledging something was amiss and that she was doing her part to clear the air. Grandmother was now supposed to show her good breeding and civility by telling some soft little lies minimizing the incident just to get the uncomfortable out of the way. Then everybody could pretend to be friends again and the affair could remain smothered until something else happened to warrant breathing life back into it. Most people strove to nurture this protective pretence. But dishonest niceness just wasn't in Grandmother sometimes.

There wasn't a quaver in her voice when she told Mrs. Doran she'd as good as turned her coat by allowing the Union Jack to hang shamelessly from her walls.

"And you'd do better to remember where the chapel is and what you are, instead of running about the British Legion remembering the poppy fields of Flanders."

Oh, God, I knew what she was at. Poppy Day! I'd known Grandmother wouldn't like Mrs. Doran joining the British Legion. It didn't matter that the woman just rolled bandages or cut pink lint and organized jumble sales for the veterans—it was a British club, therefore smacked of Protestantism and what followed that was Orangeism.

Oh, Sweet Jesus, keep Mrs. Doran from mentioning I'd offered to sell those damned imitation poppies for her when they were finished.

But Mrs. Doran didn't take things lying down either.

"Now, you just listen to me, Maggie Marshall," she said just as sharply, "my son might be under those poppies so I'll remember what I wish. I've worked my fingers to the bone to afford this house, to give Frankie a better chance than I had, and I'm not going to let diehard notions—yours or anybody else's—get me shoved back into the dregs of Belfast!"

I stayed just long enough to hear Grandmother retort, "I never *was* dregs." I took off like a hare, for Grandmother always warned, "You're judged by the company you keep," and I didn't want Mrs. Doran to judge me in the same light as Grandmother.

But more importantly, I didn't want her son biased. He was coming home sometime that afternoon. Now, I'd been dreading Grandmother rearing up in front of Frankie. "I'd smother anything belonging to me that wore that defilement," she'd carped often enough. It took me ages to discover that she'd meant to say "uniform." But, inexplicably, Grandmother had recently softened her stance regarding Frankie.

Mrs. Doran had a little get-together arranged in his honour. Mrs. Beattie and Mrs. Sweet brought a cake and a basket of imported fruit, compliments of the British Legion, and Pam's mother contributed a big tin of Cadbury's chocolate biscuits which Pam guarded with her eyes.

I couldn't contain my excitement and elected myself advance scout to watch for the taxi from the Camp pillars. I sat there a long time wondering what was bothering me. Then it hit me. Bobby McConnell would be attending with his mother and I didn't want him worming his way in between Frankie and me. I mean, Bobby and I both worshipped Constable Johnston but he was mostly Bobby's idol and, knowing McConnell as I did, he'd want prime standing with the returning hero too.

Then I saw the taxi starting up the hill.

I burst into the Doran living room a few minutes ahead of it to alert the welcoming party. After a few initial squeals of excitement we were suddenly quiet. Mrs. Doran rose from her chair at the sound of the boots on the steps. Then Frankie walked through the front door.

I expected him to be a lot younger. I was shocked. So was Mrs. Doran; she looked at him as if she didn't know him either. Then he took off his cap and it was all hugs and cries.

Frankie spent the next hour trying to coax Smokey

onto his lap, answer questions, and play down the importance of the medal Mrs. Doran passed among us. Bobby McConnell held that medal for an eternity before letting me get a look at it. And I couldn't get a word in edgeways either for the stream of questions he badgered Frankie with.

"Can I see your gun?" he asked suddenly.

"Sorry, son—I had to leave it behind."

"Oh. Why? My Uncle James didn't have to give his back."

There was a quick silence before Mrs. McConnell said something about another piece of cake and everybody began praising the quality of it, and it only made with one egg instead of the six the recipe called for.

Bobby persisted. "Why'd you have to?"

Mrs. Doran rallied. "Thank God he did," she said, laughing. "I'm afraid of those things."

"Oh, I know what you mean," Mrs. Sweet tittered. "Every time my Harry dismantles his, I'm afeared he's going to blow off his big toe."

All the ladies laughed. I didn't think it was that funny. Then Bobby turned to me. He didn't need to say anything—his leering face said it for him. "Constable Johnston has a gun." Then he gave full attention to the cake. There'd be no further competition for possession of Frankie.

I got a red face when I realised Frankie was scrutinising me. I placed the medal on its purple velvet, and Mrs. Doran put it on the sideboard for future display. I stayed just long enough to have another piece of cake and annoy Pam by taking a handful of the chocolate biscuits.

During the next few days I hung about the garden, talking to Frankie when he came outside. He asked me to lend him my old *Beano*s; he'd missed Biffo the Bear. Did he like Desperate Dan? Oh, aye, I had them all saved up. And he was delighted to learn that Lord Snooty and his Gang were still flummoxing and generally outwitting the Bash Street Kids.

Grandmother shook his hand over the hedge and said what everybody else said for a change and Aunt Madge informed us Mrs. Doran had taken Frankie up to Jackson the Tailor in Belfast and rigged him all out with price no object. Grandmother made a rude sound with her lips and said he'd need more than a suit.

"It won't take them long to get back to their old tricks," she finished up, "and if that woman"—she cocked her head in the direction of Mrs. Doran's house—"thinks they're including Frankie in their 'jobs for the boys coming home' sentiments, she's got another think coming."

I had no idea just what kind of a job a soldier would look for, but Frankie was up and out like a lark. I walked down the Whitewell with him.

"How do I look, love?" He straightened his shoulders in his new suit. It was a sort of nut-brown colour and matched his hair.

"Grand," I said, ignoring the checkered tie. It was a bit loud, but Frankie liked it because it was from a place called Savile Row and he'd plunked down a good bit of his discharge pay on it.

We took to seeing each other down the Whitewell every morning, then he'd hop a tram for Belfast and I'd head for school. Sometimes he got home before me and we'd sit in the Doran garden howling at the comic antics of Biffo, Roger the Dodger, and the rest. Frankie said it was funny the way they never got any older, were never affected by the goings on in the world. I wasn't sure what he meant, but he seemed a bit pensive.

CHAPTER
8

When I flipped the calendar page to the June scene showing Anne Hathaway's eaved cottage, the gardens on Serpentine Parade already overflowed with early yields of candytuft, forget-me-nots, and roses of every colour, and the Sommervilles clucked with delight over a particular bush bearing great apricot tea roses the size of Uncle Dan's fist. That was over a week ago and the gardens said it was already summer, but as Grandmother had predicted, they were a bit premature.

There was still this last day of school to get through and the gaping chasm of hours between nine and three yawned ahead as I plodded towards the village and St. Mary's Star of the Sea Elementary. Frankie had been late these last few days and I'd given up waiting. I turned onto the Whitewell Road, which pointed down to the lough; to the shell beach that dug and cut into our feet for the first few weeks every summer until the skin toughened; to the iron wreck grounded years ago in a winter storm which held treasure we'd never quite found. But this summer we'd find it. Just this last day—and if I wanted to get optimistic—a mere six hours to summer.

Heartened, I put an inch on my step and reached the Camp gates only to find a jeering Bobby sitting like a crow on one of the supporting brick pillars.

"Yaaaah! Jennifer has to go to schooo-ool!"

"You just wait, Bobby McConnell," I said. "You just wait until you go back a day *early*, I'll be waiting for you."

"You'll forget by then.'"

"Oh, no, I won't! If I have to spend all summer remembering, I'll be waiting. . . . What's that you've got on your head?"

In reply, Bobby pointed to the red band encircling his scalp. "This? Oh, I'm Geronimo, and Erik and the others are going to be the cavalry. . ."

I didn't have to hear the rest. I could see it. The Camp grounds were perfect for cowboys and Indians and I pictured Bobby sneaking through mazes of trenches left behind by the soldiers billeted there during the first years of the war, slinking from tree to bush and fighting a pitched battle to the last scalp.

". . . maybe we'll still be here when you get home."
Bobby's tune changed. I made a mean Indian on anybody's
team.

"Maybe they'll let you out early," he said. "We got out
an hour early."

I wished I was a Protestant, God forgive me. I don't
know why the wish presented itself in those words. I mean,
a wish is a wish, and it could just as easily have been "I wish
Catholics got out a day early."

"Anyway," Bobby continued, "you won't have to do
much work today."

That was fine for him to say. He didn't know Miss
McGrath. "I better get cracking or I'll be late," I said.

"It won't matter much if you're late on the last day," he
called after me.

No, indeed, Bobby didn't know Miss McGrath.

Long before coming under her tutelage, we gave Miss
McGrath nothing but our utmost courtesy and deference. If
we ran down the corridor like a pack of wild dogs, we always slowed down to a decorous walk until we were past her
windows, then took up the run again. The word filtered
down through the classroom generations that you'd better
mind your p's and q's, otherwise she'd remember, and when
you reached fifth class, she'd be waiting.

By the time I was in fourth class the dreaded reality set
in. It seemed I was going to live long enough after all to
enter the portals of her classroom. The outgoing survivors
took particular relish in describing the dark mahogany chair
leg she used in her efforts to instill knowledge. Nothing as
ordinary as a ruler or a skinny bamboo cane with a crook
handle for Miss McGrath! And, had she heard them, Miss
McGrath would have been proud of the picturesque adjec-
tives she'd imparted to her former students.

Long ago last September, our first lesson with Miss
McGrath was prefaced by a terse and deadly introduction.

"I'm Miss McGrath." She looked around each stiff face,

which moments before had glowed with summer carelessness, her darting eyes lingering just long enough to mark us, to let us know we were now hers. "Never are the words 'I can't' to be uttered in this room. There are no dullberts in *my* class."

Then she hit the desk with the chair leg and we all jumped. I studied the instrument of terror. Doubtless its evil gleam was kept polished by the outstretched palms of multitudes, and I was not alone in making the resolution to be an apt pupil.

We discovered, as the year went by, that no one could spit out multiplication and division tables like a McGrath pupil. And Miss McGrath's supremacy wasn't confined to reading, writing, and arithmetic either. The Christmas concert, put on by the school every year for the benefit of the chapel building fund, would have been quite ordinary had it not been for Miss McGrath's productions. We were the intelligentsia, the talented, and though the cost was very dear, we occasionally felt a fierce surge of pride in being McGrath veterans.

Well, I'd served my time and had only six more hours before summer and the merciful change to Miss Murphy's gentle ways when I went into sixth class in September.

I arrived in the classroom with a few minutes to spare, and Patsy invited me to come see the babies whenever I felt like it. We'd only see each other on Sunday mornings now, so I said I'd be at the tide a lot learning how to swim and offered to call in from there. I'd read a book about Japanese pearl divers and knew I could find the treasure in the rotting bowels of the wreck once I learned how to swim. The major upset in tradition was about to occur, and I'd relish the look on Bobby's awed face when I stood poised on the deck, arms pointed to the sky, all ready to swoop into the water like a kingfisher.

The murmur of voices ceased as Miss McGrath entered, and I couldn't help a little groan when I saw what she wore.

Miss McGrath had two twin-sets, one cherry and one mustard, which she wore on alternating days. Sometimes the monotony was broken with the wearing of a crisp white blouse. But I hated the sight of that mustard cardigan and its matching jumper, for it seemed Miss McGrath was more ferocious every time she had them on.

Miss McGrath answered our carolling "Good morning, Miss McGrath," with a polite response and a rare smile. We all thought Miss McGrath had really nice teeth. That was the prettiest thing about her—her teeth. And the smile of those pretty teeth this morning dulled the anxiety produced by the mustard twin-set.

"Take out your Catechisms. Study questions one through ten. You have five minutes," she said. Miss McGrath didn't believe in mucking about.

I knew them all off by heart so I just glanced over them until I got to number eight. There was something about number eight that always bothered me; something that I'd never really thought about before.

"Jennifer—number eight. Did God give us free will?"

And as I stood up to answer, my brain was still grasping for the elusive something; something that had to do with the avoirdupois weight tables we'd learned months ago. Now, when Miss McGrath asked a question, the answer was required instantly, and my thoughts just wouldn't disengage instantaneously. That hesitation started the fatal chain of events.

Another thing we'd learned soon after entering the fifth class was that the words "I don't know" came a close second to "I can't." Maura Malone was the only one to have erred. That chair leg had blistered her hands and "I don't know" was never heard again—until I heard myself blurting out the forbidden phrase.

"What don't you know?" Miss McGrath's voice dripped icicles.

I tried to correct myself. "Oh, I know the answer, Miss

McGrath," I said eagerly and was all ready to rattle it off when she said again, "What don't you know?" There was a distinct rise in volume this time.

"Well," I started conversationally, knowing full well it wouldn't work, "I was just thinking that it's not balanced right. . . ." I got no further.

Miss McGrath's eyes got smaller and the icy blue depths got deeper. "The Church isn't governed by earthly principles. These are Articles of *Faith*. How dare you question Articles of Faith, you impudent pup—*get out here!*"

Oh, God, I was in for it. Miss McGrath hadn't clouted me in ages, not since the Mother Nature fiasco when she said I'd made a mockery of God. Although I'd done what she asked, she took exception to God dancing through the fields with blossoms in His hair and revelling with the men and women tilling the new mantle of green. I didn't like it much either, but it was the best sentence in the whole composition and I didn't want to waste it.

I trotted out to the front of the class and she didn't have to ask me to put out my hand. The chair leg poised above, hovering like a bumblebee about to light on a honeysuckle, and I dismissed the temptation to jerk that hand away at the last instant. Experience told me the tips of the fingers hurt more. And, if she missed, the agony would start all over again—double.

"Did God give us free will?" Number eight was never asked more deliberately.

"Yes, God gave us free will to choose between good and evil, but with a strong inclination towards evil." I gasped out the Catechism answer all in one breath.

The chair leg descended with a bone-smashing whack, but I didn't dare comfort my hand until she sent me back to my seat. She didn't. She wasn't through with me yet.

"Is Jennifer Marshall's faith *strong*?" she asked the class. The room was filled with a resounding *"No!"* Miss McGrath had quite a knack for invoking the scorn of our peers. And the telegraph pole crashed down again.

A wish half formed in my pain-crazed head, its content vaguely consisting of my falling through the floor. But it was quickly overwhelmed by the remembrance of my turn-coat wish earlier that morning.

"*Is Jennifer Marshall's faith in jeopardy?*" the mustard twin-set yelled, as if privy to my very thoughts.

"*Yes!*" bawled the good little Catholic girls of Greencastle to the accompanying swish of the chair leg.

Mortified, I slunk back to my seat, my wounded hand squeezed underneath my armpit in an effort to cut off all circulation. It was only twenty past nine.

I had tried everything with Miss McGrath: extra pennies for the Black Babies box dropped in conspicuously; more than my share of flowers for the May altar—nothing worked. And there was no use complaining to Grandmother about this villain either. She considered Miss McGrath a Godsend to Catholics, a champion who turned out scholars to thwart the Orange Order's decree that Catholics were only fit for menial labour.

And it seemed the whole village agreed. I never saw any parent come to the door of that classroom decrying child abuse.

"There'll come a day, Jennifer, when you'll see Miss McGrath in a different light," Grandmother said. "Most of the wee girls in your class will be doffing in the mill the minute they hit fourteen—there'll be no secondary school for them."

But Grandmother said the Labour Government had promised some important changes if they got elected and that Miss McGrath was seeing to it we were ready to take advantage of them. She even went as far as intimating some would make it all the way to University. The word "socialise" studded her ramblings about the Labour Government, whatever that was. But it sounded friendly and if it helped me to get to University, where I knew they just read books, I supposed it was good. I didn't want to be a doffer.

I knew how much Aunt Madge hated the mill and the cloying, sour smell of flax she brought home with her.

"Well, that's what is ahead of you if they have their way," she said. "You see that?" Grandmother poked her finger at the *Belfast Telegraph*. "That's what you'll be up against—that's it in a nutshell!" Her fingernail stabbed up and down the black columns of newsprint at the repetitious "Protestant Only Need Apply" that stood out boldly over the "Help Wanted" appeals.

The phrase rattled about in my head, eventually meeting up with Bobby's contention that Northern Ireland was for them only.

"Is Northern Ireland a Protestant state for a Protestant people, Granny?"

"That's what they're trying to shove down . . . Where'd you hear that anyway?" She looked at me with sudden interest.

"I can't remember." There was no sense advertizing I hadn't watched what I said.

"Well, it's time you knew anyway," she said. "Aye, that old reprobate Craigavon boasted that one . . ." And she went into a tirade about the former Prime Minister egging on the Protestants not to employ Catholics. Grandmother was as well up on the loquacious Lord Craigavon's speeches as Bobby's daddy and I wished I'd never heard anything he said. That he didn't like us was clear, but it was the disquieting feeling he thought we were not as *good* as Protestants that bothered me the most.

Aye, Grandmother said, I'd see Miss McGrath in a different light when I was flung out there competing for jobs they didn't want to give me.

A couple of thick red welts marked the path of the chair leg. I looked up at Miss McGrath, but the light hadn't changed a bit.

Fractions and quizzes about trains coming at each other at different speeds took up the rest of the morning. Fifth class had the largest number of students, and Miss McGrath had devised a method to make her job easier. Five of us were considered McGrath "stars," and we were placed at the head of five lines of girls. When Miss McGrath introduced a new sum or another phase of grammar, the five stars were expected to grasp the new knowledge in a hurry and then impart it to the line of girls behind us while Miss McGrath spent her time concocting other crucifying lessons. Now, this bit of craftiness wouldn't have bothered me except that if someone in your line muffed it, the star was punished right along with the dope she hadn't enlightened.

I knew I was still in Miss McGrath's bad books when she added Eilish Loughran to my line that afternoon. Eilish had been in Miss McGrath's class longer than any of us and that was enough right there to brook compassion. Now, I felt sorry for Eilish, I even liked Eilish, but she was a Loughran and one of the witless unfortunates that family bred. Sometimes she drooled onto the paper she laboured over and her dull eyes had a constant baleful expression. Although she could read, it was painful to listen to her slow progress through a paragraph. But retention of what she'd read was another thing. It was enough for Eilish to remember how to pronounce each word, but it never occurred to her that those words strung together gave valuable information sometimes.

Miss McGrath chose this last day of school to prod Eilish to new heights—in *my* line. The other stars gave me a knowing look but hardened their hearts against their condemned colleague and set briskly about their task. The girls in my line rallied behind me, not because they cared if I got belted again, but because the stigma of belonging to a disgraced line clung to them too. They'd help each other, they said, and I could concentrate on Eilish.

Miss McGrath had decreed just one verse for Eilish, but she might as well have ordered the whole poem. Eilish wrung her hands and turned those baleful eyes on me as we began. Over and over it, splitting the stanzas, mending the fractured poem together again, back to the first three words. Frantic, I pleaded with Eilish, then threatened her with a good thumping when we got outside the school gates.

It was the wrong thing to do for immediately a sharp ammoniac smell spread its vapors around the room. Eilish had peed herself. Oh, God! Oh, God in Heaven, she'd peed the floor!

She just stood there in the puddle, her eyes rolling like someone possessed, and I jumped as the spreading puddle reached my shoes.

"Take that disgraceful girl out and see that she's cleaned up," said Miss McGrath.

I pulled at the whimpering Eilish, and the other girls looked at me as though I'd peed myself too.

"And bring back the pail and mop." Miss McGrath's scathing voice followed us out to the corridor.

Eilish still smelled ripe even though I'd washed her legs, and I had to do most of the mopping up too since Eilish moved slowly and we needed all the time we could get to cram that verse into her.

Miss McGrath was already examining the line next to ours. My glum failure stood next to me, no doubt anticipating our joint execution. There was nothing else for it—I'd just have to tell Miss McGrath that Eilish was simple and she just couldn't remember that much at a time.

Miss McGrath ran her fingers up and down the chair leg, caressing its fine, varnished grain. I appraised the gesture, and the mustard twin-set, and decided to shut my mouth and let fate take its inevitable course.

"Eilish Loughran—begin!"

Eilish's eyes swivelled once in their sockets and her thick tongue lay outside her lips for a long second before attempting the murder of Wordsworth.

I wandered . . . lonely . . . as a cloud that floats . . .

on high o'er vales and hills. When . . . all at once I
saw . . . a crowd, a host of golden daffodils.

No poet ever received a finer tribute, and never had my
ears heard a more eloquent recitation. I *saw* that golden sea
rippling in the April breeze, felt again the queer aching inside my chest first brought on by the bluebells, and now
knew just what Wordsworth was up to—finally.

I stared weakly at Eilish's grinning face, and it seemed
to me there was a faint glimmer at the back of her eyes that
wasn't there before. And the light around Miss McGrath
changed ever so slightly as she laid the chair leg on the side
of her desk. No, indeed, there were no dullberts in Miss
McGrath's class.

I watched the clock out of the corner of my eye as the
impartial black hands crawled towards three o'clock. Ten
minutes and I'd be free of school, free of Catechism, and
free of Miss McGrath forever.

At five minutes to three, Miss McGrath's sadism man-
ifested itself to the fullest.

"Well, girls, you're loose for the summer," she said,
showing us her pretty teeth. "I'll see you in September—
sixth class is *mine* next year."

Patsy and I stood where the Whitewell and Shore roads
formed a T. I told her I didn't think I could get through
another year with Miss McGrath. She agreed with me. What
was I thinking of anyway to dissect the Catechism; nobody
in her right mind would make that mistake. Then she
changed the subject to the dancing competition and I let
her chatter away, thankful that no great input from me was
necessary.

Nobody in her right mind—maybe I was a bit
"touched," right enough. Why did I even worry about
things like number eight? There was only one other person
in the whole of Greencastle who'd have understood about

number eight, just as he had about the graveyard clabber. If Uncle Dan were my daddy, he'd take my part against Miss McGrath too. I needed him. They just *had* to get married.

Patsy nudged me and reiterated what her mother said about Ann saying she had to get dancing shoes. Something clicked. ". . . she *had* to get married—the whole place was talking."

"Oh, yes," I said to Patsy, "you have to get dancing shoes." If the whole place said you had to get married. . . . I was awestruck for a second, then I drew a long, deliberate bead on Aunt Nin.

Aunt Nin said my visit was a nice surprise and handed me a Fox's Glacier mint from her sweetie cannister. She gave me a funny look, though, as she sat down opposite me.

"Did you know my Aunt Madge and Uncle Dan *have* to get married?" I put the special stress just the way Patsy had.

Aunt Nin's hand flew to her mouth. Then she released it.

"Jennifer! That's a terrible thing to say."

God, but she was as down on Uncle Dan as Grandmother was! I persisted. Oh, aye, they definitely had to get married.

That such talk should come out of the mouths of children.

"Oh, but it's true, Aunt Nin, I heard them talking." I didn't say what about.

Aunt Nin's normally placid eyes took on a sudden keenness and her voice was just a hint above a whisper.

"Is there a child involved?"

I beamed at her. "Oh, yes!" I said, relieved she was so understanding.

Her hand clapped her mouth again. Then she said (unjustly, I thought), "God have pity on them!" She rummaged in the sweetie cannister again and gave me another mint to see me up the road.

She watched me from the doorway. I waved and popped the mint in my mouth. Now all I had to do was wait.

CHAPTER
9

Greencastle had acquired four new souls by the second week of June. Actually, two were secondhand, but they were new to us. I met them all on Sunday. The new priest was first.

Every pew in the chapel was jammed; those that hadn't put foot in the chapel for years were there, so Grandmother and I ended up in the balcony with the other latecomers. There were only four rows in the balcony, the three back ones cut in half to make room for Ann Mulholland's organ and reserved for the choir, which meant we were right down in the front row, our elbows resting on the balustrade.

I loved the balcony, for I could spend the Mass hour gazing down on the exotic nests and flower beds the women wore, picking out my favourites. Grandmother didn't like the balcony. It was unsafe, she said, had been for years, but nothing was going to be done about it until it crashed down around our ears like so many other things.

Ann Mulholland pumped the ancient organ's pedal and whispered "One, two, three," and the chapel was filled with the "Panis Angelica." This was one of the best parts of being in the balcony—you got to see the choir. The women were in the three rows to the right of the organ and the men in the three rows on the left. Well, Molly Logan was among the men. Grandmother said that was because Ann would find herself without a contralto if she insisted Molly stand on the women's side.

Now we all knew Molly was a woman, but we treated her like a man. She walked like a man, talked like a man, hung around the Donegal Arms and the Gaelic Hut with the men, and Uncle Dan said she could play hurley as well as any of them. I said "Hello" to her in passing just to hear her raw voice answer. But Grandmother said there wasn't a finer singer than Molly Logan though those Woodbines would do her in before long. I'd never heard Molly sing except in unison with the choir. Grandmother said Molly only condescended to display her gift during Midnight Mass and that I'd never heard anything until I heard Molly Logan's solo on Christmas Eve. I wasn't sure whether this was Grandmother's attempt at a conundrum or if she was just sorry for Molly. She'd lost her father and four brothers in the big 1941 German raid. The Logan house was at the gable end of a row of houses close to Aunt Nin's. Children now jumped through its front window frames and played in its wall-free rooms. No one lived there anymore. Molly and her mother lodged in a back room above the Donegal Arms. It was a shame, Grandmother said, that Molly ran around as she did, but there was no real badness in her. Not like some others she could mention.

Molly's face was brown and speckled, like a pebble in a stream, and her light brown hair was cut short and parted at the side, throwing it into a cow's lick. She was tall and lean and had no notion of style at all. The same long, shapeless, double-breasted coat hung from her angular shoulders from Sunday to Sunday.

Grandmother dug me in the ribs with her elbow and I turned away from Molly Logan to the altar. It was banked with white and yellow gladioli, its white linen cloths glowing gold from the reflection of the stained glass window showing the glorious Assumption of Our Lady into Heaven. St. Mary's had two other stained glass windows: one depicting Our Lord sweating blood in the Garden of Gethsemane, which gave off rich scarlet and amber hues, and the other showing St. Patrick in bright emerald robes with a golden crosier in his hand and his bare foot crushing the head of a grape-coloured snake. Thanks to St. Patrick, there wasn't a snake, not even a garden snake, left in Ireland. You could have drowned in the colours of those windows. Grandmother said they were worth a fortune and the only thing that took the bare look off St. Mary's.

Well, that was all right if you were inside the chapel and God's good daylight streaming through them, but from the outside, they looked leaden and drab. The only time Protestants had a chance to see how beautiful those windows were was during dark winter evenings when the chapel was lit inside for novenas. The candles and lights couldn't do them justice, but it gave a remote idea to those looking up at the chapel that there was more to those windows than met the eye.

Grandmother nudged me away from the Garden of Gethsemane as the sacristy door opened and out strode our new priest in a swish of cream and gold vestments. Light of step, he took the three stairs up to the altar base, genuflected, then swung round with outstretched arms, and smiled all around. The gold from the Assumption window flooded his face. There was a sigh from the women's side of the choir confirming my first thought. Not only was he young, the new priest was handsome and reminded me of Tyrone Power. Actually, Tyrone Power would have liked to have had Father Murphy's head of thick, dark hair. Then he blessed us and if the rest of the faithful were like me, they forgot Father Sheridan with the first Dominus Vobiscum.

Father Murphy said the shortest Mass I'd ever heard. He was a blur of action, and the altar boys had a time keeping up with him. The only time he slowed down was at the Offering. He poised the Eucharist above his head for a long time, looking up at it, saying the Latin not in Father Sheridan's monologue, but with stress on some words, whispers on others.

". . . this is My Body . . ."

I was rigid with anticipation and went into a slump of relief when he finally lowered the chalice and drank the wine.

". . . this is My Blood . . ."

Grandmother was following the mass too. Her fingers hadn't moved a bead on the rosary, which was wrapped tightly around her joined knuckles.

Father Murphy's sermon was short too. You couldn't call it a sermon—he was really talking to us. He just said a few words about how much Father Sheridan would miss us, that he could already feel the warmth and generosity of the parish of Greencastle. The war was behind us, he said, but the challenge lay ahead; our Faith would be sorely tested; we were to pray for forbearance to keep out of the clutches of those who'd prey on national passions (whatever they were). But together we'd make Greencastle the bastion of Faith in the Down and Connor Diocese. Then he hung his dark head for a minute before lifting pleading blue eyes that looked right into mine and entreated us to pray for him that he'd be worthy of doing God's work amongst us.

I clapped. God help me, but I got out a quick burst of applause before Grandmother's manacled hands got loose of her rosary. Ann Mulholland was as quick as Grandmother and had that organ pumped and swelling out "Faith of our Fathers" before I slunk down in the seat thinking there'd be no better time than now for the balcony to cave in. That snake at the feet of St. Patrick felt better than I did.

Grandmother and I walked through the crush of people down the chapel path. Everyone was discussing the new priest. They said he was young, but God, wasn't he smart? Maynooth Seminary (that's where they made priests) was certainly turning out the scholars for us. Did you hear the way the Latin rolled off his tongue?

I was headed for a bad end, Grandmother concluded as we reached Aunt Nin's, and it'd be a month of Sundays before I attended any more of those matinees, for they were turning my head if I couldn't distinguish between picture houses and chapels.

Grandmother and Aunt Nin sat facing each other by the dead grate. It was too warm to light the fire.

"And this is John that I've been telling you about, Maggie."

Aunt Nin's lodger had taken up residence sometime during the week, but that meeting was uneventful, thank God. There was nothing to him. He was just there, a thin, grey-looking man with a pointed chin and eyes the colour of the lough in winter. He had a slight cast in his right eye—actually sometimes he had it, sometimes not. I knew that would put Grandmother off him right there for that inconsistency was the difference, she believed, between someone having the "evil eye" and a person afflicted with just plain skelly eyes.

He answered Grandmother's few polite questions with "Dublin," "A while anyway," and "No, but I've good prospects." Grandmother informed Aunt Nin that Frankie was having a time of it.

"Maybe he should have stayed in the army." Aunt Nin patted her fluff of white hair. She looked like an elderly angel.

"It's not all bad," the Lodger said, his right eye roaming inward for a split second. "The army, I mean. A man can pick up some useful things in the army—what was that fella's name again?"

Aunt Nin told him then steered Grandmother onto the new priest.

The Lodger didn't look at me at all and went back to hiding behind his newspaper. He shoved his teacup past me towards the yellow tea-cosy at Rosie's waiting hand. I hadn't seen Rosie in a while, since she'd been working all sorts of odd shifts at the mill. It hadn't done her any harm though, for she looked stones lighter and I don't know why I'd thought her hair was the colour of weak tea. It was more amber this morning and hung in soft waves around her shoulders. She poured the Lodger's tea.

"Have you seen Patsy's new brother and sister yet, Jennifer?"

I shook my head. Since school ended I'd been isolated from any form of Catholic tribal unity. I supposed I was the last one to get a look at them in the whole of Greencastle.

Grandmother's observation that "Them that need it, don't get it" affirmed itself while I was at Patsy's house. She was scraping porridge into five bowls for herself and the four other children. She'd been crying.

"I didn't!" the one called Michael shouted when Patsy said he'd ruined her dancing costume by throwing a piece of toast at Kathleen.

The costume hung on the back of the scullery door, a dark grease stain marring the bodice. A work of art, that costume was, and they said the Widow had spent weeks piping it with yellow braid and embroidering the harps and shamrocks on it. All in a good cause, people said, for Patsy was the best Irish dancer in the North. She'd walk away with all the medals, Ann Mulholland predicted, when she was entered in the championships in the Free State. Yes, Patsy would show the Free Staters that we Northerners weren't behind the back door.

"I can't keep anything good," Patsy cried. "They won't let anything alone!"

I looked around the tiny room. Odd socks littered the scuffed linoleum, clothes in jumbled piles covered the sideboard, and the sleeve of a jumper hung drunkenly from beneath the settee cushions where someone had stuffed it. The youngest—well, she was the youngest until a few weeks ago—sat naked by the scullery door shredding what was left of a newspaper.

I thought of my cherished books holding all the interesting friends a person could want; of my paper dolls—a whole family of sisters I packed away in a shoebox with all their lovely clothes. I gave a shuddering look back at Patsy's dancing costume, wondering how she'd protected it this long.

"Ask Aunt Nin how to get it out," I said, groping for the remedy I'd heard somewhere. "I think you cover it with brown paper and lift it right out with a hot iron."

Patsy looked doubtful, her big blue eyes still holding a lot of water.

"Ask Aunt Nin," I urged again. "She knows a lot about things like that."

She gave me a "nothing to lose" shrug, then took me up the narrow stairs to see the new babies.

They lay, feet together, in a cot that was jammed between the wall and their mother's bed.

"This one's Kevin and that's Theresa," Patsy said.

I don't know how she knew the difference.

"My mammy says Theresa looks just like me when I was born." Patsy's mother nodded this was so from the bed. She also nodded she was feeling better, and Patsy said the doctor would give her the "all clear" next week.

I bent down over the cot. I liked the smell of babies. Yes, Patsy had everything I wanted—even long hair. Wanting had its drawbacks, but God help Patsy, she *needed* more room.

As I walked the few steps back to Aunt Nin's I determined it couldn't do any harm to approach Aunt Nin on the subject of stains. But The News of the World was expounding to Grandmother on "taints." Rosie and the Lodger had gone for a walk and at first I thought Aunt Nin was filling us in on the distaff side of the Lodger's family.

"There were no taints on the mother's family," she said staunchly. "God rest her, but there wasn't a finer woman than his mother, Maggie. It's a blessing she was taken when she was."

Then Aunt Nin's observations took a sudden cant towards the paternal blood ties. "But I mind when his father's sister up and turned her coat—Colette had no faith, no faith a'tall—oh, there's bad blood in some families, Maggie . . ."

It was Uncle Dan they were talking about! More specifically, his Aunt Colette. I knew the story. Some said that she'd been mad with grief when her baby died without being baptised. But most maintained Colette had turned her coat because the Protestants had no Limbo. She'd no faith, they said, and where would we all be without faith?

Aunt Nin gave a dire shake of her head. "Not another man on the job would touch it. Said they'd dig every inch of the field, but they'd have to get somebody else to dig up that bush!"

My scalp shrunk. I asked, "What bush?" but deep down I already knew what they were getting at. Aunt Nin informed me Uncle Dan had unearthed a thorn tree from the centre of a field—a fairy bush!

"Ach, not that we really believe all that stuff," Aunt Nin said with a little laugh, "but isn't it funny the way things happen?" Her eyes took on a sleekit gleam. "The hurley team got beat yesterday and Dan got a rap across the skull that opened him up to the tune of five stitches!"

"Frankly," said Grandmother, "I think the man has the head staggers—always have!"

And they went into a long exchange that travelled Uncle Dan's downward path. In one desperate year, he'd thrown up a charmed life, a life procured by his mother's sacrifices.

"She went about with newspapers in her shoes to stop the water letting in—and do you mind that coat, Maggie?" Aunt Nin's chins rippled with indignation. "Sure it was nothing but a bunch of holes sewn together!"

"Aye, I mind."

He'd been the only Catholic in Greencastle's living

memory to enter that Holy of Holies, University, and he'd emerged a fully fledged Irish history professor. Uncle Dan's star soared to its zenith when the Christian Brothers snapped him up right away.

"Mind you, Nin, I think all that steeping in pagan learning had a hand in him going the way he did." Grandmother leaned forward confidentially. "He practically told me one night he *worshipped* the druids!" At this, their knowing eyes and slow nods said things to each other I wasn't privy to. "He tried to wheedle his way out of damning himself by saying if Irish women only knew how well they were protected in the old days they'd never stand for the way the priests had handcuffed them." Grandmother's eyebrows arched up. "Can you believe that? Handcuffed! Of course, I told him more's the pity they hadn't been able to cuff *him!* Sure, the last time he put foot in the chapel was at his mother's funeral!"

"And the Widow was telling me, Maggie, that from the minute the eyestrings broke on her Dan never spoke another word to his Da. Lived in the same house and never said a word—even when they were carrying the oul' fella out! Mind you, Joe O'Neill was an oul' rip. . . ." Then Aunt Nin chastized herself for speaking ill of the dead. The living were fair game though.

"No wonder the Christian Brothers got rid of him," said Grandmother. "It didn't take them long to see through him. . ."

"But that's not the way it was, Granny—remember what Aunt Madge told us that night?" They looked at me as if I were an intruder.

"All I remember," Grandmother said stoically, "is that he hasn't been associated with the Christian Brothers since."

That was true—he wasn't. But Grandmother always managed to brush away facts that didn't suit her. I remembered very well the night Aunt Madge informed us Uncle Dan had given up teaching history. I distinctly heard her phrase it that way, but Grandmother just twisted it right around and said she'd fully expected the Christian Brothers "to catch on to him." After Aunt Madge fled the living room, Grandmother sat in front of the fire staring into the grey cinders, and her face didn't reflect the triumph she'd displayed to Aunt Madge at all. There was just no fathoming Grandmother sometimes.

I liked Uncle Dan's kind of history. He was steeped in the lore and legend of Ireland and he even knew things about Greencastle nobody else knew. Sometimes, during the summer, he and Aunt Madge took me along with them on a ramble. We'd walk for miles in the scented evening air, up the Whitewell Road, cutting off on the Throne Path that would eventually lead to the Cave Hill.

"Do you know why they call it the Throne Path, Jennifer?" Uncle Dan asked me one night as we picked our way over the giant tree roots that served as stairs.

"Because it runs past the old Throne Hospital," I answered with the mild tolerance adults bestowed on me when they thought I'd asked a daft question.

"Ach, no, love"—he laughed—"the Path was called the Throne Path hundreds of years before there was thought of a hospital."

Then his eyes lifted up to the Cave Hill and he pointed to the dark purple hulk of Napoleon's Nose. "Up there," he said, "is where they used to crown the Kings of Ulster on a throne hewn out of rock and draped with fox fur."

Grandmother would have told him his head was cut and the sawdust was running out the back of it, but I just said, "Kings are crowned at Westminister in England, Uncle Dan."

"Not your Kings, Jennifer," he said ruefully. "Up there the O'Neills were crowned Kings of their own people."

"O'Neills? Are they anything to you, Uncle Dan?" I asked, intrigued that I might be talking to royalty, however distant.

"Well, *he* likes to think so," said Aunt Madge, "so we might as well humour him."

With exaggerated dignity, Uncle Dan said no one could prove he wasn't. And I was enthralled as we trod that same clay which had brushed the foot leather of the Great O'Neill and his clan on their way to the Throne; impassioned by their heroic stands against the grasping English; and devastated by the treachery and defeats that followed.

"Is the Throne still there?" I whispered, not wanting to break the spell.

He shook his head.

"What happened to it?"

Uncle Dan thrust his hands into his pockets. "It was smashed during the revels for Queen Victoria's Jubilee." His face showed lines I'd never noticed before. "A thousand years smashed to smithereens," he said to the darkening sky.

I think Aunt Madge thought I was going to cry, for she rounded on Uncle Dan. "Quit filling the child's head with your stories, Dan, if you can't put a better ending on them than that!"

"You're sounding like the good Brothers, Madge," he said and sidestepped a swing from her handbag. He laughed as he caught her wrist and pulled her up against him.

Now, I turned my head as quickly as I could for I knew my presence interfered with the kissing sessions they'd have if I weren't with them. And far be it from me to let a little kissing get me barred from future walks. But I'd seen the way he looked at her and I knew my Aunt Madge could cut his heart out for a play toy and he'd swear he didn't need it anyway.

"You see, Jennifer," Uncle Dan said, restraining my aunt's giggling aggressiveness, "the O'Neills are still being attacked!"

Grandmother and Aunt Nin bore out those words again this morning. There was a blight on his life and I was to mark their words. Those that took liberties with the fairies—well, I was just to wait and see. This last was said with anticipatory horror.

"Of course, I'm sure Madge knows what she's about"—Aunt Nin refilled Grandmother's cup—"and if anybody can bring him around, Madge can. God, but I hope so before they start counting their fingers . . ."

Grandmother's teacup hit the saucer with a vehemence that would have cracked it if I'd set it down that way.

"Just what are you getting at, Nin?" Grandmother's eyes were a queer dark green and her voice was overly gracious.

"Ach, you know how people talk, Maggie—and they've been courting a *long* time. . . ."

A new dread cut into my thoughts. Was Aunt Nin saying the fairies would exact vengeance on Aunt Madge, too? I pushed this aside though, for as far as I knew they only waxed malicious towards the principal.

"Aye, I know how some people talk, Nin," Grandmother said, still with that amiability that didn't suit her. "And I'm sure you did your best to squash this tripe."

"Sure, you know I'd never say a word . . ."

And as I went out to the water closet, she was saying Greencastle was full of rumour-mongers.

I hated to admit it, but Uncle Dan's being on the outs with both the fairies and Holy Mother Church made me apprehensive about his chances. While there was an antidote for transgressions against orthodox religion (an Act of Contrition would probably do the trick), nobody knew of anything to placate the fairies.

Since it wasn't dark, I stood up on the seat, scrabbled for the chain, and gave it a yank. The machinations gave their customary roar, my cue to jump for fear it sucked me into the lavatory. But something caught my eye at the last second. A dull black gun lay on the top of the water tank.

The violent churnings of the lavatory ended with a few

greedy slurps, then settled to a hushed sibilant hissing. I jumped down.

Wait till I told Bobby McConnell my Aunt Nin had a real live gun! He'd probably ask if I'd touched it and I briefly considered doing just that, but I could just say "Anytime I want to" and that would shut him up.

Grandmother was just finishing what sounded like a prediction.

". . . aye, Nin, the country's about to go mad again."

It wasn't until later that I remembered Catholics weren't allowed to have guns, so I made up my mind to watch what I said to Bobby McConnell, which in this instance turned out to mean, "Keep your big mouth shut altogether."

CHAPTER
===10===

The smells of cut grass and growing flowers eventually overpowered the manure compost the Sommervilles had subjected us to for the past week.

Our summer boundaries were nonexistent, and Bobby and the rest of us roamed the Castle grounds, the Camp, the fields, and everybody's garden that had anything worthwhile growing in it. Breakfast and tea were the only meals eaten at home in summer with any regularity. Lunch was almost always where we happened to be at the moment of hunger. Raspberries were free in the fields, stream water drunk from cupped hands, but garden fare depended solely on the presence or absence of adults. Nothing was sacred to us. Even Constable Johnston's apple trees got a trimming. The Sommervilles' gooseberries were our favourite until Bobby said wasn't it funny how we didn't mind eating things that had been fed by horse dung?

Rhubarb was on the menu for today. Pam and I crouched on our hunkers at the hole in the hedge, eyes intent on Grandpa McCartney's scullery window. Not a shadow there. We gave the "all clear" to Bobby with a subtle shake of the hedge. He crept out of the rhubarb bed and made a low run across the garden. He passed the greenish red stalks through to us, then crawled to the safety of Pam's side of the hedge. I counted five stalks, the very thought of the sweet tartness making my jaw glands ache.

"Who gets the one?" I said. I wasn't a McGrath star for nothing.

Bobby said he definitely got two stalks for taking the risk, so it was down to Pam and myself and each pleaded her case until Bobby said, "Have one an' a half each." Bobby McConnell could be right smart sometimes.

The rhubarb was young, more on the sour side of tart, and just a promise of what was to come later in summer. But we tucked in until the insides of our cheeks were raw. I gave Pam a fraction of my other half.

Grandpa McCartney opened his back door and we crouched lower. Pam was still crunching and Bobby gave her a thump so she had to sit there with her mouth fermenting. Grandpa was at the rhubarb bed parting the wide green leaves with his blackthorn stick.

"Hee, hee, hee." He didn't have his teeth in. "Heee . . . heee . . . heee," he chuckled again, looking over at the hole in the hedge. He knew! He'd had his eye on us all the time; either that or that sleekit, snottery-nosed William . . .

Grandpa wiped his slabbering mouth with his cuff and chortled afresh. Apprehension set in. He pointed his stick at the hole.

"The buggers that ate that rhubarb'll skitter themselves to death. Haaaa . . . haaa . . . haaaa . . . it's not ready! *Haaaaaaaah* . . ."

We ran.

My insides got a good wrenching that afternoon but I was all right by teatime. I went over to Pam's house. She hadn't fared as well and was still confined within close proximity of the bathroom. Mrs. Boyd was livid with Grandpa;

mothers weren't at all like Grandmothers. She told the story to Mr. Boyd when he came home from work, which was my cue to leave. Just before I shut the door behind me, I heard her exclaim, "God, but I'd rather have the Pope of Rome living next door to me than that wicked oul' blert!"

Her choice of neighbours puzzled me.

There was a quickening during the first few days of July. An imperceptible flurry of excitement permeated Serpentine Parade. Sagging bunting was nailed back into place, and Bobby's mother saw fit to put a large coloured photograph of the Royal Family in their front window. I walked past several times and studied the nice face of King George. Bobby and I had made a list of "People I'd like to meet." The King was at the top of both our lists along with Roy Rogers for him and Dale Evans for me. Bobby added Superman and I argued that Superman wasn't real, but Bobby said that had nothing to do with him wanting to meet him, did it? So I added the Secret Three to mine. I also listed Pope Pius—not so much because I wanted to meet him, but somehow it seemed disloyal to have the King on it without the balancing presence of the Pope. Naturally, Bobby didn't know about this addition. But though the list was changed often, the King was permanent.

King George looked handsome in the uniform. He wore a cap slung with gold braids and rows of coloured ribbons on the breast of his jacket. Everybody looked better in uniforms. Even Frankie Doran didn't look nearly as handsome in the ordinary clothes he now wore. The Queen wore a hat that was just one big flower posy and a sweet, plump smile. A couple of Welsh corgis sat at her feet. Princess Margaret gave a laughing wave, distinctly at variance with the serious face and clasped hands of the elder Princess Elizabeth. They wore ordinary coats and matching hats, which was quite disappointing as far as Princesses went.

"Are they going to ask us to put up bunting this time, Granny?"

"No," she said, "no, they'll not."

"What are they celebrating?"

"The Twelfth."

"What's it for?"

She gouged out the eye of a potato. "To show their loyalty."

I told Grandmother that the Dorans and the McKays weren't putting up any bunting this time, and neither were the Sommervilles. Grandmother dismissed the Dorans and the McKays with a disdainful snort, but not the Sommervilles. They weren't low people, Grandmother said. I thought she might have forgotten they were English, but she hadn't.

"The English don't understand what Orangemen are. But the few that live here soon get their eyes opened."

And Grandmother was jittery. "Where are you going?" and "Who are you with?" replaced "Keep away from those dams." Unnecessary demands that I be home on time for tea became routine and I'd finish the injunctions with "I know—I know—watch what I say!"

Mrs. Doran was cross, too. I heard her yelling up the stairs at Frankie, "Get up, Frankie! The morning's gone." She waited for an answer and then shouted, "Have you a future? *Have you?*"

Pam and Bobby suddenly had similar instructions to be home on time. Pam had joined the Girls Brigade and Bobby the Boys Brigade, and both had meetings to attend every night but Sunday for the next fortnight.

I sat on the kerb scratching designs in the dust with a twig. Pam marched through her gate all turned out in a white blouse, a very short navy skirt, and a navy beret with the Girls Brigade badge on it. Freshly whitened sandshoes completed the uniform. Even the word "uniform" sounded crisp and smart.

She waved a bright "cheerio" to me and I scowled at her back. I'd look a lot better in that uniform than she did. Short skirts didn't go with bandy legs.

Pam's brothers congregated with other older boys at the lamp-post. They all wore the long grey pants and black blazers they wore to church, but white sashes were now girdled diagonally from left shoulders and anchored to white canvas belts. To top it off they had strange little black pillbox hats with a few white stripes running round them. Elastic chinbands kept them in place.

They must have been waiting for Bobby, for as soon as he reached them they all headed down the street and turned onto the Whitewell. I wanted to laugh at that pillbox hat. It looked like a sweetie. "Take off the licorice allsort and eat it, Bobby!" I could have shouted that. I threw the twig at the lamp-post and stared down at my mucky sandshoes. They were flecked with so many stains it'd take a whole bottle of whitening to cover them. Grandmother kept whitening under the sink . . .

A rush of enthusiasm hit me. I still had that navy blue pleated skirt Grandmother insisted I stop wearing in the interests of modesty. It'd be just right for the Girls Brigade. The Girls Brigade! It had a ring of good-fellowship about it. Girls' clubs were wonderful things and I followed the adventures of the Secret Three in the *School Friend* every week. They were loyal and true and I was in constant apprehension that they'd never bowl over the wicked prefect of the sixth form. I could spot the wicked prefect long before she planted forged evidence of cheating in The Secret Three's locker. Her name was usually Zoe or Zelda or some equally exotic concoction. I'd be onto anyone who had a foreign name in the Girls Brigade.

Within the hour I placed a dazzling pair of sandshoes on top of the biscuit tin. They'd be dry long before Napoleon's Nose hid the sun. The whitening bottle was almost empty.

Bobby's elaborate "picture of the day" was being enacted in the second field. These productions were usually based loosely on whatever we'd seen on Saturday at the matinee, and I had strong supporting roles to his star status. I played Annie Oakley to his Kit Carson, Guinevere to King Arthur, and Pam and Erik alternated as foot soldiers and chief villains. Occasional farces were performed in the interests of fairness (more accurately, though, the villains threatened to quit playing) that cast Erik and Pam in heroic parts and Bobby and I as Prince John and the Sheriff of Nottingham. But these scenarios never lasted long.

Erik had to go somewhere with his mother so Bobby had created a rather hollow miscellany involving an unknown Prince Robert the Valiant at the head of thousands of Crusaders and Sultan Saladin and his Grand Vizier.

The Grand Vizier gave me the bad news as we defended a breastwork against an onslaught from Robert the Valiant.

"I don't think Catholics are allowed in the Girls Brigade," Pam gasped, hurling a sod at Bobby.

He must have sensed the mortal wound inflicted on Sultan Saladin and took advantage of my paralysis by storming the citadel. I sank down and lay back against the captured mound.

"What's the matter with *you*?" Bobby leaned on his sword.

"I've got sweat in my eyes."

"No she doesn't," Pam said. "She's mad because she can't join the Girls Brigade."

"I'm not mad!" I shouted.

"You are!

"I'm *not!*"

"You are so—you're mad because you're a Catholic!"

The wicked prefect had planted Catholicism in my locker; it wasn't forged; her name wasn't Zelda, but she had the same smug look. I swallowed water that was rushing up my throat to become tears.

Bobby said the Girls Brigade was nothing anyway. All

they did was learn how to tie knots and give first aid. It was the Boys Brigade that was important.

"Jennifer can tie a knot better'n you and she's not even in the Girls Brigade," said Bobby the Valiant as he sat down beside Jennifer the Grateful. The wicked prefect went into a huff and stalked off home.

I listened to Bobby's talk of the rigorous training they were going through in the Boys Brigade. You had to be able to march for miles, learn how to play the flute or beat the drum. Oh, he supposed they had *some* fun in the Girls Brigade. Yep, it was a shame I was a Catholic.

We followed the path out of the second field, jumped the stream into the first. Something jiggled around in my memory all the way home and surfaced before I got to our gate.

It's a shame you're a Catholic. He'd used the same tone we used when speaking of Eilish Loughran's imbecility. "Poor thing—it's a shame she's a dope."

The fairies struck with a vengeance the first week in July. God have mercy on me but Uncle Dan and Aunt Madge, without any egging on from Grandmother either, had a terrible argument.

I didn't catch it all since I came in on it late. They were right outside the back door, so I stayed around the side path, not wanting to interrupt.

"You should have put the kibosh to it all right away." Aunt Madge was nearly crying. "It's all over the place you're refusing to marry me since it's not your—ohhhhh . . ." Aunt Madge was sobbing now.

"I thought it was a joke!" Uncle Dan said. "When Mick says, 'I heard you're getting married' all I said was it was the first I'd heard of it. Christ Almighty, I've never seen a place that can get things so bollixed up!" His voice was harried.

I didn't know what was going on.

"You should have stopped this, Dan O'Neill," Aunt

Madge cried. "I'll never be able to hold up my head here again. . . ."

And the next thing I heard was the back door slam, so I ran round the front and was sauntering back up the steps as Uncle Dan bid me a terse greeting of some sort and vaulted right over our gate.

Aunt Madge increased her volunteering at the Mater Hospital, and Grandmother had the good grace to keep her lip buttoned when Uncle Dan didn't show up for tea on Sunday. I don't know what we'd have done if he had, for Aunt Madge was again at the hospital and when she came home she was angry about some band practising outside the hospital.

"They're at it already," she said to Grandmother. "God, but this is going to be hard to take."

I didn't like the new bitterness in her voice. My world was in tatters and I thought I'd do a novena petitioning that she and Uncle Dan would kiss and make up, but other things got in the way.

Greencastle went mad the second week in July.

"It's business as usual," said Aunt Nin, passing the teacup to Grandmother. "You should see the town." She shook her head slowly. "Painted from one end to the other."

Belfast needed painting, I thought, for when I'd made one of Grandmother's black market runs with her I was glad to get out of "the town's" bustling grey streets and bleak buildings.

Grandmother said decent people couldn't ride the tram into Belfast anymore without having their sensibilities offended.

"Mind you, I've only to go out my door to get slapped in the face. The bloody bunting's taken root in the bricks." Grandmother took a pinch of snuff and sniffed it angrily up her left nostril. "And you," she said, giving me an unjust glare, "keep away from their bonfire—do you hear?" *Snuff* went the right nostril. "If they get riled up enough I wouldn't put it past them to throw you in it!"

I don't know how Grandmother got wind of the plans to build a bonfire in the fields at the top of the street. It was one of those things she just *knew*.

But I didn't pay much heed to her remonstrances. It was a bit late for that anyway. In fact, I couldn't wait to get home to continue the forage for fuel. Pam had voiced her aversion to my helping with the bonfire, but Bobby had decreed me worthy enough to haul branches, bracken, and any other burnable debris to the bonfire site in the centre of the first field. Bobby knew all about bonfires. His daddy had told him how to build the biggest—like he did when he was a boy—and Bobby marshalled us into an efficient team.

Oh, God, Grandmother didn't know the half of it. Not only was I instrumental in building the bonfire, I'd pledged some of her new potatoes for roasting when it died to embers. Bobby said his daddy told him it was tradition to roast potatoes on the Eleventh Night. Eleventh Night! The night the bonfires would be lit all over Northern Ireland. It had a fine druidic ring to it. Uncle Dan said they used to gather the oak and gorse for burning on the Cave Hill in pagan times. Wildfire, it was called, an offering to the Hill God in the hope of bountiful harvests and freedom from evil and sickness. And the ancients added the wild agaric, sweet-smelling camomile, and penny royal so the fires would give off a thick smoke and aromatic smell. I mentioned this to Bobby, but he said what the hell was wild agaric? I dropped the notion right there, wishing I'd questioned Uncle Dan more thoroughly.

Rosie and the Lodger came in. Grandmother always made a point of asking the Lodger if he'd found employment. Aunt Nin was always ill at ease with this solicitude. He always said, "Any day now," and Grandmother always gave Aunt Nin a look I wouldn't even try to interpret. But tonight she added, "Frankie Doran's still out of work, but, mind you, I don't know that anybody ever got situated hanging around the Donegal Arms to all hours."

The cast showed up in the Lodger's eye for a split second, or maybe it was a glint of light as he picked up the newspaper and crackled it open in front of his face.

Grandmother, Aunt Nin, and Rosie took up a discussion on the trip to the Free State. Normally, I'd have been just as enthusiastic as they were, but by some unlucky coincidence the Gaelic Hut had hired the buses to take us on, of all days, the Twelfth of July. Worse still, I'd have to be in bed early on the Eleventh Night since they wanted to leave by six in the morning. Something about not being able to get through Belfast at all once the parades started. That meant I'd miss the lighting of the bonfire too. But with a bit of planning, maybe I could sneak out. The coal bunker was right beneath my bedroom window—an easy drop from the sill.

"Pull it, Jennifer, pull it!" Bobby commanded from his perch high in the bush.

"I *am* pulling," I said, giving another hard yank on the rope, which produced the desired result twofold. A scratched and sulky Bobby disentangled himself from the fallen branches.

"You didn't have to pull it *that* hard," he said. "C'mon, grab this end and help me drag it back."

I hesitated. "Suppose somebody sees me?"

"Hell's bloody bells! Do you want to help or not?"

"My Granny'll kill me if she finds out," I said, but I lent my weight to his.

All paths led to the ring of tamped-down grass. The bonfire stood in the centre, surrounded by children. Amidst hearty cheers, Bobby and I flung the last offering to the top and plopped down on the grass. I lay there milking the stem of a bit of foxtail grass—the foxtails were the juiciest—gazing at the dark hulk of tangled branches, old boots and shoes, and wooden fruit crates. We'd worked in busy conviviality for the most part; petty grievances were quickly hushed as we children of Serpentine Parade strove to make our bonfire bigger than any of the others sprouting up on surrounding streets. We'd posted guards to prevent pilferage after we lost a few choice crates we'd swiped from Morton's shop. There was no honour among thieves right enough.

I turned myself inside out to be worthy that week, and this state of being was assured when Bobby asked for a sheet. I offered the one from my bed; I'd think of some explanation for its disappearance later. Any bit of wariness stemming from Grandmother's warnings promptly dissipated when Bobby pronounced me a "bloody good sport."

An unaccountable sadness filled me. Tomorrow night the bonfire would blaze in glory for a brief while, only to end up an ignominious pile of ashes. My welted hands and scratched legs said it wasn't worth it. I sighed a long sigh and turned towards Bobby.

"Did you bring the sheet?" he asked.

"Yes. It's over there."

"Well, go get it—I'm making the Pope now."

The question "What?" never got out of me. My jaw unhinged itself and just hung there while Bobby tied a stick to a mop in the shape of a cross. A cheer rose from the others and Erik shook the hair of the mop, made a grotesque face, and started dancing. An infinity passed until the chant brought me out of my stupefaction.

"Burn the Pope. . . . Burn the Pope. . . . Burn the Pope . . ."

I'd fallen into a dreadful fairy ring. The chorale pressed closer. Don't listen, Jennifer! Close your ears and don't let them touch you in their wild enchantment or you'll be a captive forever.

Bobby brandished the cruciform and the mop-hair came to hideous life.

"Burn the Pope. . . . Burn the Pope . . ."

The high priest joined in the chorale. They'd all gone mad. Mad!

Like a wild thing I broke through the ring.

"That's it, Jennifer," Bobby urged. "Bring the sheet and the Pope's ready!"

The implications weren't lost on me; *nothing* was more Catholic than the Pope, and if they'd burn him . . . I lifted the sheet—*my* sheet was to clothe the effigy—and walked slowly towards the circle. The blurred faces of Pam, Erik, and the others milled around the bonfire and Bobby. Grandmother was right. I shouldn't be near their bonfire. *Their* bonfire. It was *their* bonfire! I could help them build it for a hundred Twelfths and it would still be *their* bonfire.

My heart hurt with a terrible sadness that was all jumbled up with humiliation. Hot tears threatened, but suddenly a murmuring droned through my head and the High Kings of Tara, the Great O'Neill and his proud chieftains whispered urgently that *they* weren't to be let think they could insult *us* with impunity. Their wrathful blood rose in my veins and with a stinging swipe I hit Bobby's surprised face. A fierceness possessed me and I lunged at him, knocking him to the ground—kicking, scratching, punching. I felt no pain, and the efforts of the others to drag me off him were in vain. Then I was in the clutches of some monster which ripped me off him and deposited me on the ground.

Constable Johnston was telling the others to keep back. Gasping through bared teeth, I accused the group. "They're going to burn the Pope!"

But Constable Johnston didn't understand. He just swivelled me round and herded me through them and pointed the path home.

"You shouldn't be here," he said grimly.

A second shock rattled through me. He wasn't going to stop them! He was ordering *me* home! I stared up at him. The brows were a bristling black line and I couldn't fathom his eyes. Fear hit me then. Policemen were the protectors of rights; if you got lost you told a policeman; the policeman was your friend . . . *B-Specials are the same men who pose as policemen during the day . . .*

I started running, my sheet flaring out after me, the retreating standard of a routed army.

"You better guard your bonfire all night," I screamed over my shoulder, "for I'll tear it down branch by branch—you wait and see!"

I sat on the biscuit tin, my face muffled into the sheet, and gave vent to some mighty howls about them and their bonfire for a long time. I *hated* them.

"Here's your *Beano* back, love."

I almost fell off the biscuit tin at Frankie's voice over the hedge. Then he said he'd bring it through and I was mortified, wondering if he'd heard.

He had. Frankie put the *Beano* down beside me and knelt on one knee. "Don't say anything, Jennifer, just listen." His eyes were all mixed up—I mean, I couldn't see what all was going on in them.

"I've an idea," he said, "but it's just to be between you and me. Okay?"

I snuffled and gave him a half-hearted nod. Then he lowered his voice further and told me he was going to arrange a surprise for the bonfire watchers. I only had a moment's hesitation at his proposal—then I grinned. Bobby McConnell could have Constable Johnston on his side—Frankie Doran was on mine!

CHAPTER
===11===

I watched the morning spread across the bed. It inched up the sheet which I was eventually forced to pull over my face. That's the way Grandmother found me, and it set her off good and proper about people in general and me in particular.

She didn't like me tooling around with my porridge either (was I trying to scrape the rim off the bowl?) and would I hurry up and get out, she had work to do.

"I think I'll stay in today," I announced, pushing the bowl at her, its blue rim still intact. I didn't look at her, but I could feel her eyes scouring my face.

Now, I didn't want her to ask the usual "What's up with you?" that accompanied aberrant behaviour, but when she didn't, my surprise was mixed with a faint feeling of abuse. Not that I could have told her anyway. She wouldn't understand in the least and I'd end up getting a good wigging for being at the bonfire in the first place.

I moped about from the scullery table to the front window, emitting huge sighs, but Grandmother paid more attention to the porridge pot which, she claimed, had dried out waiting for layabouts to rouse themselves. I wanted to shout, "I don't want your pity" at her, the way the hero always did at the pictures. But I never could understand that phrase. When something awful happened to me I wanted pity, and if I couldn't get any out of Grandmother, it was easy to inveigle some out of Aunt Madge. She was always good for a bit of pity. She'd fix whatever was wrong with me and I could sit back consoled with two ounces of brandyballs while she did the fixing. I banished a quick vision of a snuffling Robin Hood curled up with two ounces of brandyballs, whining to his Merry Men . . . So that's what the hero meant! That's why he *was* the hero—I couldn't admire him otherwise. I slunk out the back door. There'd be no pity-seeking today—I felt sorry enough for myself, thank you very much.

Smokey Doran eyed me from the fuchsia bush and I gave him a few placating "Nice pussy" sentiments, but he left anyway. The garden was in full flower now and I watched the bees grow fat with pollen. Grandmother had abandoned any attempts to keep the beds neat due to a particularly rambunctious batch of cottage pinks. The birds had got at the seed and scattered them indiscriminately amongst snapdragons, lupins, and sweet Williams. To make matters worse, in Grandmother's eyes at least, flowering bindweed had a good hold of the back hedge. Fluffy white flowers on the potato patch signalled it was time they were dug up. I had the good grace to flush at the thought. Well, they'd be dug up all right, but they wouldn't provide roast potato fare at any bloody bonfire. God take care of me—if Grandmother had ever found out the fate I'd planned for her spuds, she'd have disowned me.

Grandmother came out once to hang a dishcloth on the hedge and told me I'd get sunstroke if I sat there much longer in this heat. I wondered briefly if sunstroke killed people. I'd never heard of anyone being afflicted by sunstroke in Ireland. I sat there with my head in my hands for a long time before remembering the deck of cards hidden inside the biscuit tin. I retrieved them and fanned out the forbidden fifty-two.

Bobby had given them to me when he'd taught me to play Patience, but when I showed them to Grandmother she'd promptly tossed me and the "Devil's cards" out of the house with orders to get rid of them. She wasn't implying that Bobby was the Devil either. No, she meant the real Devil. The Devil took full advantage of gambler's greed, said Grandmother, and more than one had sold his soul for a win.

Our coalman, Johnny Brannigan, had had a run-in with the Devil owing to his penchant for playing cards. That was a winter yarn. Johnny, said Grandmother, had never gone near a pack of cards since. He was younger then, and to the distraction of his wife, he was gambling away the coal business. If there was a pontoon game going anywhere in the village, Johnny was there.

The fateful game was held up at the Gaelic Hut one

winter night, and Grandmother could bring goosepimples to the nape of my neck just by her description of the moon's rising and the wildness of the wind in the trees as the group sat down to play. Somebody had brought a stranger. Darkly handsome, he was, and dressed to kill.

It seems Johnny was having the game of his life and the pound notes were mounting at his elbow. The cards were dealt again and as Johnny picked them up, one dropped to the floor. Here, Grandmother's voice softened to an ominous whisper.

"He bent down beneath the table and footered about looking for it when God Almighty"—she threw her hands up in the air and my heart with them—"didn't his hand touch the stranger's foot. But it wasn't a *foot*." Her voice darkened and slowed. "It was a cloven hoof!" Grandmother gripped the arms of the chair. "The mark of the Devil!"

Johnny up and ran, left winnings and all, and fled down the Whitewell. I was always right on Johnny's heels as we took the Whitewell.

Uncle Dan was in our house one night when Grandmother told that yarn. "For Christ's sake, Maggie," he said, "it was just one of the lads having him on with a cow's foot from the butchers!"

But Grandmother said to me, "You believe him if you like" and followed it up with a look that distinctly said "at your peril."

I held the bunker lid open for Johnny every week when he lugged the heavy bags round the side path and emptied them. If ever there was a man risen from Hell, he was it. He was black with coal dust and his eyes, irritated with years of it, glittered redly, like two burning cinders. I'd never had the gumption to ask him about that night.

I hid the cards back in the biscuit tin and went into the house. It was too warm for Patience.

The only other time I've fallen asleep in the afternoon was when I had scarlet fever, but I'd stayed awake till all hours last night listening for Frankie to make his move.

Maybe he'd got cold feet. When I woke up, Aunt Madge was home from the mill.

"This heat's terrible," I heard her say. "It's no wonder the chile's sleepy."

"It's not just the heat that ails her," Grandmother said. She flummoxed me. How she knew some things was—well, she bore watching.

Aunt Madge said quietly, "Aye, it begins with the children. I wouldn't want mine to go through this. . . ." She stopped mid-sentence. "Oh, God, Ma, can't I say a simple thing without you pandering to rumours too?" She went upstairs to change out of her mill clothes. Then Grandmother tried to dissuade her from going to the hospital, but Aunt Madge said there'd be enough not show up tonight. Grandmother said that was right—those with good sense, and I could see it was going to natter back and forth so I went back out to the biscuit tin.

There was no peace anywhere, though. Over the hedge Mrs. Doran's voice pleaded with Frankie to stay home tonight; to forego the Donegal Arms; to let things blow over—they always did. Frankie shouted something about other people that had the same sentiments and the only thing that blew over was ashes—all over bloody Germany. And with that he came out and said a very bad word. The bin lid was lifted, then slammed down again before he headed down the side path. Mr. Doran came out muttering, gave the bin a kick, and shouted for Frankie to hold his horses and wait for him.

A few minutes later I heard somebody rummaging through the bin. I crept towards the hedge and watched Mrs. Doran salvaging the blood-red poppies one by one. I put my head in my hands. I didn't understand anything anymore.

Grandmother and I were spending the evening of the Eleventh Night at Aunt Nin's. As we left Serpentine Parade, I took a furtive squint up the street, but Bobby and Pam weren't in sight. Hah! They must have taken my advice to guard their bonfire.

This bit of ego-bolstering, dubious to begin with, received a thorough pasting as we passed street after street of bonfires. Children tossed old mattresses, baby cots, and junk of every description onto the towering structures with feverish last-minute resolve to make theirs the biggest. Each was crowned with a mitred effigy. I turned my hot face towards the lough. The lough had its moods and I thought I knew them all. But it just lay there in unfamiliar indolence, a heavy blue, waiting for a breath of wind like the rest of us.

God, but I didn't like this weather. It was sultry and unnatural. The tar was still soft on the Whitewell, and Creswell's cows' clap had dried as it dropped.

A crowd of men lounged up against the wall of the Donegal Arms. Frankie Doran was in earnest conversation with some of them, but just as we got up to them, Frankie nodded at me and gave a quick, dark grin. Then they filed through the open door into the secret recesses of the pub. I sneaked a look in as we passed, for I knew Grandmother wouldn't approve of my interest. But I just got a whiff of what I assumed was stout and a fleeting glimpse of hordes of people, all anonymous.

The doors at Aunt Nin's were all open, too. The little white row houses looked cool and refreshing and distinctly at variance with the hot red bricks we'd left behind. And they were, blessedly, as bereft of bonfires as they were of bunting. I thought back to the time of the Victory Party, when I'd felt sorry for Patsy living here where they didn't celebrate anything. It was funny the way things turned around. Patsy didn't know how lucky she was.

It was also a relief to me that the Lodger was, as Rosie put it to Grandmother, "Away up to Belfast to see a mate about a job." Not only did his dour presence put a dampener on conversation, but there was the difficulty about the chair.

Our basic seating arrangements consisted of two armchairs flanking the hearth and a settee, set back a bit, between them. In normal families, one armchair was the daddy's (inviolate) and the other the mother's (vacated occasionally, depending upon the importance of the guest).

Now, Aunt Nin's house didn't have the usual mammy and daddy situation any more than ours did, so it was her chair that was never usurped, while Rosie's was proffered to visitors of venerable age, like Grandmother. The same thing went on at our house; when Aunt Nin visited, Aunt Madge lost her chair. We were funny like that about chairs.

All that changed after the Lodger came. He'd managed somehow to ensconce himself in Rosie's chair, and Grandmother was relegated to the settee. Grandmother said privately that it was terrible what Nin Rafferty was fostering under her own roof. Why she blamed Aunt Nin wasn't explained; I said if Rosie wanted to give the Lodger her chair that was her own fault. But Grandmother said I was too young to understand.

I'd been embarrassed more than once when Grandmother made a great fuss about not accepting Rosie's new place on the settee, for I knew her spurious remarks were intended to shame the Lodger into giving her the armchair. But he had no rearing at all and remained absolutely nonplussed by Grandmother's theatrics. Since he'd taken himself off to Belfast, Grandmother would get the favoured chair and we'd all be spared this jousting tonight.

Rosie sat on the settee, and I dragged the wee stool over by Aunt Nin's chair. Aunt Nin patted my head.

"Are you all ready for the trip?"

"Oh, aye," I said, with so much emphasis I surprised myself.

Aunt Nin laughed and said she didn't think Patsy would sleep for excitement tonight either. I just put on my idiot smile and said nothing. Patsy might be all het up, but I was more *grateful* than excited: grateful I'd somewhere to go while the Twelfth celebrations were going on. Last night had scunnered me on anything to do with the Twelfth.

"D'you mind the time," said Aunt Nin, "ach, it was before the war, we got Mick McKenna to sling some extra butter down his trouser legs?" Aunt Nin's chins jiggled at the memory. Everybody started laughing, except me. I didn't remember anything about Mr. McKenna except that he was Patsy's daddy.

"What did you want him to sling the butter down his trouser legs for?" I asked.

"Well, you see, Jennifer," Aunt Nin explained, "you can't go to the Free State and not come back over the border without a few luxuries." She gave a sleekit grin. "But since the authorities up here take a dim view of that—well, we've no choice but to *smuggle* the stuff in."

My eyes must have grown twice their size. Smuggle! I squeezed my legs together, savouring the same thrilling tingle I got during hide and seek when the soft approach of the seeker threatened discovery. This trip sounded better all the time. Rosie rolled her eyes. "But never trust anything to the bold Mick . . ."

"What happened?" I was all ears.

"The daft bugger dropped it right at the custom man's feet and got the whole busload of us searched. Everything was confiscated!"

Aunt Nin said Grandmother would be hung from one end to the other with rashers and butter—all under her coat.

"Ahhh," sighed Grandmother, "you've never tasted butter till you get your mouth round Free State butter." Grandmother smacked her lips and she and Aunt Nin went into raptures about Free State produce. Their rashers were thick and lean and not saltpetered to death like the bacon up here. And their sausages . . .

Fortunately, Rosie could stand it no longer either and fluttered into the scullery to make the tea.

Aunt Nin asked me to help her keep an eye on Grandmother so she didn't overdo herself and get us all caught. I entered into the conspiracy wholeheartedly. And Grandmother confided, to my delighted anguish, I was to play a central part in the actual smuggling since Aunt Madge had let it be known she wouldn't be going on the trip after all. We'd leave the edibles to her, and I was to lean my efforts towards yards of dress material. Now, I didn't remember this, but it seems Grandmother used to bind my stomach with red flannel every day for over a year when I was between two and three years old. This, said Grandmother, was Great-grandmother's remedy for ensuring flat stomachs for life on the family females. Well, this same "binding" would be done, on a grander scale, of course, under my clothes, and the customs men would be none the wiser!

Rosie brought in tea and a plate of soda bread. I was in grand form again and voiced a few elaborate plans of my own for getting huge sticks of peppermint rock through.

Uncle Dan came in about nine o'clock. I hadn't seen him since he and Aunt Madge fell out. He'd been to Belfast to pay the bus people, and the three buses would be ready and waiting at the bottom of the Whitewell at six in the morning. He mentioned something about not being sure of the head-count, but that he'd paid for a full load anyway. He was looking at Grandmother. I got it then—he was sort of asking if Aunt Madge was going on the trip. But Grandmother wasn't about to give him any "ins" where Aunt Madge was concerned.

"You're sure those buses will be on time?" she said. "They were late the last time, I remember."

The accused reassured her we'd be headed for the border long before the high jinks started.

"How is it in Belfast?" Aunt Nin wanted to know.

"It's warm up there," he said, fingering the rim of his cap, "and about to get warmer."

There was a quick silence and I should have taken that

opportunity to steer this mundane conversation away from the weather and back to the smuggling. But Rosie got ahead of me. "I feel sorry for those that can't get out of it," she said. And I knew then that it was no coincidence that the Gaelic Hut held its trip on the Twelfth of July.

Rosie glanced at the clock often, then she went to the door and peeked out.

"It's started," she pronounced. "There go the bonfires."

I thought there'd be a mad rush to the door to see the spectacle, but nobody moved except me. Rosie pointed up the hill, then left me alone.

Spectacle, it wasn't. I was too far down the hill to see anything but an odd lick of flame against the now shadowed hillside. But the myriad white streamers of smoke showed clearly against the dominating black mass of Napoleon's Nose before dissipating into the lavender night sky.

I watched for a long time, zeroing in on one thick plume I was sure came from the fields at the top of Serpentine Parade. I imagined Bobby and Pam, dancing hand in hand with the others around the crackling inferno, felt the stinging smoke in my eyes. . . . I squeezed them shut. But the vision of Frankie's beribboned army uniform and peaked cap, concealed under the effigy's sheet and mitre and representing the King, just made my eyes smart all the more. I was contrary like that sometimes.

"It was the same then as now," Uncle Dan was saying, "good and evil. With or without modern religion, it all comes right back to that—good and evil. And what's good for some"—he took a long pull at his pipe—"is evil for others. Take the bonfires, for instance. In ancient times they were used to drive away the enemies of the crops—the vermin. Very practical, the old Celts were, and you could say"—he grinned suddenly—"the Protestants have the same intent."

I agreed with Grandmother. Uncle Dan must have overdone himself at the Donegal Arms. There were no crops in the fields at the top of Serpentine Parade. No, he said, but it sounded like a grand idea at that. He left for the pub.

"I'm afraid that's the way of it right enough," said Aunt Nin, like she was afraid someone would hear her. "There's been trouble in the shipyard, and Mick McKenna was advised to stay home from his work today." Patsy's daddy was given the word by friends, Aunt Nin told us, and I didn't like the way she said "friends."

My mouth had dried up. Grandmother's hadn't. "Well, now, aren't they a decent bunch?" she said. "I saw the time not too long ago when he'd have just found himself accidentally"—she accented the word—"feeding a furnace at Harland & Wolffs. My, but they're getting civilised—a warning, no less!"

Rosie was pouring more tea into Grandmother's cup when Uncle Dan again darkened the open doorway. My heart gave a lovely turn and I just tingled at his words.

"Where's Madge?" The eyes were very blue. I'd known all along he'd really come to Aunt Nin's to see her and not about any old buses.

Grandmother's cup wavered before she answered. "She's at the Mater."

Uncle Dan ran his hand through his black hair. "They're getting very forward up there," he said. Then he plunged the talk right into summer yarns. "I remember the last time they planned to march through the Market." He looked from one to the other of us, but settled on Grandmother. I squirmed closer to Aunt Nin, all ready for the story. It was one of my favourite yarns, for there was an element of siege about it.

The Market was a small Catholic enclave right in the heart of Belfast, and one year the men of the Market took it upon themselves to stop the Orangemen passing through. They barricaded the street! Oh, it was a grand battle, they said. . Of course, the Orangemen eventually got through but—and here we all got a good laugh—they *limped* rather than marched! I'd only heard Grandmother and Aunt Nin's version of this one, so I was hoping Uncle Dan would freshen it up a bit.

Summer yarns took a dreadful new twist that night. By a simple change in tense, they ceased being yarns.

"They're barricading the Market tonight." Uncle Dan was grim.

"The Market!" Rosie clutched at her apron. "Oh, Dan, there'll be open murder!"

"Aye," he agreed. "And there's more. I hear tell at the pub the Falls and Ardoyne are up in arms about the resumption of the Twelfth, and there's a call out to back up the men of the Market."

"Jesus, Mary, and Joseph protect us," Rosie intoned.

"I'm going up to get her, Maggie," Uncle Dan said. He made it sound like a question. And he looked just the way Grandmother felt about him—a bit pagan. They clung grimly to each other's eyes for a minute, and I was ready for shattering the silence. Then Grandmother nodded assent, but somehow I got the impression fealty had been wrested from her.

Uncle Dan hurried away.

The lovely tingle had become a pressuring urge to go to the bathroom. "I have to go," I said with a touch of hysteria, and I raced through the scullery out to the water closet.

It wouldn't be dark for ages yet so I stood up on the seat to pull the chain. I'd taken to fingering the barrel of the gun, which was just a working up to the eventual lifting of it. My hand was raised before it was shocked into withdrawal. There was nothing there. The gun was gone.

I jumped down and ran back into the house where the talk had again turned to the trip. But we couldn't seem to capture the earlier gay mood. Grandmother and Aunt Nin sighed a lot and Rosie glanced at the clock often.

It was fortunate I'd had a bit of sleep in the afternoon, for we stayed at Aunt Nin's until after midnight. The Widow Byrne and Patsy's mother came in. And as the bonfires roared their message across Northern Ireland, the somnolent embers of nationalism were fanned to life in me around Aunt Nin's hearth.

The ignominy of past Twelfths was relived, then salved with counter-stories of the great civil war which resulted in the birth of the Free State, the glorious land of heroes songs were sung about; pastoral land of milk and honey, of rashers and butter.

"I wish they hadn't stopped until they got us free too," I said peevishly.

"Some haven't." We all looked at Rosie.

Grandmother hadn't said much, but when Aunt Madge came in just ahead of the Lodger and Uncle Dan, she perked up.

"I thought you said he never touched a drop," she said to Aunt Nin and motioned to the Lodger being helped up the stairs by Uncle Dan and Rosie.

Aunt Nin stoutly said a saint might be induced to imbibe with the carry-ons around us.

The Widow and Patsy's mother left and Uncle Dan said he'd walk us up the Whitewell. What he really meant was he'd walk Aunt Madge. They dallied far behind Grandmother and me, Uncle Dan's head inclining down towards Aunt Madge's, just the way I liked it to.

It was quiet except for the gentle scuffing of our feet and the odd raucous cry of a corncrake in the fields.

"Did you know nobody's ever seen a corncrake, Jennifer?"

I nodded up at Grandmother, depriving her of my usual response. She said this every summer at the sound of the first corncrake. Corncrakes were too fast for us and kept to the long grasses. Uncle Dan said corncrakes were birds, that naturalists had long since exposed this old wives' tale with photographs, but Grandmother said how would they know—nobody had ever seen a corncrake.

I didn't know who to believe. I'd never seen one. But I knew they were there in the long grasses just by their cries. Uncle Dan said they weren't cries either, that they were love songs to each other.

A faint tinge of burnt wood hung about.

"I hope it thunders and lightnings all day tomorrow," I said with sweet bitterness. "I hope the rain comes down in buckets . . ."

"Ach, no, love," Grandmother chided. "Pray for a heat wave!" She smiled at me, the green chips in her eyes dancing in the lamplight.

I thought she'd lost her senses. Then it dawned on me! We were used to dealing with rain. Heat waves were a different story. The Orangemen would drown in their own sweat, drop in their tracks of heart attacks!

Grandmother saw I was getting her meaning and nodded her head. "It's a long way to Finaghy Field," she sang, and simultaneous sleekit smiles broke on our faces. Our eyes locked in wicked glee and what had taken Grandmother many years and countless incidents to acquire emanated from those burning eyes into mine in that one night. I was at one with Grandmother!

I linked arms with her the rest of the way, neither of us aware that calamity, in the form of Constable Johnston, was on Mrs. Doran's doorstep.

CHAPTER
12

We saw him close the gate as we rounded the corner of Serpentine Parade. Grandmother's arm stiffened and she slowed our pace so Constable Johnston was already on his way up the street by the time we reached our house.

"What was he . . . ?"

Grandmother rudely hushed me, and we scuttled silently up the side path.

"But Granny—"

Grandmother shook her head and firmly closed the back door on the long primal scream of Mrs. Doran. Someone walked over my grave again.

"Get up to bed, Jennifer, you've to be up in a few hours—and no buts," she said, further sullying the purity of our recent alliance.

Aunt Madge came in and I heard the low murmur of voices for a minute, then our back door opened and closed again. I didn't need to peer over the windowsill to know it was Aunt Madge who'd gone over to the Dorans. Aunt Madge didn't have any grudges.

A petulant yellow moon glared through the window, looking like a fat baby about to cry. Grandmother said a full moon went hand in glove with lunacy. It affected the tides and men's minds. The asylums went on nervous alert; madmen had to be trussed in straitjackets. She warned me never to stare at the lough when there was a moon on it for it could lure me in out of my depth. Sometimes I tested this, dared the moon to enchant me. I'd even take a few steps forward, letting it draw me, glazing my eyes. Then, before it had a chance, I'd stick out my tongue, put my thumbs in my ears and wiggle my fingers, and run like hell. But I wouldn't have taunted this one. The whole world had gone mad. Goosepimples rippled up my arms.

Aunt Madge tied the bow at the back of my blue organdie.

"Frankie Doran has gone away," she said.

Eleven years of the village code chorused, "Oul' Fitzpatrick left us last night," "The Widow's sitting up with him," "He knows the Grand Secret now." But before I had time to sort out my emotions, Aunt Madge swung me around to face her.

"He'll be gone for a while," she continued. The code had nuances.

I threw my arms around her in relief when she told me Frankie was in Crumlin Road gaol and gladly agreed never to mention words like "prison," "gaol," or the "IRA" around Mrs. Doran. Mrs. Doran was very upset, Aunt Madge said, and I wasn't to ask questions because Aunt Madge had filled me in with everything I needed to know.

There had indeed been trouble at the Market last night. God alone knew how Frankie Doran got mixed up in it. But there it was, Frankie had been one of many lifted by the Royal Ulster Constabulary, she said, and I wasn't to confuse his arrest with the activities of thieves or the like.

"To some, Frankie's a hero, Jennifer." Aunt Madge's eyes pleaded with me to understand her. "Then there's others who'll brand him a criminal. It all depends what foot you dig with," she finished, pushing her hair back with a weary hand.

Oh, I understand fine! But I wasn't sure about Mrs. Doran. She dug with the right foot all right, meaning she was a Catholic, but her sentiments leant towards them rather than us. She'd feted them, strung her house with their flag, joined their clubs. . . .

My insides suddenly turned to water and my stone-flinging arm withered in its socket. Bible history had been well thumped into us by Miss McGrath and I could have recited that whole story for you verbatim, right down to "Let he who is without sin cast the first stone." I flung no more stones at Mrs. Doran.

Grandmother shouted from the scullery for us to quit the dilly-dally or we'd miss the trip. Aunt Madge had changed her mind.

Grandmother and I got our wish. The lough was glassy and still and the sky was the deep summer blue which I now knew presaged a scorcher. The three buses waited at the bottom of the Whitewell, their fronts pointed up the Shore

Road towards Belfast. I ran ahead to make sure I got on the same bus as Patsy. She was hanging out the window of the lead bus calling, "We've saved your seats."

There was a lot of jostling and seat-swapping since Grandmother wanted to be by Aunt Nin; Aunt Madge, at Uncle Dan's request, moved back to be adjacent to Rosie and the Lodger; and I squeezed in with Patsy and her daddy. Patsy's mother couldn't go on the trip since somebody had to stay with her brothers and sisters, and John, that meant the Lodger, had decided to go on the trip at the last minute. I assumed this information meant he'd originally offered to watch the children. I couldn't suppress a tinge of resentment that he'd let Patsy's mother down. Him visiting the Free State was a great example of what they called a "busman's holiday." I drew my mouth into a spiteful line and glared at him. The effort was wasted. He had his head back on the seat and shaded his face with his hand, bearing out Grandmother's opinion that his was a face not used to seeing the light of day. I think Rosie was a bit miffed at him too, for she kept giving him sharp looks and only spoke to him in quick whispers.

A faint skirl of bagpipes sounded in the distance and a low murmuring rumbled through the bus. Everyone turned to look out the windows on our side. A long banner, unfurled between two poles, crested a dip in the Whitewell Road. Higher and higher it went before hundreds of black dots appeared which turned out to be black bowler hats. Then a blur of orange spilled over the ridge and a great *baroooom ba booooom boooom* startled the flutes into momentary silence before they took up the tune again.

The huge assemblage ambled towards us with a peculiar shuffling gait.

"What's the matter with their legs, Granny?"

Grandmother said I was seeing the "pad and shuffle." That's the way Orangemen walked, she said, and couldn't Uncle Dan get these buses moving or we'd never get through the town. The angry drum rattled out another tattoo and there was a loud cheer from the black and orange ranks as they stopped outside the Orange Lodge.

Uncle Dan swung himself out of the bus and got into a harried conversation with the three drivers.

I looked back to the Orangemen. There was a bit of shifting and barked ordering before the throng got on the move again behind the banner. The banner was beautiful. It was made of silk and, as Grandmother said, nothing took a dye like silk. Its vibrant purples, oranges, reds, and blues showed a man with long curls, flowing cape, and drawn sword astride a stamping white horse; a blue river meandered at the back of him and a lone red hand contrasted against a shimmering white sky. It was marred, I thought, by the stoic red print across the top declaring Greencastle LOL No. 956. Now, I could tell myself the banner was beautiful, but I had enough savvy to know not to praise its material beauty to anyone on the bus. You had to watch what you said to your own, too. The world was full of snares.

It was the licorice allsorts that hypnotised me, especially the one in front carrying one of the banner poles. *It's the Boy's Brigade that's important.* . . . Unruly red hair sprung from the pillbox and clashed violently with the orange sash around its wearer's neck. I stared into the face of the first Orangeman I'd ever seen, but Bobby McConnell didn't see me, absorbed as he was in keeping the banner hoisted at the same level as the other polebearer. I looked up at the pulsing blue sky. You've a long way to pad and shuffle, Bobby McConnell, and it's going to be a scorcher. Now, if I were the other polebearer, we could pretend we were in the French Foreign Legion, battling our way to a desert outpost in the Sahara. . . .

A commotion at the back of the bus brought me out of the reverie. One of the hurley team grabbed Mrs. Conway's new puce hat, blew out his cheeks and belly, and strutted up the aisle, pumping his arm up and down the way the man at the head of the Orange procession did. Everyone laughed and egged him on. Patsy gave me a dig. "Isn't he a cod?" she giggled. I could only muster a wan smile. I couldn't put my finger on it, but I was more embarrassed than amused. There was something unsettling about adults mimicking other adults.

The buses revved up, only to be drowned out by a furious barrage of drums, flutes, and bagpipes and the swell of stentorian voices. They sang a short-versed song, the repetitious last line of which was all I could get because it became a roar. ". . . *the sash my father wore.*"

Patsy's daddy stood up as the bus inched forward. "Right, lads"—he jerked his thumb in the direction of the Orangemen—"that's enough of that muck! Give us a note for the Soldier's Song, Molly," he shouted to the back where Molly Logan and half the hurley team sat in a cloud of Woodbine smoke.

Suddenly the bus resounded with the rousing "*Soo . . . old . . . jers are we. . . .*" Oh, it was grand. Now, I didn't know all the words, for we didn't get to sing this song often, so I just followed Patsy's lead and stood up, right arm across my breast, and thundered out what I knew of the forbidden words; words that magically would lose their fetters the minute we crossed the border and would become the National Anthem of the Free State.

We wouldn't have stood a chance in a face-to-face confrontation with the Orangemen, but inside the bus the din we created kept us from hearing the insults Grandmother said were contained in "The Sash My Father Wore."

But we'd have needed blindfolds, I discovered, to get through Belfast unoffended. Large groups of bowler-hatted, orange-breasted men gathered on waste ground, in streets, and at Orange Lodges. Bobby belonged to a huge fraternity. The Boys Brigade was everywhere as were the lilt of fifes and the deafening cannonade of the mighty Lambeg drums.

Every stretch of wall was plastered with red, white, and blue slogans. NO POPE HERE. . . . REMEMBER 1690. . . . KICK THE POPE. Gable ends of houses proclaimed with chilling brevity, KILL THE FENIANS. . . . GOD SAVE THE KING. Catholics were Fenians. Some houses were painted red, white, and blue from top to bottom. Banners and flags hung deathly still. No wind dared breathe on them.

The man on the white horse pursued us all the way through the streets of Belfast well out onto the Dublin Road. I asked Grandmother who he was.

"King Billy," she said. "William of Orange." Then she told me he was a Dutchman who'd helped the English defeat us. And what the red hand signified was sickening. King Billy had cut the hand off a soldier and thrown it into the River Boyne, symbolising his intent that the river run red with blood.

We passed towns and villages all seething with black bowlers, sashes, and the rest of the Orange paraphernalia; then on to lone farmhouses flying Union Jacks.

I hadn't realised we'd all been quiet, that the clamour of Belfast was all its own, until bottles clinked at the back of the bus. I should have kept it that way. Grandmother always said my mouth would get me into trouble.

"They shouldn't be allowed to do this," I said. It was just a timorous aside to no one in particular.

"Allowed!" Patsy's daddy was incredulous. *"Allowed!"* he said again. "Ach, chile, have you no learning a'tall?" Then he stood up and told the whole bus there was a wee girl up here who said the Orangemen shouldn't be allowed to do what they're doing. The whole bus was filled with cackles. I was mortified.

"Allowed, hell, the bastards are encouraged," someone yelled.

"Watch your language back there!"

"Up the IRA!"

"Watch your language! Let the dead rest!"

Another round of derisive laughter. I didn't get the joke, but I laughed anyway since it wasn't me anymore.

The back of the bus remained boisterous, and Grandmother said they'd brought the Donegal Arms with them and that the people running this trip—she cast a contemptuous glance over her shoulder at Uncle Dan—should bar the booze.

Uncle Dan didn't hear her. He was bending over Rosie and the Lodger. I could have smacked the Lodger. He was still hiding behind his hand, barely nodding his head at Uncle Dan's attempts at conversation. Somehow his "hide-behind-the-hand" rudeness to Uncle Dan bothered me more than the "hide-behind-the-newspaper" version he practised on us.

Uncle Dan came up to the front and tapped the glass behind the driver. He cupped his hands. "How many miles to the border?"

The driver held up three fingers and Uncle Dan went back to Rosie, who put her arm around the Lodger and snuggled up to him in a fashion that would have disgraced Aunt Nin if she'd looked back at them. Ach, maybe I was miffed because Uncle Dan and Aunt Madge looked so tense sitting together.

Patsy and I counted every field from there to the border. We rolled up to a few shed-like buildings at the side of the road. Now, I hadn't expected the Great Wall of China, but a few yards of empty road and a couple of big sheds put a bit of a strain on the imagination.

A policeman held up his white-gloved hand.

The other two buses were ahead of us, and when the policeman went on board the first bus my heart flew to my throat until I realised we weren't smuggling anything yet. Another policeman just walked around the outside of the bus in front of us looking up at the windows. We got the same treatment. I wished he'd come on board so I could practise keeping my face blank—a dry run, so to speak. The policeman waved us on. Then the bus was filled with wild cheering. We were in the Free State!

Uncle Dan tapped the glass again and asked the driver to stop. He jumped off the bus and had a quick conversation with the driver which resulted in an unscheduled stop in Dundalk, a few miles down the road.

Uncle Dan told everybody to stretch their legs. Patsy and I took him literally and chased each other around the perimeter of the bus. Only Grandmother and Aunt Nin stayed aboard; everybody else went off to find toilets.

Fifteen minutes later we were on the road to Dublin again. Perhaps I expected too much: I'd seen it rain on one side of Serpentine Parade while the other was spared, so there was no reason to doubt Grandmother's laudation that the grass was noticeably greener on the other side of the border. But the furrows of cabbages and potatoes fanning out in mesmerising waves, the clusters of cows and sheep speckling the grassy slopes of the Free State, were no different from those in the North. Only Miss McGrath's testimony that Ireland's chief industry was agriculture was borne out.

I'd counted a lot of fields before I noticed we were missing three passengers.

The four of us sat at a window table in the Gresham Hotel picking at roast beef Grandmother said was mummified.

"They saw us coming," she rasped at Aunt Nin.

I'd never eaten at a hotel before; they could have served me anything and it would have been delightful. The waiters all wore black uniforms with starched white shirts and balanced silver trays with the ease of circus jugglers. They called Grandmother and Aunt Nin "madam," Uncle Dan "sir," and me "miss."

"Everything to your satisfaction, madam?"

Aunt Nin murmured yes, and Grandmother used the

village code, saying she'd never seen beef like it in her life and couldn't find words to praise it. Grandmother had no praise for Uncle Dan either.

"You could have got us all branded as sympathisers," she told him.

Grandmother had sunk to new lows. Now, I didn't like the Lodger either, but I thought anyone doubled over with what Uncle Dan diagnosed as acute appendicitis deserved some sympathy. Rosie and Aunt Madge had felt the same way and elected to stay in Dundalk to make sure the Lodger came out of surgery all right. I knew it wouldn't cost Rosie a thought to sacrifice the trip to Dublin—she liked the Lodger—but it was to Aunt Madge's everlasting credit that she'd stayed to keep Rosie company.

Then Grandmother confounded us all. The Lodger was, she said, used to making himself sleight; it was only innocents like Frankie Doran who got left holding the bag. What one had to do with the other was beyond me and I wasn't the only one.

"Frankie Doran! What's he to do with this?" said Aunt Nin with a bleak look at Grandmother.

Grandmother blatantly admitted she'd clouded the issue. "I don't know," she said, "but he's in Crumlin Road gaol this morning for possessing a firearm in that melee last night."

Uncle Dan ran his fingers through his hair and muttered something about Frankie being lucky he wasn't holding a bullet instead of a bag. I had a feeling the village code had been exercised to the hilt all the way from Dundalk.

The waiter came and swept the crumbs of our dessert off the tablecloth onto the floor and handed Uncle Dan the bill.

Grandmother shook her head. "They saw us coming," she said again.

Uncle Dan said he'd take me to get some peppermint rock and that Grandmother and Aunt Nin could get their shopping done; we'd meet back at the bus by five. Grandmother took Aunt Nin's arm and told her to keep a firm grip on her handbag.

"Pick whatever you want, Jennifer," Uncle Dan said. The confectioner's shop was filled with the biggest, thickest sticks of candy rock I'd ever seen. Postcards showed various beauty spots and landmarks, and knicknacks of every description were either printed with "Come Back to Dublin" or something in Gaelic that Uncle Dan translated as "A Hundred Thousand Welcomes."

But I knew what I wanted the minute I saw them.

"Could I get a flag, Uncle Dan?"

Uncle Dan reached over to the tin cannister, plucked a little green, white, and orange flag, and handed it to me. It was only the size of a handkerchief and stuck onto a flimsy stick, but I felt like a standard-bearer. I had a stirring vision of Bobby McConnell on a white horse holding a large Union Jack. I rode a huge black stallion and bore the green, white, and orange. We sat facing each other from opposite ends of the first field.

Uncle Dan interrupted the scene. "Pick some rock too, love," he said. "You can't come to Dublin and not get a stick of rock."

We stepped back out onto the crush of O'Connell Street and maneuvered our way to what Uncle Dan said was the birthplace of the Free State. It was here at the General Post Office that the men of 1916 had proclaimed Ireland independent of England. It wasn't much to look at, and its sooty walls were chipped and scarred.

"Bullet scars," said Uncle Dan, and I hastily withdrew my finger from a hole. "They ran up the first tricolour here," he said, pointing to the top where a huge replica of the flag I held hung listlessly against its pole.

"Do you know the meaning of those colours, Jennifer?"

I didn't know the colours meant anything other than to distinguish one flag from another.

"The green was for Catholics, the orange for the Protestants, and the white"—Uncle Dan squinted up at the flag—"symbolised the peace between them."

It took me a minute to absorb this. The first reaction was one of admiration; what that flag said was that all the people of Ireland were "We." We were all "We!"

Then I was overwhelmed by anger. *They'd* spurned it. I said so to Uncle Dan.

"They shouldn't have been included at all!"

Uncle Dan put his arm around my shoulders. "Then you'd have excluded many of the leaders of all the fights for independence, love."

I swung around to face him, speechless. And he rattled off names like Patrick Pearse, Wolfe Tone, Roger Casement, and somebody called Yeats who wrote poetry. Dumbfounded, I questioned him with my eyes.

"Yes, Jennifer, they were Protestants. But you're not likely to hear that brought up much in yarns." His face shadowed. "They were a special breed, Jennifer." Then he muttered something about "either dead or fled."

We walked on down O'Connell Street towards the Liffey Bridge, not speaking. I was visualising Bobby McConnell's sniggering reaction if I told him we had a Protestant poet on our side. I dismissed the whole thing, hoping nobody else would tell him either.

I don't know what Uncle Dan was thinking, but he looked—well, he looked lonely. Perhaps it was because Aunt Madge was stranded in Dundalk, for he cheered up as soon as I mentioned I wanted to get her a present, something saying "Dublin" on it. That reminded him, he said, he'd a present to get her too. Then he looked hard at me, his eyes sizing me up.

"How'd you like another stick of rock?"

I gave him a look too. "Why am I getting it?"

Uncle Dan laughed and called me a wee twister. Then he got serious. He was going to buy Aunt Madge a ring, but I was to tell no one about it. The last part was why I was getting the extra rock.

"What kind of a ring?"

"A special kind."

"Uncle Dan," I said, "if it's what I'm thinking it is, I'll keep my mouth shut for nothing. Just tell me you'll marry her no matter what Granny and Father Murphy say."

"Why, Jennifer!" He sounded incredulous. "I'd marry Aunt Madge tomorrow if she'd agree."

I gaped at him. "If *she* . . . you mean, it's not Granny and Father . . .?"

Uncle Dan gave a deep sigh and looked to heaven. "Put it like this, love, they're only helping her stick to a negative answer."

God help me, but I'd been working on the wrong people all this time.

We met Patsy and her daddy sitting at the foot of Nelson's Pillar. None of us felt like making the climb up the stairs inside it. Patsy had a flag, too, and Mr. McKenna was loaded with paper parcels. A boy of about thirteen sidled up to us. He had, as Grandmother would have described it, a face like the map of Ireland. A truculent chin squared off the lightly freckled face which was dominated by fierce blue eyes. He wore a man's cap and his clothes all looked too big for him. Two smaller children hung behind him, one holding onto a rope which was attached to a little dog Smokey Doran would have made two of.

There were different kinds of dirt, Grandmother maintained. Dirt on my knees after a day's Indian scouting was "clean dirt," but a tide mark around the neck was something else again. A high-water mark lapped at the boy's chin. He had his hand out.

"Give us a sixpence, misther, for to feed my wee brothers." The two children peeked around him at us. Uncle Dan fiddled in his pocket and gave him some pennies.

"Me mother, God bless and take care of her, has TB," he said, moving to Patsy's daddy, who had apparently anticipated the boy's intentions. "Would your wee gurl be wanting a dog, misther?"

Patsy's daddy told him no and to move on, but the boy persisted in the soft, wheedling accent.

"You can take him for t'ree shillin's."

Free Staters were contrary, Grandmother said. If a word started with the "th" sound they made it a strong "t," but if the "t" sound was called for in the middle of a word, they perversely made it come out as "th." I looked at the little dog. Matter oozed from its eyes and its coat was patchy.

"I must have t'ree shillin's to feed . . ."

Uncle Dan told the boy to take himself off, and the boy's voice changed from a gentle whine to exceed Uncle Dan's strident tone.

"Dirthy Norterners!" He spat on the pavement and I flinched. One of the children tugged at the boy and received a quick cuff for his efforts.

Something gnawed at me. Didn't this boy know we were . . . ? I looked at the flag making convulsive twirls between my fingers.

"Dirthy Norterners!" The boy was sneering. "G'wan away back were you came from!" He made a shooing motion with his cap.

People stopped to look at us, attracted by the commotion, and we scurried off to the Gresham Hotel. Uncle Dan told Patsy and I not to fret. That boy was a professional beggar and made a good living at it, he was sure. It was an accepted trade down here. No, the boy's wee brothers wouldn't starve.

That tourism was Ireland's second most important industry was proven by the amount of merchandise, both seen and unseen, we were hauling home with us. Packages stuffed the overhead racks, bulged out under seats, and turned the aisle into an obstacle course.

Grandmother had a bosom as big as Aunt Nin's by the time we reached Dundalk, where Rosie and Aunt Madge rejoined us. Rosie assured us the Lodger was recovering nicely, and I wondered why she looked like she might have a good cry. To Aunt Madge's horror, Grandmother threw a parcel of sausages back to her and, in effect, suggested Aunt Madge alter the contours of her body. When it came to smuggling, Grandmother had no reserves. Uncle Dan whispered something to Aunt Madge, and her face got even redder despite the fact that he'd rescued her by putting the sausages down the sleeve of his shirt.

"If you want to keep your flag, Jennifer, you'd better do something about it. The border's coming up!" Grandmother said with unrestrained delight.

I pressed my forehead to the window, but it wasn't any cooler. My flag. My eyes stared back at me, reflected in the darkening glass, and the beggar boy gave a nasty little tug at my insides. He'd blighted the whole trip and continued to goad me.

I shifted my gaze to Grandmother's reflection. It showed the back of her head. There was something bothering me about Grandmother too. I was used to her contrariness; I knew she sometimes took an opposite tack just for the sake of getting an argument. But from the minute we crossed the border she'd acted like the Free State was only wonderful from the northern side of the border. Its scenery, while impressive, she agreed, couldn't hold a candle to the Glens of Antrim; and what was there to compare to the Mountains of Mourne? It was strange, this sudden loyalty to the North.

The beggar boy loomed over my left shoulder in the glass, challenging me. Oh, no—not on your life, I told the spectre, far be it from me to up and shout "The Emperor has no clothes"; that we didn't belong to the Free State and its people; that we neither liked nor trusted each other . . .

Oh, God, I could just see all of Greencastle looking at me, sadly shaking their heads at this poor creature who'd just proven, irrefutably, she was possessed of low wits.

"Half a crown for a pound of sausages!" Grandmother was saying to Aunt Nin. "You can only trust a Free Stater to rob you blind."

There you are! There's your answer, I said to myself in the window. That beggar boy had tried to rob us blind and when we wouldn't let him—well, anybody who'd stoop to begging couldn't have any principles left. Dirty Northerners indeed! The cheek of him, and him with a tide mark! What did he know anyway? He didn't even have enough rearing to wash his bloody neck, for God's sake!

I shut my eyes and told that beggar boy to take himself off. All the Catholics of Greencastle couldn't be wrong anyway. He might as well have called them all liars. The window steamed up and I shifted my head.

I rolled the flag around its thin stick and slipped it up inside my dress all the way to my armpit. Provided I didn't have to bend to the left, my flag was safe.

There were certain commodities, I discovered, which could be brought over the border openly and without penalty: things like rock, ashtrays, and tea towels smattered with shamrocks and depicting Blarney Castle or Tara's legendary harps. Clothing, jewelry, foodstuffs were allowed, but if the stiff duty imposed couldn't be paid, then they were confiscated. So the whole busload of us sat suffering under layers of coats and cardigans, rashers, sausages, and butter.

Strictly forbidden was the smuggling of guns (which we didn't have to worry about) or anything smacking of nationalism (like flags, which I did have to worry about). But my main concern was Uncle Dan and the ring. It wouldn't matter if he was caught with it, Uncle Dan had said, as if his name was Carnegie.

I was pressed into service by Patsy's daddy and wore a corduroy jerkin intended for one of the brothers. Patsy wore new Irish dancing shoes with silver buckles and shrank in a bilious green cardigan bought for her mother.

If we were grilled by customs men, we were to say we'd brought them with us from Belfast. No, we had nothing to declare. Nothing at all.

At any other time I'd have been flattered at being inducted into this exclusive liars' clique of adults where amnesty was a foregone conclusion. But the dismal state of my soul was really beginning to worry me. I hadn't been to confession since Father Sheridan left a month ago. I'd taken a mathematical approach: The more venial sins you committed, the more time you spent in Purgatory. I'd plenty of venials accumulated and one more couldn't make that much difference in the sentence computation except . . .

A blackness descended upon me. Except that I'd got that whopping big mortal sin of helping to build a Protestant bonfire. And I was hoping for mercy on that one, basing my defense at the Judgement on ignorance of the bonfire's purpose, thereby reducing it to venial status.

If you died with a mortal sin staining your soul, you went straight to Hell—no ifs, ands, or buts. The smart thing to do was get right to confession and get the matter out of the way. But there was also a tenuous escape clause. If you said an Act of Contrition for your sins and died between confessions that was supposed to practically eliminate the necessity of the middleman. I'd said one every day since the bonfire.

I came to a decision. I couldn't afford any more mortal sins.

"Is it mortal or venial?" I asked Patsy's daddy.

Grandmother gave me that look which signified she thought I was being cheeky. I ignored it.

"What?" Patsy's daddy was now convinced I was an idiot.

"The sin."

Patsy's daddy widened his eyes and rolled them around. "Ooohhhhh," he said, before giving a rather inept demonstration of the workings of the village code. "Well, now—ahh—y'see, Jennifer, there's no harm in a wee white lie that—uhh—we're forced into now and again to protect the innocent . . ." He looked around, inviting help with his eyes, but Uncle Dan's chuckles infected the rest of the innocents on the bus and he threw up his arms and sat down.

Oh, aye, I said to myself, it's all right for *you* to laugh; *you* didn't provide the fuel to burn Christ's Vicar on Earth.

The jerkin felt like a balaclava as we pulled to a stop near the customs shed. The hurley team was shaken from a deep sleep induced by their tour of the Guinness Brewery. Everyone else composed themselves and beatific expressions abounded as the great venial sin got under way. I stuck an enormous hunk of rock in my rapidly drying mouth.

I watched the customs men wend their way up the aisle. They were selective in who they asked the vital, "Do you have anything to declare? Any butter, tea?" Some declared a half a pound of sausages here or a few rashers there to put them off the scent of the larger hoards like the one in Grandmother's chest.

Perhaps Uncle Dan didn't look like a rasher-runner, for by the time they got to him it was, "Any jewelry?" I needed to go to the bathroom.

"No," Uncle Dan said steadily, looking the customs man right in the eye. The customs man returned the look for what felt like minutes, then blessedly moved to Aunt Madge.

Now, Aunt Madge hadn't even been to Dublin, hadn't even been coerced into hiding the sausages, but she just wasn't any good under duress, I found out. She'd never been shifty-eyed until faced with the customs man. The word "no" acquired about four extra syllables the way she said it, and her eyes were in her lap.

"That's a lovely ring," said the friendly customs man.

Ring! Oh, God, God. I closed my eyes, knowing my knickers were going to be soaked any second.

"Where'd you get it?" the customs man said. The mild interest in his voice didn't match his eyes.

"I . . . he . . ." Aunt Madge cast a pleading look at Uncle Dan. "We . . ." There was a long look between them and Uncle Dan's eyes were anxious. Mine darted back and forth as if I knew what the silent conversation consisted of.

The babble of voices trickled to silence as tension communicated itself back as far as the hurley team.

"We're engaged, man," said a grinning Uncle Dan. "Have been for six months." This last was said like he was leaking a confidence.

I'd have thought it impossible to make the word "congratulations" sound like an insult, but that's the way it came out of the customs man as he moved to Grandmother.

"I've a pound of sugar and a few rashers." She kicked the bag at her feet. Grandmother was an expert under duress. The customs man hardly acknowledged her, ignored Aunt Nin, and abruptly marched down the aisle and jumped off the bus.

As the "all clear" sounded, everyone whooped and people started congratulating Aunt Madge and Uncle Dan.

"You're a quare fella, Dan O'Neill," said Patsy's daddy, his eyes mischievous. The hurley team slapped his back, pumped his arm, and bottles chinked in toasts. Aunt Nin had tears in her eyes and cried, "God love you both." Then she said, "When's the big day?"

"Oh, not for a long time," my Aunt Madge told the whole bus. "It's not like we *have* to get married or anything." If the same tone had been used by anyone other than Aunt Madge, I'd have said there was a jag in it.

Grandmother said nothing. That's when I realised it wasn't a farce. My Aunt Madge and my Uncle Dan were really engaged. That meant engaged to be *married!* Oh, he was a fly man! Grandmother couldn't very well up and say she didn't approve with half the village of Greencastle celebrating the event. I ran back to them, gawked at the ring and draped myself across Uncle Dan's legs, and whispered in his ear, "You're a big twister, Uncle Dan." He laughed and rumpled my hair.

No, indeed, it wouldn't have mattered if they'd found the ring on *him*. I wondered how he'd got her to agree.

The bus sped to the North and home. The trip to the Free State was over. So was the Twelfth, but its effects were only beginning.

CHAPTER
====13====

Friday, the thirteenth, dawned ominously. Napoleon's Nose had disappeared and the sky was just one big slate cloud threatening to burst. That was all right with me as long as it cooled the place down. I'd never make it in the tropics, I knew now.

The smell of frying bacon cheered me out of bed, and Grandmother was humming to herself as she tended the spluttering smuggler's feast on the pan. Aunt Madge had already left for the mill. Grandmother gave me a plate of fried soda bread, dip-in eggs, black pudding, and rashers so streaked with lean that only the edges curled. That would stick to my ribs all day, she said. She had errands for me to do down in Greencastle and I could play with Patsy for a while. Either I was particularly hungry or Grandmother was right that Free State stuff was better than ours, for I did justice to her efforts.

"Take your Burberry. It'll be coming down in buckets before you get back."

I tied the laces of my sandshoes. Last winter's Wellingtons were much too small now and I didn't see the point of her caring about the top half of me getting wet if my feet were letting in. But care she did. "You can't read newspapers if they're turned back into pulp."

I got a bit of a jolt passing Mrs. Doran's front window. Her blinds were at half-mast. There were two occasions when we employed this position: If the sun was particularly bright coming up over the lough, the blinds deflected the glare on our side of the street, or if someone on the street was being buried, this was the traditional posture of respect. But the sun wasn't visible and nobody had died. I quickened my pace until I reached the Sommervilles' gate. Mrs. Sommerville, on her knees at the foot of the big Queen Elizabeth rose bush she worshipped, waved her trowel at me.

"Rain today, Jennifer!" she called cheerfully. "Not good for them, you know." She fondled the big perfect pinks that had brought first place honours to Serpentine Parade from the Royal Belfast Horticulture Society two years in a row. "Too much sun—not good for them at all." Another wave of the trowel and she bent towards the earth again. I turned onto the Whitewell. Leaves that had darkened to the deep green of summer now had a thirsty gray sheen to them, and a sullen grey lough said rain, too. A few people scuttled past me, homeward, and away ahead a woman had a girl by the hand. It was Patsy. I started to run, then stopped. I didn't want to catch up with the Widow Byrne. They turned into Creswell's dairy.

It hadn't been Patsy anyway. I found her on the fractured remains of what once had been a sea wall. The tide was on its way in, washing over the wavy furrows that past tides had etched in the sand.

"It's not like it's forever," Patsy said, "but to hear my mammy you'd think it was. 'Things will die down, Mick, they always do,' she says. She says they'll let him back in the shipyard after a while, but he says no, not after what he told the foreman. My mammy says he should have kept a better houl' of his tongue. But he says he's not waiting for *them* when he's sure of a job in Birmingham with Joe Kane now—that's a friend of his," she filled me in, "who's made thousands since he went to England last year."

Patsy's daddy had made up his mind and was leaving tonight on the ten o'clock boat. I agreed with Patsy's daddy; if you could make thousands in England, then it was stupid not to go. Of course, if it was up to me, I'd have headed for America, where they make millions. But I didn't say so to Patsy in case it got back to her mother, who would, I was sure, forbid Patsy's ever speaking to me again.

The tide made an eddying swirl at our feet. In another fifteen minutes we'd have to swim, for it was sneaky, the tide was, and poured through chinks in the wall and cut you off from the beach. There was no question about it, it was time I learned how to swim. Besides, the clique on Serpentine Parade would still be smarting from the bonfire fight.

"I'll be down again tomorrow," I said, scrambling down onto what was still dry sand. I reminded her of the tide.

"Okay," she said. She was just going to stay for another few minutes. "I get my daddy's place in the bed while he's away," Patsy said, telling me where her mind was.

Aunt Nin gave me a couple of biscuits in passing to see me up the road. I had two stops to make: Katie Keenan's for the *Irish News* and Morton's for the *Belfast Telegraph*.

The first big drowsy splats hit me at Creswell's and I stuffed the newspapers inside the Burberry. By the time I rounded Serpentine Parade it was a steady rain, without the intensity of a shower, the kind that eleven years had taught me would last for days without let up.

I played paper dolls at the bay window and Grandmother settled herself in the chair with a mug of tea, her glasses, and the newspapers. The rest of the afternoon was punctuated with what I thought excessively loud crackles of newspaper, accompanied by snorts and sighs.

A simple statement like, "Did you enjoy your wee

sleep?" was considered a declaration of war by Grandmother. Couldn't a person close their eyes for a minute without being accused of sleeping the day away? Aunt Madge and I pretended she never took any naps. So, when part of the paper slipped from her fingers around four o'clock, I crept over and tested my stealth by removing the rest. Grandmother continued to close her eyes. I had a sinister search to make. I wanted to see how many heart attack and stroke victims the heat had claimed of the Orangemen.

The front page of the *Belfast Telegraph* had more pictures than it usually did, and a banner of print shouted, THE GLORIOUS TWELFTH. Orangemen smiled, scowled, danced, and marched from one end of it to the other.

The word "Greencastle" stopped me on page three.

GREENCASTLE MAN ARRESTED—IRA SUSPECT. The small print followed:

> Francis Doran of Greencastle was arrested late last night during a riot in the Market. The 23-year-old suspected IRA gunman is being detained in Crumlin Road gaol at His Majesty's Pleasure charged with numerous offences ranging from attempted murder to disruption of seasonal marches.
>
> The Royal Ulster Constabulary reports another gunman wounded at the scene, but checks of local hospitals failed to turn up anything, leading the RUC to believe the gunman has already crossed the border aided by friends.

I gave a low whistle. Frankie would indeed be away for a while. I was away on to wondering how the other man fared, the one who escaped the dragnet, when the enormity of Frankie's predicament hit me. Poor Mrs. Doran was disgraced!

I checked the *Irish News* to see if it spread the word. Now, Mrs. Doran didn't read the *Irish News*. She, like Grandmother, felt it was a bit provincial. But Mrs. Doran would have felt better about the *Irish News* version of the affair. It referred to Frankie as a recently decorated member of the British Armed Services and exhorted Stormont, the seat of our Government, to ask itself why Frankie now resided in Crumlin Road gaol. (I thought that the height of naivete.) And they substituted "man" for "gunman," "riot-inciting" for "seasonal," and just said another man, perhaps wounded, had given the slip to the RUC.

I marvelled at the deviousness of the English language. Right then and there, I decided to keep the two reports for further study. If I could master the knack—oh, the possibilities were endless!

I rummaged for the scissors in the sideboard drawer and went back to the *Belfast Telegraph* and started cutting before I remembered Grandmother's admonition not to desecrate the paper before Aunt Madge had read it. You never knew, she said, if people wanted to read what was on the back of what you cut out.

I turned the page to see what I'd be cutting through and spent the next few minutes reading one sentence over and over. It was under a picture of a man wearing a little fez hat and the ubiquitous sash. He held a sheet of paper. The caption under him read, "Grand Master Armstrong reads text of King George's telegram expressing congratulations and good wishes to the people of Northern Ireland for their magnificent show of loyalty to the Crown—full text page 6."

There was a roaring in my ears as I struck the King of England off the list of "People I want to meet." Then my rage turned inward. I was stupid; I knew nothing about Protestants and not much about Catholics. *They shouldn't be allowed . . . Hell, they're encouraged. . . .*

I sat studying Grandmother. In the peace of sleep it was a nice face, a face that hadn't forgotten her own grandmother's struggle to survive the great famine. She'd told me that story often. "Oh, aye, Granny Connor watched the English ship the beef out of the country to grace English tables while the Irish people dropped dead on the roads. It stuck in my mind," she said, "if Granny Connor had died, I'd never have been born!" Grandmother could make a hundred-year-old grievance personal. Then I turned around and did the same thing. I took after Grandmother sometimes.

"Granny," I whispered so she wouldn't hear me. "I'll never, never, *never* stand up for the King again." And the whispering wasn't because I knew she'd take issue with the adverb either. Vowing just seemed more potent somehow when your vehemence wasn't distracted by reactions.

I twisted the *Belfast Telegraph*, minus the article about Frankie, into a torch and subjected it to a trial by fire in the grate.

Mrs. Doran took to her bed, Mr. Doran stretched his weekends, and the scalloped fringes of their blinds remained at half-mast during the day.

I spent most of my days at the tide with Patsy. Aunt Madge offered me a bribe: sixpence and an E sweetie coupon every Friday if I'd check with Mrs. Doran every day to see if she needed any errands done. That our milk and bread was brought to the door lightened the burden, but she'd need someone to bring other foodstuffs from the village.

A paying job appealed to me, but I discovered that the responsibility of leaving Mrs. Doran's ration book, money, and shopping list at Aunt Nin's while I was at the tide hampered my freedom. Mrs. Doran's needs were sporadic, so I couldn't establish a routine. Twice, I was halfway up the Whitewell when I remembered and had to run all the way back to Aunt Nin's, retrieve the book and money, purchase the groceries, and then lug them all the way home. But Aunt Madge had given me such lavish praise on how well I'd performed, I just couldn't say, "I quit."

My conversations with Mrs. Doran during the first few

weeks of this arrangement were confined to stilted questions on health—"How're you keeping this morning?" and tomatoes—"Do you want home-grown or Guernsey?" and weather—"It might rain." Her attempts were met with just plain yes and no because each word of a lengthier reply had to be defined right down to root meanings. To say I was fearful of letting something slip that might bring more pain to Mrs. Doran is a mild way of putting it. The same brevity was in my answers to Grandmother's sleekit pries about the state of the Doran household; the only difference being I took a certain amount of pleasure in yes-ing, no-ing, and maybe-ing her. If she wanted more news, let her ask Aunt Madge or declare a truce and go straight to the source. I had her there, though; had her stumped; and we both knew it.

Grandmother had gone around the house crowing that she'd been right. "I warned that woman to have no truck with them. Sure, an infant could have told you they were just biding their time until the war was over to get back to their tricks. They couldn't afford any trouble in their own back yard."

Aunt Madge agreed with Grandmother. Certainly she had won her point. But then Aunt Madge walked out the back door saying she'd no stomach for triumph over our own.

Grandmother was also basking in triumph over the defeat of Winston Churchill and his Tories just a week ago. Aunt Madge and I had been shushed into silence so many times we just gave up talking about anything worthwhile and gave Grandmother and the wireless free rein. The whole election had been confusing to me. Churchill had brought us through the war and I thought it very ungrateful of the people of Britain not to vote for him. But whatever else the English were, Grandmother said, they weren't stupid and the man in the street wanted a better wage for his labours so he voted for Labour. Who "the man in the street" was she didn't say, but she did say that the Labour

Government had ordered the Unionists who governed us in Northern Ireland to reflect the same changes they were instituting in England.

"They're furious, of course," Grandmother said of the Unionists. "They're used to a free hand and a blind eye from the Tories."

"But if we don't like the Unionists, why can't we just vote for someone else to run things over here?"

Grandmother said that was a very good question and that although I now knew what inciting sectarianism was it would take her forever to explain what gerrymandering and business and plural votes meant. I didn't let on I didn't know what she said I did.

Mrs. Doran came up with an errand I didn't relish doing. Why she'd waited a whole week wasn't apparent until later.

"Jennifer, I'm not able to work on these anymore. Could you bring them over to Mrs. Sweet, love?"

She handed me two boxes of cloth poppies and two pieces of folded material, one red and one black. Another small box contained the slim wires and green tape used for the stems.

"What'll I say if she asks when you can start again?"

Mrs. Doran said she didn't think so and I didn't know if she meant she didn't think she'd be able to start again or if she didn't think Mrs. Sweet would ask.

Mrs. Sweet didn't ask, so the dilemma solved itself. She just took the poppies and said some fluttery things about being *soooo* busy and how nice I was to bring them over and save her the bother. And then I knew why Mrs. Doran had waited. Never a week went by without Mrs. Sweet, Mrs. Beattie, or one of the other British Legion ladies stopping in. Their constant visitations, which riled Grandmother so much, had stopped.

And I knew another thing too—those poppies were

Mrs. Doran's resignation from the British Legion. I decided to leak this information to Grandmother.

I avoided the fields, the Castle grounds, and those who frequented them. All my energy was devoted to mastering the intricate coordination of the breaststroke in two feet of water.

Uncle Dan had calculated the tides for me and I knew exactly when the level of water was at two feet on the beach side of the sea wall. He said everybody could swim, that the only thing really needed was *confidence*. And he gave me safety rules we both knew I'd follow.

I'd got the rhythm right, but the confidence part continued to elude me. It was do or die, I thought, my choice of words putting off the doing for another week. This fear was eventually overcome by yet a greater fear. Bobby McConnell had taken to sitting on the brick pillars of the Camp gates again. He looked the other way when I got close, but I knew he was watching me. And the towel I carried gave away my destination, so it was only a matter of time before he made some rotten remark about me never being able to swim. And I couldn't lie; he'd make me prove it.

Patsy, her brother Michael, Dierdre, and Noreen stood in thigh-high water at strategic points around me. They'd make sure my head was pulled out in case confidence didn't show up. Do or die time had arrived.

I was down on my hunkers, chin just at the surface, finishing an Act of Contrition. Then I gave the little push with my toes, going into the glide I'd practised. And when I'd normally have put my feet down, I went into a furious breaststroke, hands making small circular motions in front of me. I was just ready to put my feet down when I realised that it was *my option* whether I put them down or not! Confidence flooded me. I put my feet down in the sand and stood up, acknowledging the cheers.

"Nothing to it," I said, "all you need is confidence."

God, but I wished Bobby McConnell was there. Then I took on the job of swimming instructor.

Grandmother announced she and I would start a novena for Frankie Doran, so we went to chapel every night for a week and spent the evenings at Aunt Nin's. I learned a lot about Catholics and was privy to summer yarns I'd never heard before. These stirred up a fierce sense of nationalism in me and I was all for us opposing them any chance we got.

Patsy's Uncle Joe came down every Thursday night to see how they were getting along now that her daddy was away in England. He lived up in Belfast on the Falls Road. That Uncle Joe lived on the Falls Road turned out to be significant. Patsy said it ran parallel with the Shankhill Road and that the two were bastions of IRA men and B-Specials, respectively. And she was full of the great stories Uncle Joe told them. It was this immersion in all things Catholic that led to the uncovering of Grandmother's darkest secret.

That Thursday evening Uncle Joe was besieged with coaxes to tell the children more. I'd been invited in by Patsy and sat quietly, legs crossed Indian fashion like the rest.

"Is it Jennifer, you say?" he asked me.

"Yes, Jennifer Marshall," I replied.

"Ohhh," he said slowly, nodding his head. "And where do you come from, Jennifer?"

"Up the Whitewell Road." I was flattered Uncle Joe showed such interest. Then everyone barged in on our conversation, requesting what appeared to be the general favourite, the story of Kevin Barry.

Uncle Joe pulled Patsy's head down and whispered something to her. Patsy straightened up, laughing. "Oh, aye, Uncle Joe. She's as Catholic as you and me. She takes after her mother's looks."

Uncle Joe turned up the side of his mouth in a wry smile. Then he told us all to pay attention. The room was hushed and the children huddled closer around his chair.

"Now this story begins back in the time of the Troubles," the singsong nasal twang of Belfast began, "when the Sons of Ireland rose against the English upstarts one Easter Sunday morning." He nodded to Patsy, whose lilting voice took up the tale. Everyone's eyes held a strange uniform light when the British soldiers offered Kevin freedom if he'd tell the names of his comrades. We all gulped with relief when Kevin proudly answered, "No!"

Under normal circumstances the ballad of Kevin Barry would have had immense appeal for me. I mean, I would have been all for storming Crumlin Road gaol to free Frankie! As it was, I suffered through Patsy's singing with only slightly less discomfort than Kevin himself.

Uncle Joe thought I was a Protestant! I was glad when he shooed us all outside.

"Well," said Patsy to my question, "you can't blame him. I mean you have to be careful of your company when you're talking about the Troubles."

I agreed you couldn't be too careful.

"You've got a real Protestant name, Jennifer," Patsy said earnestly, "and—well—you *look* Protestant!"

Protestants didn't want me in their clubs because I was Catholic, and Catholics, suspicious of my origins, had to be careful of me in their company because of my fair-haired Protestant looks. My name was on a par with Zoe or Zelda too.

I wasn't adopted. My mother and father weren't the King and Queen of Mandalay. Now I knew the truth: I was some changeling the fairies had left in everyone's unwanting midst.

I spent the vast portion of the next day gazing at myself in the mirror, but the outward signs like premature aging or sickly appearance didn't show up. In fact, I'd never seen me look healthier. Perhaps this was a trick of reflection though.

"Am I all wizened up?" I asked Grandmother. Change-lings normally were wrinkled.

Grandmother's eyebrows shot up. "No," she said, sprinkling a muslin cloth with vinegar.

I almost crumpled at her feet with relief. It was a firm, comforting no.

Then she added, "There's no danger of that for quite a while yet." She spread the muslin over a tray of potted herrings and put them in the larder to cool.

"The rain's stopped," she changed the subject. "I'm away out to pick a lettuce." I followed her down the shell path.

"Take a sniff," she invited, "just take a whiff of that!" She inhaled and let out a sigh of pleasure. "There's nothing to beat the smell of wallflowers after a summer shower." And indeed the air was sweet with their unique and pungent scent.

"People won't grow them, you know—or if they do, they shove them away at the back by themselves up against walls."

Just like me.

"That's why they call them 'wallflowers,' by the way," she rambled on.

Grandmother hadn't segregated them. They were mixed with dahlias and sweet Williams. Clusters of brilliant yellow petals crowded on long stems; others were a dark wine color or a peculiar subdued shade of scarlet.

"That's why they call girls that don't get lifted for a dance 'wallflowers.'" She gave a hoot. "They're left standing by themselves up against the walls!"

Was I a scarlet wallflower or a yellow one?

We moved to the lettuce bed. They lay like bright green roses, petals spread, lapping the goodness from the rain. Grandmother got down on one knee, picking over them.

"Why do we have a Protestant name?" There! It was out!

The smell of wallflowers clung heavy in the silence. Grandmother's fingers had stopped inspecting leaves.

"Your grandfather was a Protestant," she said, finally. She wrenched a lettuce from the earth, its naked roots bleeding soil.

"But . . . but you *hate* Protestants!" In for a penny, in for a pound.

She stood up and turned to face me, the green eyes as bright as the lettuce she held.

"Ahhhh, now, love," she said softly, "but *he* was different."

I'd never understand this woman—*never*.

CHAPTER
14

The emotion the Twelfth had stirred did indeed die down around the middle of August. Serpentine Parade's bunting was a thing of the past and stony nods again took on neighbourly "Think we're in for some rain" conversation starters.

But though there was no more visible evidence that there was a deep division between them and us, I now knew it was there. Like the corncrake, you didn't have to see it to know it *existed*.

Protestants cloaked themselves in the robes of largesse they could afford, and Catholics—well, we just slithered back into the long grasses of "Watch what you say."

Bobby and I exchanged a few tentative "Hiyas." He'd grown an inch. It was a shame to waste the last few weeks of the summer holidays on nothing more than chance "Hiyas."

"Where'd you get them?" Bobby did the first real speaking.

"Get what?"

"You know what—the squibs."

"What squibs?"

"Don't pretend you don't know—the bangers!" Then his mouth turned up at one corner. "You blew the arse out of the whole thing, y'know."

I tried to look intelligently aloof.

"All that work—the greatest bonfire ever built," he sighed, "and it was over in minutes. Karrroooom—sticks flying." His arms warded off unseen objects. "I knew it was you." He narrowed his eyes. "God, if I could have got a hold of you right then I'd have murdered you." He grinned at the thought. "No kidding!"

I decided to start walking.

"Where'd you get them?" he called after me. "Can you get some more for Halloween . . ."

That Bobby McConnell was more interested in squibs than peace pipes didn't bother me at all. We were even! I sat rocking on the biscuit tin and gave way to peals of laughter that Grandmother said were hyenic.

Bobby and Erik had a football game going right outside our gate. Pam stood goalie between a blazer and a pullover. I stood well back on the sidelines watching—not that I had any intention, mind you, of wheedling my way in, although I must say Pam Boyd wasn't a goalie I'd like to have had to praise.

"You didn't even *try* to get that." Bobby had his red, sweating face very close to Pam's.

"I did too!"

"You did not!"

After a few more bars of this dialogue, the game resumed and I stood kicking the dust in the gutter. Suddenly, the ball trickled to an almost dead stop at my feet. It was the slowness that alerted me. Never in a million years would Bobby McConnell have missed *that*.

I looked at him and his eyes told me the rest. I drew my right leg back and gave that ball a belt Stanley Matthews would have envied. Up it soared towards Pam, who decided it was useless to even try blocking it.

"Goal!" shouted Bobby. "That's three to two!"

It was official! I was too happy to hear anything else. But Pam had apparently screamed "Run!" and the three of them ducked down behind Pam's palings. When I saw what the ball had done, I was too sick to run. The Queen Elizabeth was still shuddering, its prize blossoms' life blood dripping away in front of me, petal by petal.

I just stood there for an infinity while the Sommervilles surveyed the damage, too wretched for fear.

"Jennifer—come over here," Mr. Sommerville said. My feet had taken root. "Come on. You must face the damage you've inflicted."

That his temple veins weren't pulsing with righteous wrath, that he wasn't screaming mad, was worse. Worse still, they were kind. My eyes bubbled.

"There, there, now, Jennifer." Mrs. Sommerville put an arm around my shaking shoulders. "Don't distress yourself further, dear. We know you didn't *mean* to do it."

We were at their front door. "I was just saying to Mr. Sommerville"—she gave him a companionable smile—"wasn't I, dear, that the Queen Elizabeth wasn't a patch on what it was last year. Roses just don't take to heat waves." She gave me a quick squeeze and told Mr. Sommerville over her shoulder not to forget to throw the ball back onto the street. She was sure its owner was anxious.

And I spent the next half hour sipping tea and munching exquisite little tea cakes in happy bondage to them body and soul. The soul part was forever, and the body part was every Saturday morning for a month. They had plenty of weeding, raking, and lawn mowing; they were sure I'd be a marvellous help.

What with my errands for Mrs. Doran and one Saturday morning's weeding for the Sommervilles behind me, I'd acquired a certain amount of self-discipline. Just do it and get it over with was the motto. But it didn't apply very well to blackberry gathering.

"Don't eat them before they're washed," Grandmother had said earlier. I inspected the plump blackberry for maggots and promptly ate it, remembering not to wipe the purple juice on my dress. Grandmother had given me a paper bag which was only slightly heavier than when I'd started. There'd be little jam at this rate.

The brambles dropped low with blackberries as big as damsons, and I set to work feeding the bag instead of myself. There was a faint rustle behind me. Bobby McConnell was catching bees somewhere in the fields this morning and I wouldn't put it past him to let the bloody things take their wrath out on me.

But it was only a sparrow darting from a hawthorn bush into the next field. I squinted at the hawthorn bush. There'd be a nest in there! I set the bag of blackberries down and skirted the bush, parting thorny branches and hardy white flowers. The nest was just a dot of mud-coloured grass high in the dark interior.

Grandmother didn't like pets, she said. She'd never go through again what she went through with my father's greyhound for all the tea in China. Aunt Madge said that was just words, that Grandmother had loved Trixie and she'd lived the Life of Riley until she was twelve and died of overweight. Aunt Madge said she'd been ashamed of Trixie, who ended up looking more like a donkey than a greyhound.

I looked at the nest again. I could keep it at the bottom of the garden and no one would know until I had the birds trained to sit on my fingers. Grandmother liked birds, I reasoned, or why else was I sent out in the snow to scatter breadcrumbs about the garden? And while she'd bark at me for drinking the top of the milk, it was "Ach, God love the wee craturs," when birds dug through the cardboard top of the morning milk on our doorstep and slurped half the cream before we took it in. They only got bold during a bad frost, she said, when all their water was frozen.

Yes, I'd be good to the little birds; feed them bread-crumbs dripped in milk and maybe worms.

Birds were a bit tame for my taste and I'd much rather have a pet lion like Lion Boy in the *Beano,* but there weren't many lions running around loose in Ireland. It was amazing the bullies you could subdue if you rode around on the back of a lion.

After one bad scratch I reconnoitered, tried another approach, and got two more for my pains. The mother bird had done her work well. I retreated to the blackberry bush, found my solution, and started running towards a patch of buttercups in the centre of the field.

"Bobbeee . . . Bobbeeee!"

Bobby, armed with a jam jar, looked up. "What's the matter?"

"Nothing. I've found a nest and I think it has baby birds in it." I fluttered my eyes the way film stars did when they wanted something from the leading man. "I can't get near it—it's too high for girls."

My sickening appeal wasn't working. Bobby was stalking a bumblebee sucking drowsily on a flowering clover. *Snap!* The lid of the jam jar clicked crisply and Bobby held up his conquest still clinging to the clover bud.

"Bobby," I simpered, "would you get the nest for me?" Bile rose in my throat at his indifferent eyeing of another bee.

"What'll you give me if I get it?"

Partial success! Then I had a terrible time wrestling between a paper lion and real birds.

"My old *Beano*s."

"I get them."

Potential failure.

"Well—what do you want?"

Bobby straightened up. Maybe he'd grown two inches. "Take down your knickers and show me."

Oh, God, God! I looked up at the sky, wishing I could fall into its calm blueness, and a funny little tingle just wouldn't be suppressed. Grandmother only mentioned knickers as items of laundry, but eleven years of inference and euphemisms had left their mark.

"Will you?" Something seemed to have gone wrong with Bobby's eyes. I bent down and started plucking at my socks. This was an emergency and "Watch what you say" just didn't apply.

"Oh, Bobby, I'd do it, but I'd have to tell it in confession. It's all right for you, you don't have to go."

"Even if I did, I just wouldn't tell," said Bobby.

Uncle Dan was right. Catholic conscience *was* exclusive. It didn't matter for Bobby; he didn't know any better. But I was an enlightened creature of God and I'd be haunted by guilt. Father Murphy! It would all come out. I saw it all . . . the girls in my class pitying and shunning me . . . Miss McGrath . . . and Grandmother . . .

"Do you want the nest or not?" Bobby looked at me with his strange new eyes.

"Okay—okay," I said crossly.

But he was crafty, Mr. McConnell was. "You'll take your knickers off and let me look?"

"Yes," I snapped and turned my back on him to stride across the field to the hawthorn bush. The unwanted tingle was still there.

"Up there," I said, pointing through the bush.

"Here—hold this." Bobby thrust his bees at me.

He held the nest gently and walked towards me. The tingle was gone and something else had taken its place, something only Grandmother could have put a name to. My forehead was moist. The nest, cradling four bald birds with outsized beaks making noiseless squawking motions, was placed into my waiting, blackberry-stained hands.

"There's your jam jar," I indicated with a nod. Then I tore off across the fields, the nest clutched against my chest.

I placed the nest in the hedge at the bottom of the garden and sat on the biscuit tin staring at it, my face a slaughterous red with shame. I wanted to put it back in the hawthorn bush, but the mother bird would never come back . . . and oh, God, but I wished I'd taken my knickers off.

I put my hands over my face and sat there for a long time not seeing anything but the pictures of my mind.

Smokey Doran settled himself under the fuchsia bush and turned his two yellow eyes on the hedge. Then he rolled over, stretched his legs in the air, and spread his claws before beginning the ceremony of his daily wash.

I occupied myself with preparations for my defence in the confessional. I'd run the gamut of the Seven Deadly Sins, and broken every Commandment, save one. I was sure what Bobby had proposed was the adultery one which overlapped the neighbour's wife one in some way. And Miss McGrath left no doubt that even to *think* evil things (let alone agree to them) was tantamount to commission of them.

"I've told lies." Blanket statement. Father Sheridan had never asked me questions, but I didn't know about Father Murphy so I made Smokey be him and ask "What kind?" just for the practise.

"Oh, like when Granny asked me if I'd ate the last potted herring and I said I didn't." Venial.

"And what lies have you told that might be mortal sins?" The confessional was getting a bit stuffy.

"Well, there was this promise . . ."

"Yes?"

"Well, I wanted . . . something . . . this boy said he'd get it for me if I'd . . . let him see something."

"Something?"

"Well, it was *somewhere*."

"Whearrow!" "Father Murphy" lunged past my stran-gled, fainting, *"There."*

The biscuit tin crumbled beneath me and I lay para-lysed as the unbroken Commandment was ripped asunder.

It was all over in seconds, I think. I stared at what was left of the carnage: a few glistening strands of rubbery mat-ter clinging to the shredded nest. Murder had been done and there was blood all over my hands. Hysterics propelled me through our back door, through to Grandmother and Aunt Madge.

"Jesus, Mary!"

"Jennifer! What's wrong?" Aunt Madge was screaming.

". . . blood on my hands . . . killed . . . murdered!"

Grandmother shook me hard and my mouth clamped shut.

I ended up in bed, caressed with hot milk and biscuits from Aunt Madge and nothing but guarded looks from Grandmother.

Grandmother daubed carbolic lotion on my hair—that was to keep the National Animals off—combed it until it fluffed around my head like—well, like a halo! I couldn't have felt that way last night, but I was now shriven, my soul a white shining shield again.

Saturday morning had been spent driving nails in hydrangea roots, which Mrs. Sommerville said turned them a different colour, and trimming long yellow-flowered streamers of what Mrs. Sommerville said were "creeping loose strife that had crept far enough." I'd enjoyed it more than the weeding of last Saturday. I got more tea and a sugary gravy ring too.

Confessions were heard from four to seven o'clock. I studied the language in the articles about Frankie, but I just befuddled myself more and would end up telling Father Murphy I'd shot and killed someone.

I was quaking as I said the Act of Confiteor. I knelt beside Dierdre, who was next to go in. The sinner's door opened and out came Noreen, who went on up near the altar to say her penance. It seemed to me Dierdre just went in long enough to say "Hello" to Father Murphy and come back out again.

I closed the sinner's door behind me and knelt down. Blackness. Then what I assumed was Father Murphy's profile materialised through the grille.

"Bless me, Father, for I have sinned. . . . I've lied, stole, cheated, helped to burn the Pope by accident, caused baby birds to be eaten by a cat, and if I've forgotten anything, you can be sure I did it and I'd like to be forgiven for that too."

It was the most rapid, most complete sentence I'd ever uttered. Father Murphy just said I'd given him a lot to think about, that I must try harder not to give in to temptation. Then he gave me a surprisingly lenient penance of three Hail Marys and, contrary to everyone's opinion about his command of Latin, gave me an absolution fraught with stutters.

I walked out of that confessional into the now empty chapel and knelt facing the Garden of Gethsemane. The refracted scarlets, yellows, and purples glowed all over the alter and me. I said more Hail Marys than necessary.

So here I was, snuggled up in the big armchair feeling shiny, fragrant, and *good!* This was the last night I could legally stay up late, for Miss McGrath loomed ahead on Monday morning. I shrugged her off and turned to Biffo the Bear in the *Beano*.

Grandmother ironed and I read until the back door opened and closed and Aunt Madge came in from the pictures. She looked white and worried and the look that passed between her and Grandmother was, I knew, village code for "Get rid of Jennifer."

"Jennifer, there are some biscuits up in the tin, love." I was already getting up. "You go on in the scullery and read your comics at the table."

Unlike Aunt Nin's, our walls weren't two feet thick and I culled enough of Aunt Madge's news to start me trembling.

". . . young Patsy . . . run over . . . killed dead. . . !"

Patsy McKenna?

". . . Bridie was in the Donegal Arms . . . a few jars too many since Mick's been away . . ."

It *was* Patsy. Oh, God have mercy!

". . . running across the Shore Road to the Widow Byrne . . . mother to come home . . . at the corner of the Whitewell Road."

I saw it all before I went in to face them.

"Patsy was the best dancer in Ireland" was all I said, and I went into a terrible keening wail I'd never heard before.

On my way to Mass the next morning, I let Grandmother get ahead of me and stopped at the corner where the Whitewell and Shore Roads met. I looked over at the Donegal Arms, then at the road, tracing Patsy's running steps. The morning sun glittered on the three little pearls that still lay in the rust-coloured stains near the middle of it.

"Wear the darkest dress you have—no, not that navy skirt, it's too short—the bottle-green one." The words came softly from Grandmother. "And remember, there is to be no carrying on between you girls. You go in, kneel down, and say a decade of the rosary, then leave quietly." Grandmother buttoned her black cardigan. "And another thing, don't speak unless you're spoken to. The less said at a wake the better."

Yes, Grandmother had seen dead bodies before.

I hadn't.

No, you don't get used to it.

No, kissing the corpse's forehead was optional.

I was to pay my respects. That was all. I didn't have to look.

Patsy's house was crowded. The Widow Byrne sat in Patsy's daddy's chair. Uncle Dan was too big for anywhere and sat on his hunkers at the scullery where Aunt Madge was helping to keep the tea going. Neighbours, and I supposed relatives, made up the crush.

All the little groups whispered amongst themselves and occasionally they mouthed sombre words of dubious comfort to Patsy's mother, who sat unmoving, staring into the fire with red-rimmed eyes.

Dierdre and Noreen sat on the floor at their mother's feet, peculiar prim smirks fixed on their mouths. I was glad it had been arranged that Dierdre, Noreen, and I were to go upstairs together. There were more people coming in and the Widow beckoned us to the foot of the stairs.

"Patsy's in the front room. And don't touch anything," she whispered.

"I get my daddy's place in the bed while he's away."

"Go *on*," Noreen hissed and gave me a shove.

"No! You!"

"Okay—I've seen her already."

"Is her face all bashed in?" There was no use trying to keep the anxiety out of my voice.

"No, but the back of her head is."

I stifled an anguished gasp.

"Ach, it's all right, Jennifer, you can't *see* it. My mum says they had to stuff it with cotton wool."

Patsy's dancing costume hung on the wall, its graceful cape flared over the right shoulder, and, standing to attention beneath it, the silver buckled shoes that could flash through a hornpipe. The room was lit only by tall white tapers at the head of the bed, the same room where not too long ago I'd been invited to see new life.

I tried to close my eyes, hoping to keep that memory, but they'd frozen and were fixed on Patsy's motionless white face, where the only visible evidence of violent death was a tiny, jagged bruise on the left temple. But there was something new, different, about Patsy's face. The flickering candlelight played on her long dark ringlets, on the long white linen shroud, on the mother-of-pearl rosary beads entwined about her joined hands. She looked as beautiful as Blessed Maria Goretti, whose picture hung in my room. Blessed Maria, only a few years older than Patsy, had been stabbed by her uncle for refusing his advances. I didn't know what "advances" were, but Grandmother said Blessed Maria's virtue and innocence were an inspiration to young Catholic girlhood in these wicked days. That's why she'd bought it for me.

My heart lurched. *Wise,* not innocent. Patsy's face was *wise!* She knew the Grand Secret; she now *knew,* really knew for sure, if everything the Catechism said was true.

Oh, God! If it were, I hoped she'd gone to confession on Saturday.

"Oh, Patsy, I hope you're happy." Tears tripping me, I dropped to my knees and joined Dierdre and Noreen in the middle of a Hail Mary.

Grandmother hurried me out to Aunt Nin's. There was an argument brewing, she said. People had no respect, no respect at all—it was just another excuse for a drink. I let her ramble on. I didn't care anyway. I felt drained, like I'd been awake for a week and all I wanted to was sit down and close my eyes.

"Here, love, you just put your head down there on the settee." *Thank you, Aunt Nin.*

I didn't sleep, just lay there with my eyes closed. Something kept nipping at my memory.

"There were eight drunk men in that car," said Aunt Nin, "and that's murder in my book!"

"Aye, that's what the Widow was saying."

"Mick's been told. Somebody rung up the rooming-house but he can't get a boat tonight—no Sunday sailing. But he'll be here Tuesday morning. They've put the funeral off until Tuesday."

"I just hope Mick isn't told too much." That was Grandmother. "There'll be ructions, Nin. A wake troubles consciences right enough."

Aunt Nin let out a long "aaaahh." "She's not been a well wumman since those wee twins came. Ach, I don't know, Maggie, a man has to work wherever he can." Aunt Nin left it there, then wondered aloud if Rosie's train would be on time. Rosie had taken to visiting the Lodger in the Free State every other weekend. "I dread her coming in. She was awful fond of wee Patsy. Poor wee Patsy. Isn't it the God's truth the innocent always suffer?"

Imps, armed with red-hot tridents, prodded my memory. Who *had* I seen going into Creswell's?

"You asleep, Jennifer?" That was Grandmother. I didn't move a muscle. I couldn't; my closed eyes were still fixed on the remembered flash of a silver buckle. . . . Oh, Jesus, Mary, and Joseph protect us!

"She's taking it bad, Nin—and I'll tell you something else—that chile had a *vision!* She *knew* this was going to happen!"

"God Almighty!"

"Aye, Nin. May God strike me dead if I'm telling you any word of a lie. She came running in in hysterics the other night. Sitting as right as rain in the garden one minute and the next—Oh, I tell you, Nin, I've never seen anything like it! Screaming somebody's been killed and murdered and there was blood on her hands! And it nothing but blackberry juice."

I was fascinated. There was nothing I could do but lie there and let Grandmother compound her error. I couldn't have told them the whole story anyway; besides, she'd think

I was lying, just like I was about being asleep.

"Couldn't get anything else out of her. We had to put her to bed."

I was on my way to becoming as famous as Aunt Nin. A new winter yarn had just been born.

CHAPTER
15

The first day back at school was uneventful. We were all in our old desks, except Patsy. Miss McGrath had on a white blouse and a black skirt, and the mahogony chair leg was in its usual easy-to-reach place. We said a whole rosary for the repose of Patsy's soul instead of Catechism.

Miss McGrath said we were starting a new school year and that the sixth class was a critically important one—one that would determine the paths each of us would choose through life. We'd all acquired the fundamentals, she said; now she'd see how we applied them. None of this made much sense to me, but she could have talked this way all day and I'd have listened happily.

Then she called Eilish Loughran up to the blackboard and handed her a piece of chalk. Eilish was instructed to write "How I Spent My Summer Holidays," the subject of our composition, while the rest of us hauled desks around to make four rows instead of the three longer ones of last year. Patsy's empty place was lost in the shuffle.

I started the yearly chronicle four times. "It was a summer I'd rather forget" my first attempt began, begging for an altercation with the chair leg. I just didn't like the sound of any of them, and I'd have had to omit most of "what I did on my summer holidays" or make up a lot to put me in a better light.

God, but I was glad I wrote it the way I did, for she chose a few to read out loud, mine among them. Two were about visits to the Free State, but most told of days at the tide.

Then the class was treated to my visit to the Highland Glen at the base of Ben Nevis, the highest mountain in Scotland, and the adventures I had with Robert, son of Robert the Bruce, who wore a kilt but wasn't a sissy. There was a sad farewell at the end when my grandfather, the Highland Chief, presented me with the Cairngorm Brooch, which meant I'd rule the Clan one day.

Miss McGrath said the class had just received a fine example of the difference between factual and fictional writing, which turned out to mean that she didn't believe a word I'd written except that Ben Nevis was the highest mountain in Scotland.

Before we went home she gave us all a sealed envelope and told us we'd be getting out early tomorrow for Patsy's funeral.

We were all stopped by Miss McGrath at the entrance to Our Lady's Acre. Only an intimate family group of adults was at the graveside. No women were allowed. We sat on the low wall watching as Father Murphy shook Holy Water from a brass stick with a round part at the top which acted like a salt cellar.

". . . Dei Gratia . . ."

He wore purple and black, the Church's mourning colours. Purple was a strange colour. If you put it alongside yellow or crimson, its vibrance was unequalled, but coupled with black it just died.

". . . mortis nostris . . ."

Men lifted the coffin from its trestles. Patsy's daddy's chin quivered. "There's no death like the death of a child," Grandmother always maintained.

". . . ora pro nobis . . ."

I'd light some candles. That was all I could do. Patsy knew the Grand Secret; she knew I couldn't return in kind the favour she'd once done me.

The grass verges and mounds seemed even greener in the fine mizzling rain. Graveyard grass always was more lively, Grandmother said. When someone was being buried, it was a good sign if it was raining. "Happy is the corpse that the rain rains on," Grandmother quoted sometimes. I'd always felt this was a form of surety, given our weather's preponderance for rain.

But as I sat on the wall at Our Lady's Acre watching the shovels, listening to their mesmeric *shluff thud* sounds, I wanted to believe it was true. "Happy is the corpse that the rain rains on," I whispered, looking up into the drizzle.

It fell on my face, light as a fairy's kiss, but it *was* rain. ". . . Dominus vobiscum, Amen."

That Rosie chose to marry the Lodger scarcely a week after Patsy's death was a fresh target for Grandmother's disapprobation. We got the news from Aunt Nin. "Ah, Maggie, I suppose we should resign ourselves that children'll up and go away."

"You resign yourself all you want"—Grandmother pointed her spoon at Aunt Nin—"but my Madge will have to be on the boat and it out to sea. . . ." Grandmother stopped and gave the warning eye to Aunt Nin that enough had been said in front of me. Aunt Nin paid no attention, though, for she said Patsy's daddy was putting his foot on a boat for England and Bridie and the children with him.

Aunt Madge and Uncle Dan accompanied Aunt Nin to the Free State for the wedding, and Grandmother and I received accountings of the affair secondhand. And while it wasn't a big do as far as weddings went, it pleased me to hear Aunt Madge describe how well Rosie looked, Aunt Nin express relief that the Lodger's family were respectable people who'd taken to Rosie as if she were their own, and Uncle Dan say that the Lodger had been in better humour than the last time he'd seen him.

Grandmother had said, "Is that right, now?" and "Well,

isn't that grand!" at all the right places and blithely avoided showing her true colours until Aunt Nin and Uncle Dan left.

"Pink!" she said. "Oh, Mother of God—pink!" Then she formed a contemptuous dimple by sliding her mouth to one side. "Oh, God forbid that any daughter of mine had to get married in pink!"

Curiously, Aunt Madge didn't light on Grandmother for this display of pettiness.

"What's wrong with pink?" I said. "I thought you liked pink, Granny."

"It's a disgrace—a disgrace!"

She ignored my request for clarification and went right into the merits of Aunt Nin being horse-whipped, of God bringing the world to a swift end, and of the depraved being sentenced to eternal damnation.

Speaking of eternal damnation, I thought, it was time I did the mountain of homework meted out by Miss McGrath.

Miss McGrath had been challenged by the new Labour government and I rued the day they were ever voted in. If we could pass what they called the "qualifying examination," we could go to secondary school and the Labour government would pay our way. And there wasn't any doubt in anybody's mind that pass it we would—provided we lived to take it. June was a lifetime away.

That envelope she'd sent home with us contained a note that shanghied us for an extra hour every day after school. I was nothing but a drudge and I lodged my complaints with Grandmother.

"And just how am I supposed to lug all those books *and* Mrs. Doran's shopping?"

Mrs. Doran still hadn't ventured beyond her back garden. The blinds still rose to only half-mast each morning and Aunt Madge and I were the only outsiders who saw her. Aunt Madge tried to get her out and about. "Get yourself busy. There's a lot to be done in the parish and the new priest needs help." Aunt Madge patted her hand. "And Frankie's young . . ."

"Ach, Madge, love, he's marked—even if he doesn't go whole hog. . . ." She changed the subject suddenly. "My mother had nine children!" She whirled her head around towards me. "Nine children! I was always ashamed of us." Then she focused on Aunt Madge again. "When Sammy won the pools, I saw a glimmer. . . ." Then her eyes just sort of wandered. "I knew it when the bunting didn't come down, but I didn't want to believe . . ."

I was about to ask what she knew but Aunt Madge said Grandmother was waiting for me so I had to leave. But I took my time getting to the back door in case they said anything of import.

Aunt Madge told us Frankie's case wasn't coming up till November, but that Mr. Doran, aided by a collection taken up at the Donegal Arms, had hired a real Philadelphia lawyer from Belfast to get him off. She also said, before she left for the Mater Hospital, that people were just plain ignorant. This was in response to Grandmother's revelation that there were those in the village who were asking Aunt Nin what kind of a mother was that that wouldn't go see her son?

"I'll make a bargain with you." Grandmother's eyes narrowed slightly. "You do the studying and I'll do the shopping. You give me the list before you leave and I'll keep the stuff here till you get home and you can run through the hedge with it."

It sounded good. I agreed. I'd study. But what about my sixpence and sweetie coupon? Grandmother said she'd never thought about that, but if I wanted to keep it going I'd better not let on she was helping me.

I agreed to that, too, but I had a distinct feeling she'd bent the rules for reasons other than kindness to me.

Miss McGrath proceeded to drive us down the endless road of fractions, decimals, subordinate clauses, and predicate verbs—whip at the ready. She also got a government notice requesting that she recommend students with low intelligence quotients for placement in special schools. The only reason she let us in on this was because there was an inspector coming to observe us sometime and she was depending on us to shield Eilish from discovery. Privately, a few of us laughed and said we'd outdo Eilish in the idiot category if it would get us away from Miss McGrath.

But I got to thinking about Eilish—about whether she should be shielded. If anybody could teach her, it was Miss McGrath—but maybe she'd be better off in one of those new places—oh, God, I didn't know. Maybe I'd know more by the time the inspector showed up. Miss McGrath said it could be tomorrow or next year. Then I put the notion of exposing Eilish as a dullbert out of my head completely when I saw myself thwarting Miss McGrath.

The smoky pink and lilac hues of autumn skies were much in evidence the third Saturday morning in September as the last summer lawnmower droned its final cadence in the Sommervilles' side lawn. I told Mrs. Sommerville I'd be back next Saturday and, astonishingly, felt a bit of a letdown when she said my time was up. I said I'd probably look in next Saturday just to see how the chrysanthemums were coming along. I'd tended these myself and Mrs. Sommerville said we'd get a splendid showing.

We were tackling the rudiments of algebra and I knew right from the start Miss McGrath was going to have a field day with the chair leg. But it was heartening to have Grandmother's assurance that anybody who could convince people x plus y equalled whatever they came up with wouldn't have any trouble getting a job. That I was going to be a spangled trapeze artist and wouldn't need algebra was kept under wraps since it would only have made Grandmother bar the matinee for a while.

Bobby was studying for the qualifying, too, and that made it paramount that I pass. But by the time the ruddy tinge of October flared on the trees, we saw less of each other. It was almost dark now when I got out of school at four o'clock, and Old Coffey had the lamps lit before I got to Serpentine Parade. When it wasn't raining we all got together for kick-the-tin. We huddled under bushes in twos and threes, for the gardens we knew so well in summer became sinister in darkness.

I found out what Bobby's daddy's "Gration" was a few days before Halloween. Grandmother came down with rheumatism that night, too, the same night Uncle Dan and Aunt Madge dropped a bomb on us.

Uncle Dan had friends in high places and one of them from his university days had offered him a job conducting Celtic studies in a Jesuit college in Boston. The job was opening up in the spring.

"It's a good chance, Maggie," he said, "and we're applying for emigration."

Grandmother and I both picked up on the plural. I couldn't get over how the news that Aunt Madge and Uncle Dan would be getting married—and that's what it meant—turned sour at the mention of America.

Grandmother grabbed at the hearth brush and swept unseen ashes into the grate. "What brought this on all of a sudden?"

"It's not sudden, Maggie, "I've been thinking about it for a long time. There's no future here for us. . . ."

My mind snapped to attention, recalling the tail end of the conversation I'd heard between Mrs. Doran and Aunt Madge when I'd hesitated in the dark of the scullery. It didn't seem important at the time.

". . . there's no life here, Madge—no future. Get out while youse are young. God knows I tried to get Sammy to go to England, ach, it was before Frankie was even born"— Mrs. Doran let out a few racking sobs—"but he said it was here he was born and here he'd die." Mrs. Doran covered her face with her hands and shook her head. "The best of a bad job is all you can hope for here, Madge"—the hands came down—"the best of a bad job. . . ." And they'd continued to stare at each other until I left.

Grandmother and Uncle Dan were staring at each other, too, and Uncle Dan's eyes had the flinty blue cast which signalled he was all ready for an altercation.

But it didn't come—at least not the way we thought it would. Instead, Grandmother turned the dreadnought away from Uncle Dan, the Protestants, England, and the rest, and pointed it at America.

They were a bad bunch, she said, and we were to look at the way they treated the poor darkies—wouldn't let them eat with them, made them give up their seats in the buses, and that wasn't the half of it.

All this puzzled me for when Uncle Dan took Aunt Madge to dances at Queen's University, the last words out of Grandmother's mouth were, "Don't you be letting her dance with any darkies, now." Uncle Dan had once told Grandmother he admired her stance; that it wasn't many mothers who'd forbid their daughters dancing with the sons of kings. But Grandmother just said she didn't care whose sons they were, Aunt Madge wasn't to dance with them.

But I didn't say a word. I backed her new championship of the darkies to the hilt. I saw what she was up to now—she was just trying to scunner them from going.

But Uncle Dan was unmoved. The job in America was a godsend. Grandmother jumped on that one.

"Godsend! Now, that's a mouthful coming from you!" Then she started on Aunt Madge. Had she lost all conscience to bring children up in a heathen home?

"They'll be brought up Catholic, Ma," said Aunt Madge.

Then I discovered how important Aunt Madge and Uncle Dan's children were going to be. They'd been discussed with Father Murphy already and Uncle Dan had signed a paper that turned them over to the Church. All this fuss even before they were born! I was all ready to shout, "But what about *me*?" but Grandmother sort of did it for me.

"I don't know what'll become of this poor chile with only me to rear her," she said to the fire.

The poor chile huddled closer to Grandmother and I knew we looked a woebegone pair. "I'll never leave you, Granny."

"Don't lean too heavy on that side of me, love. My rheumatism's awful bad."

I shifted. So did Aunt Madge, and as they left for the pictures, Uncle Dan gave Grandmother a look that ended up being a hybrid of a smile and a scowl. That's what the Sommervilles would have called it anyway. My vocabulary had been enlarged. "Propagation" was no longer used exclusively with "of the Faith"; I dug "dibbers" for certain species, large holes for others; and I could discourse for twenty minutes on the merits of adequate staking in herbaceous borders.

A spasm shook me as I remembered I was indeed going to leave Grandmother. How was I ever going to state my case for attendance at an English boarding school with girls like the Secret Three, where religion didn't matter and the wicked prefect never won?

I'd quizzed the Sommervilles about life in England. There were Catholics there, weren't there? Did *all* the people like the King and the flag? Somehow "Watch what you say" didn't apply with the Sommervilles.

"Does the King like *us*?" I asked them one day.

Mrs. Sommerville gave me another tea biscuit. "I'm sure if he knew you, Jennifer, he'd like you very much." She passed the plate to Mr. Sommerville, who stood by the mantelpiece. "Yes, I'm positive about that," she said.

I decided that maybe the King just didn't know—I mean, he had an empire to run—and that when I got to England I'd find a way to enlighten him.

But first I'd have to win over Grandmother, and putting an English boarding school over on somebody like Grandmother was—well, it was too soon to fret about it anyway.

Halloween was miserable. I'd dressed up in Aunt Madge's old taffeta but we were all drenched before we ever got to the "and if you haven't got a farthing, then God bless you" of the traditional jingle at the first house. Grandmother contended that that wasn't the right song, that it was an English Christmas ditty, but never let it be said the Irish did anything the way they were supposed to.

Normally we'd have received pennies, sweeties, or candied apples, and nuts for our singing efforts, then cavorted for hours setting off squibs. Bobby was a great one for Jumping Ginnies, the kind that exploded six or seven times and chased you like imps. I preferred the colourful Catherine's Wheels (somebody said they were called that because St. Catherine was martyred on a spinning, flaming wheel), glowing Roman candles, and sparkling fountains. But the rain spoiled everything and we gave up and went home. I griped to Grandmother about it. She didn't like fireworks, and anyway, she said, we let them off on the wrong day, too; November 5 was the day for fireworks, commemorating Guy Fawkes' vain attempt to blow up the English Parliament. She thought they hung him. "Pity," she added.

Grandmother's rheumatism worsened that night. Her back was killing her. Aunt Madge did everything to lessen the discomfort: cushions at her back and her feet up on the stool. But Grandmother said she'd been dreading November. November was the month for deaths, she said, for its dank vapors just worsened every ailment. People with nothing but bronchitis suddenly drowned of pneumonia in November; those bedridden for months lingered until November took them; and old people like herself breathed a sigh of relief when it passed them—if it passed them.

Aunt Madge and I exchanged stricken looks. It was the

first time Grandmother had ever referred to her age.

"My sister went in November," she sighed. "Poor Annie. That she was taken and that profligate she married spared! Well, we warned her—warned her up to the last. But you can't get anybody to see through who they're marrying. There's no accounting for taste." Grandmother sounded far away and fear bubbled up in my throat. "Married the McCracken from Cushendall that lay himself down on the railroad tracks so the train would cut off his arm. Low cur! It was for insurance money!" She said this last with her usual verve, then took up the lament again. "Annie went into a decline away up there in Cushendall. We didn't get word of it for months—till November—her being so far away and all. Aye, it was November Annie died too."

She put me up the pole with that one. But Aunt Madge said she'd never heard of anyone dying of rheumatism, and Grandmother wouldn't say anything else for the rest of the night except piteous requests for tea and a shift of the cushions.

The rheumatism cured itself during the night. It must have been the rain she'd got caught in last week, she said.

All Saints Day was bright and clear, and after school Bobby, Pam, Erik, and I hung around the lamp-post bemoaning last night's Halloween weather. Nobody wanted to play kick-the-tin since the hiding places were particularly mucky.

"I wish we had some conkers," Bobby said. "They're ready now."

The game of conkers had been handed down to us last year by Pam's big brothers. The chestnuts were left on the hearth to dry, then pierced, and a string with a knot on the end threaded through. The object was to crack and eventually disintegrate everybody else's chestnut. I think it was called "conkers" because you held the string in one hand and the chestnut in the other and with a snapping motion conked the stationary and defenceless one held by the opponent. When you missed, he got to conk yours. But last year the chestnut gathering had been done by Morris and Reggie, and Pam said there was no chance of them continuing this philanthropy since all that seemed to interest them anymore were their skinny Raleigh racers and the plump girls from the Royal Academy.

A pragmatic Bobby brushed the bad news aside. "We'll get them ourselves. Anybody want to come with me?"

Pam had an ironclad excuse; she was going to Belfast to get new ballet shoes. Bobby ignored her. Erik went into a long rigamarole we all knew would mean no, so Bobby shut him up and turned to me. Now, I didn't want to go, but since the nest catastrophe I was still walking on thin ice where Bobby was concerned. And here he was staring me down with that "What's your excuse?" look that goaded me into saying, "I'll go right after I finish in the Sommervilles' garden." Bobby's slap on the back helped smother the misgivings for a minute before all the complications crowded back.

Our boundaries shrank during the short winter days; the lamps were lit by four o'clock now and Old Coffey didn't snuff them until eight in the morning. The tide and the Castle grounds became forbidden territories. Grey's Lane was automatically included with the Castle, and Grey's Lane had the chestnut trees. It didn't take Bobby long to overcome the obstacles. Saturday afternoons were normally spent at the matinee. We were going to the matinee so we'd just arrange to get sidetracked, gather the chestnuts, and be home in time for tea as usual. Nobody'd know the difference, he insisted, if nobody else told. He looked at Erik and Pam, who hastily pledged silence.

If I'd gone to the Sommervilles' earlier the next morning Mrs. Doran couldn't have conscripted me when the ragman trundled his barrow down the center of Serpentine

Parade. The blue, yellow, and red balloons enticed children to coax their mothers for offerings. I should have been happy; Grandmother seldom gave me anything to exchange for a balloon. Our old clothes were given to the Widow Byrne for jumble sales and the like.

"Any oul' rags . . . any oul' rags . . ." the chant went. "Any oul' rags to-daaaaay-aaay." I gripped the big cardboard box Mrs. Doran had given me and stood motionless in front of the ragman. His peaked cap hid his eyes. It upset me. I felt a bit disloyal to Frankie when I finally handed the box over to the eyeless ragman and he hoisted it onto the barrow. He gave me a red balloon. I mean, I wanted the balloon and all, but it upset me—and the damn balloon burst.

A robin made a glutton of himself on the Sommervilles' elderberry tree while I raked the dead leaves beneath him. The feast before the famine ahead. Other birds headed for milder climes, but the robin stuck it out with us all through winter.

I kept an eye on the weather. I'd no intention of going away up to Grey's Lane if it was going to rain. Napoleon's Nose played hide-and-seek all morning. Sometimes just the tip of it appeared, a skirt of mist swirling about the lower slopes. But there were no definite rain clouds.

It was Bobby's idea that I should wear my Burberry. It had deep pockets. We rounded the corner of Serpentine Parade, made sure we said hello or waved to anybody in sight, and promptly took the first turning and doubled back towards the fields.

The paths were mucky now and stalks of rusty dock had sprung up amongst the wet grass. The fields weren't pleasant in winter. The hawthorn bushes were dark blotches and the odd tree spread stark black boughs against a dreary grey sky. The only real colour around was the deadly reddish berries of nightshade mingling with the brambles, beckoning the unwary. We cut through the links and took off like hares at the "Gettoutahere" shouts of a group of golfers finishing their rounds.

Grey's Lane was ankle deep in chestnut leaves, but they were damp and didn't crackle anymore. A few yellowed, curling leaves still clung to the branches, gamely camouflaging clusters of remaining chestnuts. Bobby was all for climbing to get some, but slippery moss had formed on the twisted trunks making it next to impossible to get a footing, so we contented ourselves fishing among the leaves for fallen ones. Finding them was easy. The lime green outer shells were prickly. These we cracked open and pocketed the smooth, gleaming brown chestnuts within. My Burberry sagged at the sides.

"I can't walk with any more," I said. "Let's go, Bobby."

"I've still got room."

No wonder, I thought, the bulk of the harvest had been dumped in *my* pockets. I sat down on a root and decapitated toadstools for a while, wishing I was in the safe dark of the Troxy rather than the now eerie light of Grey's Lane.

"Bobby, we better watch the time. How long do you think we've been up here? Bobby? Bobby!" He'd disappeared. So had Napoleon's Nose and the tops of the trees in the Castle grounds.

"Bobby McConnell! You come back here this minute!" I struggled to get up; the chestnuts felt like rocks. "Bobbeeee . . ."

I listened, then dragged myself down deeper into the lane and the muffled, though clearly belligerent, "Over here!"

"Come *on*—I'm leaving." But he knew I was bluffing. I wasn't about to make the trip by myself. He rubbed the last of the chestnuts against his blazer lapel, looking very much like the bulging Tubby Tucker in *Schoolboys Own Weekly*.

"We've got enough to last for weeks," he beamed.

"Right," I said firmly, "so let's get home. I don't like the looks of the weather." I looked up the lane and the direction I'd come was blotted out at twenty yards.

We scrambled up the bank and the soft greens flowed all the way to the fields. A ten-minute run, twenty with the chestnuts—all night if the mist caught up with us. Oh, sweet Jesus, I'd forgotten—not *this* night! Not All Souls Night, Lord . . .

We reached the fifteenth hole and stood holding onto the pennant pole, gasping. I was all for jettisoning the chestnuts, but Bobby said he'd kill me.

"Hurry." He pointed diagonally towards the ninth.

I clutched at the pocket linings to keep them from banging against my thighs. Bobby stopped suddenly and I barged into him.

"I can't see it!" That there was alarm in Bobby McConnell's voice set me trembling. The mist closed in on all sides leaving just the small clearing we were in. The mournful blast of a foghorn carried up from the lough.

Bobby grabbed my arm. "At least we're pointed in the right direction." But by the time we'd gone a few yards, we weren't in the least bit confident of our navigation.

"Let's go back to Grey's Lane," I pleaded.

"Okay." His quick agreement only made it more apparent he was frightened too. We stumbled wildly through roughs and sand traps we hadn't encountered before. The mist became a damp woolly fog, perhaps even a killer fog from Scotland.

"It's no good," Bobby panted. "We better wait a while till this lifts a bit."

"If you'd come when I told you," I whined, "we'd be home by now." I tried saying a silent Hail Mary, but Bobby went straight to the source. "Oh, God, please call off the fog."

I don't know how long we sat in the rough before the fog became mist again. Suddenly, a grotesque headless figure just appeared in front of us and I was on my feet, but

Bobby let out a husky "No!" and grabbed me. It was only the petrified remains of a swamp tree—and we were too near the dams for comfort. I moaned. "Oh, Jesus, Mary, and Joseph protect . . ." but Bobby shushed me.

"Listen!"

I listened, but all I could hear was the drumming of my blood, not the hoofbeats of Galloper Grey's horse I expected.

"Over there," he whispered, pointing through the swirls.

I didn't *want* to see anything, but Bobby insisted.

"Someone s coming."

I saw her for a moment, just long enough to recognize the tweed costume and felt hat before she was gone again.

"It's Mrs. Doran!"

"What's she doing up here?"

I couldn't have cared less and told him so. "Mrs. Doran! Mrs. Doran!" I called as we picked our way very cautiously.

"Mrs. Doran!" I shouted again just as she came out of the mist. She didn't hear me, for she just kept walking and didn't look like she was having any trouble seeing where she was going. She held a burlap sack in one hand. What on earth . . . ? Then the mist crept over her in patches and the sack seemed to jiggle just before she was swallowed up again.

"Bobby . . . ?"

He was away ahead of me. "Smokey must have died. She's going to throw him in the dam." He'd gone a bit green around the gills. "We should help her," he said.

"But . . ." I shut my mouth. Then we both plunged forward at the tremendous splash that followed.

"Oh, Bobby, be careful!"

We crawled over the embankment and met Bottomless face to face for the first time. I knew it was Bottomless instinctively. Mist licked at the surface where chilling grey ripples still wavered. But there was no sign of Mrs. Doran.

"Bobby!" I screamed. "She's fallen in!"

Bubbles came from the middle of the circling ripples and the felt hat was pushed farther out. Bobby was shouting at me.

"Take off your coat! Hurry . . . here, you hold this end and I'll hold the other!" Panicked, I did as I was told. "You can swim, Jennifer, but you won't need to. Just see if you can grab anything and don't let go of the coat." He crouched down, feet dug in, one hand firmly grasping a clump of pussy willows. My mouth opened but nothing came out and I stood there pointing at myself. He wanted *me* to . . . Oh, God, but I wished I'd let well enough alone and never attempted to best Bobby McConnell at anything.

"I . . . I *can't!* Oh, Bobby, I can't!"

"Yes, you can. You said you could! I won't let go!"

The next thing I knew I was in water, very cold water, and sinking like a stone. I came up gasping and Bobby was shrieking, "There! There!"

I made a few flails with my free hand. I didn't want to find anything. Then I touched something. *I wouldn't lay hands on that cat again if my life depended on it.* . . . Terror blinded me. I could see nothing but black water. Bobby was screaming again.

"Jennifer! Jennnnniiiferrr . . ." But he sounded far away and I didn't really care what he wanted anyway. And then I was holding on to an anchor of chestnuts. I let go and a huge wave swamped me. I dimly remember the frantic underwater breaststroke just before the weeds got me and pulled . . .

I was lying face down and something huge was sitting on me. I coughed, hoping to rid myself of its crushing pressure, and was promptly flipped over, sat up, and my head pushed down between my legs. Up again, down again, like a pump handle. I threw up.

"Jennifer? You all right?" Bobby McConnell looked like a drowned rat.

"What happened?" My voice scared me.

"You bloody well near drowned," a voice roared behind me, "that's what happened!" Constable Johnston, brows bristling, coatless, hatless, and shoeless, glowered down at me.

I began to cry. "My Granny'll kill me—where's my Burberry . . . ?"

"Any more stunts like this and she won't need to go to the trouble," growled the Constable. "Bloody stupid kids!"

Strangely, he didn't go into a tirade about us being where we shouldn't be. He put on the only dry garment left, his jacket tunic, braced his shoulders, and gave his sopping trouser legs a few shakes. Then he put his bare feet into the shoes and wrung his socks out and stuffed them in his pocket, grabbed both of us, and the long march home began.

We'd walked a long time before I realised that this hand that held me so tightly had saved my life. And Bobby McConnell's too. The pussy willows hadn't held, Bobby told me later.

CHAPTER
═══16═══

They never did find my Burberry, or perhaps they just didn't look, bent as they were on finding Mrs. Doran. Bobby said never mind, he'd managed to salvage some chestnuts in his trouser pockets.

The Widow Byrne was cheated of Mrs. Doran. They'd taken the body to the morgue and it came back to Serpentine Parade already coffined. But, undaunted, the Widow was sitting up this wake night with the corpse.

Constable Johnston sat on our settee beside Uncle Dan. Let's see if he had this straight, he said, and repeated what Bobby had told him. It was important that we didn't lie about this, he said, and I replied, "No, sir, that's what happened." And he appeared to believe me. He wrote "Death by misadventure" down on his notepad.

Grandmother folded her arms and leaned back in the armchair. I sat on the fender of the hearth at Aunt Madge's feet.

"I've a cup of tea boiling, Mr. Johnston," said Aunt Madge.

Constable Johnston nodded his thanks as she went into the scullery. Then he focused on me again. "You're sure there's nothing else you can tell me, Jennifer?" I shook my head as emphatically as I could and I thought he looked relieved.

Anyway, I wasn't sure that the mist hadn't played tricks with my eyes. Grandmother took the edge off for a change.

"They should have filled in those dams long ago," she said. "Sure, nobody can even remember what they were ever used for and they're nothing but a dumping ground for dead animals. It's enough to cause the plague."

Aunt Madge served the tea and handed round a plate of buttered tea biscuits.

"How's young Sarah, Mr. Johnston?"

"Oh, fine . . . fine." The black brows tangled and met. "She's getting a lot of attention at Whiteabbey Hospital. Nurses are making quite a pet of her." He smiled at Aunt Madge the way he smiled at Sarah in their garden.

"Oh, that's grand—grand. Mrs. Boyd was telling me the other day she'd been down to see her and she looked much better." Aunt Madge was an expert when it came to the village code. I was with her when Pam's mother gave us the findings of her visit to Sarah at the sanitorium.

"God in heaven, Madge, to look at her you'd think there wasn't a thing wrong with her," Mrs. Boyd had reported. "You know they say they take a turn for the better right before the end."

"Aye," said Constable Johnston, "the nurses were telling me she'd eaten all those big Jaffa oranges I brought .

down—every last one of them. And"—his eyes brightened—"she put in a request for more!"

"Oh, that's wonderful," said Aunt Madge and we all kept the Jaffa oranges buoyed up as long as possible. They were scarce, but if there was one to be had, it would be commandeered for Sarah. Then Grandmother gave a cough. "I was reading the paper the other day—ach, it was just a wee paragraph or two—where they've had great results with a new medicine in the sanitoriums in England."

I jostled this around in my head, but couldn't see any evidence of the code being employed. In fact, the use of the word "sanitoriums" was a big deviation with Constable Johnston sitting there. I think everybody else did the same mental exercise and came to the same conclusion.

"What paper was it in, Mrs. Marshall?" Constable Johnston's voice had an edge to it.

"I think it was the *Belfast Telegraph*. Now, it was just a paragraph or two, mind you, but that's what it said."

"Did it give the name of the medicine?" That was Uncle Dan.

"Aye, but it was one of those big long things I couldn't even pronounce."

"You could go up to the *Telegraph* office in Belfast, Mr. Johnston," Uncle Dan said, puffing his pipe. "They're making breakthroughs all the time right enough."

"They used it on soldiers first to see if it worked," Grandmother said, adding to the authenticity of her statement.

I was so proud of Grandmother I could have burst. In effect, she'd given Constable Johnston the first honest ray of hope for Sarah. Even I knew that. Maybe she was right that you learned all you needed to know from newspapers. Constable Johnston wolfed down his biscuit and slipped his notepad into his tunic. Then he looked at me and said if he ever caught us near those dams again, we'd feel the weight of his boot on our backsides. Other than that it was a cheerful parting. Grandmother and Aunt Madge thanked him again for saving me and Uncle Dan shook his hand and walked him to the door. The front door closed.

"You're sure you read that, Granny?" I just had to ask it.

"Aye," she said, consoling me. She gave the coals a turn with the poker. "But no matter what medicines they come up with, sure everybody knows there's no cure for bad care."

A winter yarn came into my head, one Grandmother told about a girl in Greencastle who took to her bed and didn't get up for twenty years. Boy ran off and left her and she never put a foot outside. He must have had his reasons. Poor mother lifted and layed her. Possessed, she was. Father Sheridan had just come to the village then and had paid a visit to the afflicted household. Some said he must have performed an exorcism, for whatever he'd said, that girl had raised herself. Mind you, nobody'd have any truck with her, so she took herself off to England. . . .

The fire settled in the grate. *Nobody'd have any truck . . .* Father Sheridan's powers had been limited to devils; even he couldn't exorcise stigmas in Greencastle. And I knew even if Sarah Johnston was cured, she'd be described all her life as "the wee girl that was in bad health."

The blinds of Serpentine Parade were lowered to half-mast. Father Murphy stood behind the hearse dressed in the purple and black I used to associate exclusively with Lent. Ranks had been formed, the men four deep. Most of them were strangers to us, relatives of both Mr. and Mrs. Doran. Frankie had been given what they termed "compassionate leave" to bury his mother. Uncle Dan represented us and Constable Johnston stood beside him "to watch Frankie," Grandmother had said. Protestants didn't usually attend Catholic services and it was a mortal sin if we went to theirs. Mrs. Boyd and Pam peeked under their blinds.

The sky was heavy with rain it callously hoarded. *Happy is the corpse that the rain rains on.* Mrs. Doran wasn't happy and I prayed for rain before the cortege reached Our Lady's Acre.

Getting the coffin down the front steps was hair-raising and I wished shoulders like Uncle Dan's were bearing the brunt of the front end instead of Mr. Doran's. The men from the funeral home laid out trestles and Mrs. Doran was placed on them.

Mr. Sommerville came over with a big wreath and laid it beside the others. Grandmother had gone to Belfast for ours. I didn't like it and neither did she. It had flowers on it that should have been dead seasons ago. She said they were artificially grown in hothouses, that there was no smell to them. But the Sommervilles had fashioned their wreath themselves with mauve chrysanthemums on a bed of ivy—a living, breathing thing amongst the falsely bright iris, lilies, and carnations. As Mrs. Sommerville had predicted, we got a splendid showing.

Mrs. Sweet and Mrs. Beattie carried a huge wreath studded with red cloth poppies and placed it beside the bank of flowers.

"A tribute from the British Legion," Grandmother said dourly, as they scurried into Mrs. Boyd's house and joined her under the blinds.

Frankie cocked his head up at me. He looked like he wanted an answer to something, but I didn't know what the question was. Finally, I just mouthed a silent, "I'll save the *Beano*s for you!"

He smiled and looked at me for a long time. I'd said the right thing somehow.

Father Murphy said something to the funeral home men that triggered the few last actions before Mrs. Doran left us forever. The men closed the straggled ranks behind the hearse and Father Murphy. Grandpa McCartney, black-thorn stick in one hand, his black bowler hat in the other, shuffled out his garden gate and melted into the last row.

"Granny . . ."

"Shush," she said fiercely. Her glittering eyes were on Grandpa, Aunt Madge's tearful ones on the slowly moving hearse that turned the corner of Serpentine Parade. I watched Grandpa too. He was a Protestant, one of *them,* but he was walking behind the black biretta of Father Murphy. Mrs. Doran would have liked that.

Thunder rumbled somewhere at the back of Napoleon's Nose and I made a promise to be more respectful of Grandpa McCartney's garden.

Aunt Madge went through the hedge to Mrs. Doran's; she'd offered to have the tea ready for the mourners when they got back from Our Lady's Acre. Grandmother and I went into the house.

"The old bugger forgot his sash," Grandmother hooted as we got inside. "He must have got his parades mixed . . . Jennifer?"

"I'm away to help Aunt Madge," I shouted, and left her with no audience.

CHAPTER
17

Grandmother complained that the winter butter was so white this year it could have passed for lard. She said she'd known we were going to pay the piper for the grand summer we'd had. There wasn't much rain, but a black frost sucked the moisture up out of the ground, puckering it into puddles of dark ice. I helped the Sommervilles mix a winter mulch from the grass cuttings and leaves stored in the tool shed.

"The holly bush is the only thing that'll thrive, Jennifer," Mrs. Sommerville said as we blanketed roots and bulbs with burlap. "Berries galore this year."

Then came the bright mornings of Jack Frost. He made the sun red, the sky pink, and crusted the ground and roofs with white hoar frost. Ice buds glinted on the nubs of trees. By Christmas Eve the holly bush was bright with berries. Mrs. Sommerville pruned off a bunch for me to take home. But I got my tea first.

Mrs. Sommerville sliced through the snowy landscape of the Christmas cake, and a mound of Christmas trees, sleds, and snowmen ended up on my plate.

"Mr. Sommerville and I have a present for you, Jennifer." She smiled, giving a nod to Mr. Sommerville. He handed me a package from the mantelpiece all wrapped like the Christmas presents in comics.

"Open it, dear," encouraged Mrs. Sommerville.

I'd never had a real Christmas package to open before, and the thought of disassembling the tartan ribbon and ripping the beautiful paper . . .

"Ohhhh! They're just like yours!" I cried, holding up a pair of fawn gardening gloves.

"Now you'll be able to tackle the thorns better," said Mrs. Sommerville.

Mrs. Sommerville gave me a kiss and said they'd appreciated my efforts.

"Happy Christmas," they called after me. I clutched the holly with no trepidation. The gardening gloves worked. I also saved the red tartan ribbon for my long hair when I got it.

Grandmother was skimming grease from the drippings of the goose. She wouldn't buy turkey because it was too dry; yet she spent a lot of time getting rid of the very thing she wanted. I didn't comment, just showed her the holly and the gardening gloves.

"Your presents are on the piano," she said; "you might as well have them now since you know what they are." Santa Claus was only a memory. "And the new biscuit tin is empty now—throw out that other rusty oul' thing you've been sitting on."

The *Girls Crystal* and *School Friend* annuals were inscribed as follows:

To Jennifer, with Love from Aunt Madge
x x x
Christmas 1945

and,

From Granny

I spent the early afternoon savouring the adventures of the Secret Three by the bay window. Bobby McConnell walked past and I flourished the books at him.

He pointed to himself and cocked an imaginary rifle to his shoulder and shot me. Then he took a run at the slide we'd made at the corner and whizzed out of sight.

Grandmother, Aunt Madge, and I went down to Aunt Nin's at nine o'clock. We were all going to attend Midnight Mass. I'd never been before. Aunt Nin had been sitting in the gloaming, the light from the fire casting friendly shadows. She lit the gas lamps when we came in.

"I hear the Corporation is thinking of putting us on electricity," she said to Grandmother, "and you know what that means—they'll up the rent!" She didn't know, she said, how she could stretch her mill pension to keep up with the progress they were planning. Then she went into a string of praises for the Lodger. Rosie had done well by herself. "That Christmas card"—she pointed up to the mantelpiece—"had a five-pound note in it. They couldn't make it up for Christmas, so they want me to come down to Dublin."

Then she said Rosie was on the way, and I said, "I thought you told us she couldn't come."

"I did," she replied and without stopping she added,

"I've got something for you." She reached down into a cloth bag at the side of her chair and pulled out a lilac scarf. I knew I'd been sidetracked, but I let it slip when she handed me the scarf. The whole village had scarved themselves in a new lacy stitch that was all the rage. I'd counted twenty-nine from the chapel balcony last week.

"All you do is drop certain stitches," Aunt Nin explained, "and let them unravel all the way down."

"It's beautiful, Aunt Nin, and just the colour I wanted."

Grandmother had a funny notion that lilac was a low colour, but I loved it. I'd wear it tonight to Midnight Mass. Midnight Mass. It sounded mysterious, and a shadowy vision of cowled monks gathered around an altar stone gripped me. Midnight . . . black . . . the smell of incense . . .

Aunt Nin brought out a suet pudding steaming smells of plump currants, orange, and lemon rinds. She stripped off the white flour cloth and the spices intensified. I doused my pudding with cream and when I'd finished, I lay back on the settee bloated, content, and a bit sleepy.

The gas lamps flickered and so did my eyes. Then my stomach did the same thing as the Christmas cake sleds, and snowmen did battle with the currants and rinds of suet pudding, keeping me on the nether side of a twilight sleep.

"Seven years!" Aunt Nin was saying. "Ach, no, Madge—poor Frankie. God have mercy," she tut-tutted. "Sure, he's just a lad."

Just a lad of eighteen summers . . . I heard Patsy singing the clear, lilting ballad of Kevin Barry as we'd sat around her Uncle Joe's feet. Frankie was twenty-three and if I could rouse myself, I'd vomit. Gluttony deserved to be a Deadly Sin.

Aunt Madge sighed. "The solicitor begged him to show remorse so he'd get off lighter. . . ."

> *Turn informer and we'll free you,*
> *But Barry proudly answered "No!"*

Patsy had given us a strong, defiant "No!" and we'd all cheered.

"Far from showing remorse," Aunt Madge continued, "he did the old IRA trick of showing contempt! Wouldn't answer a'tall! You know how they pretend it's not a court of law. The solicitor told Mr. Doran there was nothing he could do—that Frankie had damned himself."

"He was damned before they opened their mouths anyway," Grandmother said. "Of course, it was all right for England to put a gun in his hand to do their killing for them—but the minute he set foot back here—oh, aye"— Grandmother's voice was mocking—"it's all right for a Protestant to carry a gun, but well dare a Catholic be caught with one! If I'd have been Frankie, I'd have made a run for the border from the funeral . . ."

> *Calmly standing to attention*
> *While he bade his last farewell*
> *To his broken-hearted Mother*
> *Whose grief no one can tell . . .*

I moaned. I wasn't well. I didn't want to think about *that*.

> *For the Cause he proudly cherished*
> *This sad parting had to be*
> *Then to death walked softly smiling . . .*

"It didn't move, I tell you!" I shouted silently to Patsy. "I only thought it *might* have."

Patsy stopped singing, but other voices came out of the shadows where I'd been keeping them at bay.

"Poor Mrs. Doran, may God rest her. Terrible accident." That was Aunt Nin.

Grandmother had stuck to the weather. "Aye, that fog's a killer, don't I well know. Sure anybody could miss a footing."

"Ach, sure, she was very upset—she'd had Smokey a long time." I think Aunt Madge said that.

Everything began to unravel, like the stitches dropped from Aunt Nin's knitting needles. They knew Mrs. Doran hadn't fallen in. I'd known too. We'd made a numbing poultice of words and slapped it on the festering truth. But there'd been no challenge from me for if the village code hadn't been mobilised, the dialogue surrounding Mrs. Doran's death would have indicted the living, us as well as them, and damned—literally—the dead.

A suicide's soul went straight to Hell, its earthly remains condemned to the other side of the wall girdling Our Lady's Acre, apart from the rest of the faithful whose deeds were judged by God himself. As it was, Mrs. Doran was buried on hallowed ground. In Greencastle we were very nice to our dead; only the living were ostracised.

God help me, but I belonged; I wasn't an outsider. I'd cracked the heart of the village code on the bus from Dublin when, after the evidence was in, I'd convinced myself Free Staters were a part of us. The baptism of self-deceit had worked because I'd already confessed the truth to myself, *then* went about poulticing the wound. And that's what was haunting me about the burlap bag. I knew something they didn't, but I hadn't been able to acknowledge it. I'd been a McGrath pupil too long; you didn't *think* you saw in Miss McGrath's class—you either saw or you didn't. And if that bag moved—oh, I was learning the ways all right—then Mrs. Doran had murdered Smokey. And if—oh, please God, no . . .

"Oh, Madge, I've been upset all day. Smokey disappeared and I couldn't find him and I just knew something had happened to Frankie!"

The village code sanctioned the juggling and weaving of words, but Mrs. Doran had taken it to extremes—she'd changed the *names!*

The coals shuddered in the grate, and my eyes flew open.

* * *

I was purged. Yes, I knew who killed the cat; knew how he'd died; but *what* inspired the killing of Smokey, with all its dark symbolism, would remain a mystery forever. Theories were just that—suppositions. And you could slant them to suppose anything you wanted.

Grandmother and Aunt Madge were on their feet, urging me up as Aunt Nin squeezed into her coat, so I didn't have time to salve myself beyond the quick thought that if he'd lived, Smokey would sorely have missed his liver stew every Sunday. But I'd have to tax the code to its limits with this one anyway, and I just wasn't up to it yet.

While I muffled myself in the new scarf, a debate ensued as to whether Aunt Nin should turn off the gas lamps. They stayed lit. It was Christmas.

Aided by the extra candlepower within, Gethsemane, St. Patrick, and the Assumption revealed their purples, scarlets, greens, and golds to all of Greencastle that Christmas Eve. I'd never seen our little chapel so festive. Curliqued branches of gleaming brass held candles that slanted upwards at each end of the altar. All the pedestal candles were lit, too, instead of the usual token few. Myriad red votive lamps glowed under the Sacred Heart on the left side, and the blue ones sparkled at the feet of Our Lady on the right. A muted amber light warmed the straw in the crib set up just inside the communion rail, the focal point of my attention.

The smell of freshly burnt incense wafted up to us in the balcony and mingled with that of past benedictions. I knelt between Aunt Nin and Grandmother while Aunt Madge made a place for herself in the row behind. Ann Mulholland had the choir all rigged out in newly acquired burgundy grosgrain robes which inspired Grandmother to ask Aunt Nin where Ann thought she was—the Opera House? Even Molly Logan had donned one, although she still stood at the end of the men's row.

I leaned over the balustrade and counted five other lilac scarves. They definitely stood out. The coughing, whispering, and feet scuffling stopped as an army of altar boys, dripping lace vestments, took their positions. For a merry minute of pure wickedness, I willed Bobby McConnell's face on that of the boy holding the incense urn. But I was forced to let him loose. Even imagination has credulity limits. If Bobby ever found out that I'd gussied him up as an altar boy . . . But I pulled myself up, realizing he never would. "Watch what you say to them" would prevail, and Bobby McConnell would never really know me. That I had this edge on him should have made me gloat.

Ann Mulholland's organ poured out the first stirring strains of "Adeste Fideles" as Father Murphy appeared before us in a dazzle of celebrant white and gold.

The choir did Ann proud all the way through the Christmas hymns. Towards the end of the Mass one of the altar boys read the story of the first Christmas. "Unto you this day is born a Saviour . . ." The Holy Infant's halo, seemingly alive in the wavering light, radiated up to me as Ann softly began the introductory notes of "Silent Night." Suddenly, a lone voice soared through the chapel. Awed, I turned to look at Molly Logan. The same speckled brown face was uplifted, eyes fixed on something unseen near the ceiling, the powerful voice climbing until I was just one big goosepimple.

I experienced a communion in the chapel I'd never experienced before. The essence of everything great in human beings was contained in that voice—it encompassed us all, them and us. A flash of insight, just a tantalising hairsbreadth from infinite understanding, was immediately watered down to raw emotion, the same kind that Eilish Loughran stirred when she immortalised Wordsworth for me; that Grandpa McCartney evoked when he paid his ultimate respect to Mrs. Doran. But I couldn't make up my mind which emotion to respond to, for although I felt like cheering, I apparently thought it appropriate to cry.

Molly's rich contralto deepened to the final *"Slee-eep in heavenly peace"* and Midnight Mass was over.

"Ahhh," Grandmother sighed, "hasn't she a voice, love?"

I looked at her through watery eyes. No answer was needed.

It was a glittering night. A hard frost had set in and covered the chapel path with treacherous diamonds. Aunt Nin and Grandmother held on to each other, picking their steps. Aunt Madge, with unsuspected sure-footedness, was away in front making for the big overcoated man we were both in love with. Uncle Dan stood waiting, pipe glowing like a night-watchman's brazier, at the chapel gates.

"You can tell him to come on up for a bite of goose," Grandmother called after Aunt Madge. I suspicioned this was Phase II of the "Kill him with kindness" campaign she'd already mounted, but she added, "You, too, Nin."

I looked up and searched the vast quivering heavens for the Star of Bethlehem. Miracles happened, they said, when it rose. The winking North Star was particularly bright, but I couldn't quite muster the lie. The Star of Stars wasn't there.

God, I'd have liked a miracle right then, but I quickly disavowed any petition, for it'd have been just my luck to end up blind, deaf, and dumb like the shepherd boy in Miss McGrath's play. There were all kinds of miracles and God took a dim view of selfish miracle-seeking. I still hadn't got over the penalties the last one had imposed. Now, Moses had had the right idea and made sure a lot of other people benefited too.

A yelp from Aunt Nin, her feet skidding out from under her, brought me back to earth. But Grandmother held on to her like Grim Death and succeeded in defying the laws of gravity. My plump Aunt Nin wouldn't be allowed to fall—not on your life—not as long as Grandmother had a hold of her. I laughed out loud and Grandmother mistook it for cheekiness.

No, I thought, I didn't need any miracles just yet—not as long as Grandmother was my ally. Even Uncle Dan himself once told me, "If fists came to blows, love, I'd want your granny on my side any day!"

I looked back up at the midnight sky. "Thank you for my granny, God," I whispered. A lot could happen from one season to the next—and it was a long time till spring.

MAEVE BINCHY

ECHOES

Ireland in the Fifties. Three children from very different backgrounds are growing up in the tiny seaside town of Castlebay. Clare dreams of escape through education and David of a dazzling future as a specialist doctor. Gerry just wants fame and success. Over the next decade their lives are destined to meet in a quite unforeseen way, but never will they escape the echoes of their past.

POST A LITTLE HAPPINESS

Post·A·Book

A Royal Mail service in association with the Book Marketing Council & The Booksellers Association.

Post-A-Book is a Post Office trademark

RUTH ADLER

A FAMILY OF SHOPKEEPERS

Around the turn of the century, Europe was a turmoil of Jewish migrations. From Warsaw to London's East End come Ada and Jacob Samuels. Leaving poverty and oppression behind them they arrive in search of a haven of freedom and prosperity; in its stead they find a strange and sometimes hostile country. The life they create for themselves, their shop, their children, family and friends, is a richly woven tapestry of community relationships. But Ada and her husband emerge as strikingly different in some ways from their fellows; in their attitude to religion, to their business, and above all to each other. Captivating, moving, and sometimes endearingly funny, their story is not only a social history of the period but a living portrait of a family striving under difficulty for civilised survival.

CORONET BOOKS

ALSO AVAILABLE FROM CORONET BOOKS